Sometimes we are born into a family, and at other times we have ties that bind us in different ways. *Family Ties: Thicker than Blood* by B. G. Howard is a genre of literature that needs to be revisited. In the vein of *GoodFellas* and *The Godfather*, *Family Ties: Thicker than Blood* takes the reader into the heart of organized crime. Willie, the main character, is a young man from the South who finds his way to New York. He befriends an organized crime family boss and, thusly, the new *Family Ties* are born. The novel is also a love affair with the city of New York. You will be transported onto the streets of New York City in all its glory and darkness.

—Professor Gwen Alexis, California State Fullerton

The *Family Ties* characters pulled me onto the pages and made it difficult to put the book down as the story is filled with action, romance, and adventure. Amazingly, B. G. Howard takes you on a ride alongside Willie LeBeaux through the streets of New York City, to the countryside of rural Georgia, and back to the city as he attempts to navigate the perils of a criminal enterprise, family drama, and opposing love interests. After reading *Family Ties: Thicker than Blood* you'll want the characters' lives to continue. It demands the need for a sequel.

—J. A. Johnson, Entrepreneur, Jacksonville, FL

FAMILY TIES:

THICKER THAN BLOOD

To: Charnet,

Thank you for
your support and
confidence.

B. H. Howard

FAMILY TIES:

THICKER THAN BLOOD

B. G. HOWARD

BGH Publishing
Adult Content

This is a work of fiction.

All the characters, organizations, and events portrayed in this novel

are either products of the author's imagination or are used fictitiously.

Printed in the United States of America

Published by BGH Publishing

P.O. Box 8103, Jacksonville, FL 32239

www.bghoward.com

Library of Congress Cataloging-in-Publication Data

is available upon request.

Also available in hardcover, softcover, e-books, and audiobook

Paperback: 978-0-578-60720-7

Hardback: 978-0-578-60721-4

Ebook: 978-0-578-60722-1

Library of Congress Control Number: 2019918186

"My first work of fiction is dedicated to the memories of the late B. G. Howard, Sr. and the late Maretha (Chank) Howard who passed away prior to realization of this lengthy effort. Gratitude is extended both, to those who believed and supported me as well as those who didn't.

Above all else, I thank the Creator for creating me to create.

Special appreciation to the one most appreciated for making the biggest sacrifice, my wife, Sandra Howard.
Thanks to Randy Sullivan at GTI, for you first believed.
Thank you Robert Johnson, Beverly Poindexter, Caroline Wade, and Deborah Steele for knowing it was possible.
Additionally, thank you Rosa and Buck for seeing the vision before I did.

Table of Contents

Introduction

Willie LeBeaux finds his way from a small town in South Georgia to the mean streets of post 911 New York City, like many, in search of that big break. Witness to an uncanny situation, Willie inadvertently saves the life of Ozwald Jenkins, or Oz, as he's known on the streets. Coincidentally, Oz happens to be an instrumental figure of a notorious crime family; one that controls illicit activities throughout the five boroughs. Oz befriends the adopted pupil who, by default, learns to thrive in the ruthless underworld he's destined to one day inherit, but harbors no desire to have.

That creates a challenging issue for Jerome, the ousted second in command, who has his sights set on assuming Oz's throne in the relatively near future. Circumstances are more complicated when Willie unwisely becomes romantically drawn to NYPD Officer Ernestina Lady, with whom he enjoys spending time but knows the true nature of his "business activities" can never be disclosed.

As if he's not having enough trouble manipulating the unfortunate cards life has dealt him, Willie then has to contend with the unexpected arrival of Tammy. She's a closer-than-comfortable cousin from back home in Georgia, who shows up at LaGuardia Airport without warning to surprise him. Willie is shuffled back and forth physically, psychologically, and emotionally between the life he desires and the one he's been forced to live, while trying to overcome obstacles constantly thrown in his scripted path.

1

Setting the Tone

It was a hot, balmy summer day in Harlem as we made our way across Amsterdam on the way to Charlie's Place at the corner of 128th Street and St. Nicholas Avenue. I remember being in the passenger's seat of the Navigator wishing I was someplace else. My preference was to still be enjoying the warm flesh blanket I had to leave before seven o'clock this morning. Any place would be better than riding shotgun to collect on a debt Charlie had allowed to fall delinquent. Ozzie, or Oz as he was recognized on the territory, was a pretty low-key, easy-going fellow. But let there be a hold-up with his cash flow, and he had no problem conducting late-night swimming lessons in the Hudson River.

Charlie, a two-bit make-believe hustler from the Midwest, had come across a pool hall in a rather shady business deal a few years back. The only thing known to be true is the fact that the previous owner suddenly left town, never to be heard from again.

Charlie's Place, most commonly known to locals as the Watering Hole, served as a legitimate front for anything outside the law. A person could view a menu containing everything from prostitution to "pre-owned" autos at Charlie's...and virtually anything else could be ordered special. His hands were shoved into whatever crooked deal he thought would turn a dollar.

Amp announced as the 'Gator came to an abrupt stop in front of a huge flashing neon sign, "The time has arrived."

I tried to sound as commanding as possible, "You lead; I'll cover the door."

Amp's voice blared like a bullhorn as he tugged his oversized button-down shirt to conceal the pump shotgun from passers in front of Charlie's, "You punk muthafucker; better get yo slow ass in the current, 'cause this shit 'bout to get serious for real."

"One more time!" I snapped. "I already told you about that Mama shit! You never met my damn mom! It'd be wise of you to keep her name out your fucking mouth."

"What 'n hell you talking?" he questioned. "I ain't said shit 'bout yo mama."

Making my way through the front door, I chastised him, "I might be a lot of things, fool," I said. "But an M-F and S-O-B I'm not. That's where I draw the damn line."

It was no secret Amp and I didn't care too much for each other. He took pride in being the biggest ass in the shithouse and resented the fact that I'd found favor in the sight of Oz, his mentor. More annoying for him was the realization that he had chosen the streets as a way of life and aspired to someday take Oz's place. I, on the other hand, wound up in the game purely by accident, and wanted nothing more than to escape the hellhole where I had learned to thrive. Not from ambition to do so, but from a simple need to survive.

I was shocked back to reality by the screams of a woman watching action at the corner pool table when she caught a glimpse of Amp's shotgun. "Daaammmnnn, that bastid got a big-ass barrel up in this joint!"

Sounds of desperation came from an older fellow as he hobbled past carrying his walking cane so as to not have it slow him down, "Let me outta dis bitch 'fore somebody cut loose up in here."

With people screaming and running in every direction trying to take cover, Amp's deep bass sounded over the jazz on the old jukebox. "Where 'n hell that punk, Charles? If this song end b'fore I get a answer, I'm gone start playin my own music up in this piece!"

I had made my way through the crowded pool hall a little easier than Amp. My 9mm Smith & Wesson handguns were a little less conspicuous and afforded me more maneuverability. Upon crashing through the stained-glass door of an office in the rear of the building, I found Charlie trying to unlock the bars covering the window that opened to the alley out back. It had always puzzled me as to how Charlie could be a respected notorious gangster but known for being afraid of guns. With all his armor caught off guard in the front of the pool hall, he was a sitting duck. I mean, who'd ever expect anyone to have the balls to try Charlie at his house?

He stammered, "I was just about to...just about...to... just about..."

"Aww, save me the song and dance, Charlie!" I interrupted. "I guess you trying to get the checkbook from your truck parked in the alley? And if you expect me to swallow that pile of... What the hell?" Charlie had reached into the top drawer of the desk and pulled out a stun gun. I almost fell over laughing. "You might wanna invest in some real firepower, pussycat. If you'd like, I can turn you on to ole boy down by the docks," I said.

Directing the taser toward me, "You won't think it's so funny when I pop yo ass with these five thousand amperes," Charlie said.

I walked a little closer, to demonstrate my lack of intimidation at the sight of his weapon of choice, "Dumbass," At that point, I was cracking up. "They're called volts. And you got to get way too damn close to use that little bitch shit." I was overly theatrical, "Now, let's save all the drama. You know damn well who I work for…which means, you know exactly why I'm in your shit. We can do this like men…or I can treat you like the whore you turned out to be and straight pimpslap your bitch ass. But either way, you gonna un-ass Oz's count."

Charlie seemed as though he was about to piss his pants, "Well…well," while eyeing the stainless iron in my right hand. "I…I got part of it," he said.

I was almost offended. "Now, Charlie, you know damn well I didn't drive all the way downtown, break into Macy's, just to be satisfied to leave with a fucking ugly-ass tie." I explained, "We're not playing this game, Charlie. To bring back part of it won't keep Oz off my ass. Knowing that… won't keep me off yours!"

Apprehensively, Charlie asked, "What I, need to do?"

I shoved the barrel of the gun up his nose, "Pay the man his due! And I mean all his due! Like that's a damn question you have to ask me. Your ass been in the game long enough to know better than to do the shit you do. Long enough to know you don't jerk Oz around like that!" It could have been that nasty-ass fish tank that hadn't been cleaned since the fish moved in, but I would bet my right ear Charlie shit his pants. He was burping uncontrollably out his ass and I was repulsed by the smell. I explained, while backing away in search of air that wasn't contaminated and checking my watch, "This is the way we gone work this. It's now twenty-two minutes 'til three. I have one other stop to make before I get back to Oz's place on the Upper West Side. By the time I roll up there, you're going to have this shit straightened out with the old man. And I don't mean with promises or part of his money. Or else, I'm going to come back for another visit. And you know how I hate to go at anything twice, unless it's a good bit softer than me."

With beads of sweat dripping from his nose, Charlie reassured, "I'll have Oz's money to him before he even know you stopped by me."

I was still about five or six feet away so Charlie had become a bit more relaxed, "That's going to be kind of difficult," I said as my 9mm sounded off, CA-CLACK, CA-CLACK, "... since Oz is the one who sent me over to see you." I shouted over Charlie's screaming, as he fell back into the chair and grabbed his foot, "Now we *all* know I was here."

"You some-bitch!" he cried. "That was my damn foot!"

Looking back over my shoulder while passing out his office, "Could've been your old greasy ass," I established. "In case you got any ideas about running...you'll be easier to catch."

Once outside Charlie's office, I walked through the crowd of nervous patrons Amp had parted like the Red Sea and headed for the 'Gator parked out front. Amp trailed behind with a frown on his face like a disappointed puppy.

"So, where the green?" he asked. "I know yo hillbilly ass wasn't sucker 'nough to take a bitchin check."

I snapped, "Get off my family and back in the damn truck before you have half the fools in this place up your ass."

It wasn't even four o'clock yet, and had already been an incredibly long day. All I wanted to do was go by Moms' apartment in Harlem and refill my tank with some of her greens, potato salad, and good ole buttered cornbread. I'd watch a little football with Poppy while 'word wrestling' and then head on back down to my sanctuary in the Village; the two places in this crazy world where I could always find some semblance of peace.

Intruding on thoughts of quality time with my surrogate parents, Amp said, "I still wanna know what 'n hell happened wit dis Charlie bullshit."

I was already frustrated. The last thing I needed was to be drilled by some kingpin *hopeful*, "There's nothing to know. He said he was gone clean the shit up with Oz in a minute."

"What you mean, *he gone clean up wit Oz?*" he persisted. "Bitch, that's why we here. We is the fuckin clean up crew! If it wasn't already messed up, shit won't need cleaning up. You done gone and lost yo godda…"

I interjected over his complaint, "That's enough of your damn babbling!" I yelled. "Now, I put up with a lot of shit from you, and mama knows I'm no choir boy myself, but what I won't have is any bastard taking the Lord's name in vain!"

Even though I was a disgrace, in every sense of the word, as far as my biological parents saw me; there was one thing that had been instilled since I was a nappy-headed little boy back on the farm in rural Georgia. I could almost hear my momma say, *"Don't never take the Good Lord's name in vain,"* as she peered through me from beneath the brim of that ragged woven straw hat. *"Alls ya doin is dammin yo soul to hell!"*

It seemed like so long ago and so far away from home down in South Georgia. I had only been in New York a few years, but it felt like an eternity since coming to the Big Apple, chasing dreams of stardom and life on *easy street*. Ironically, it's not until you arrive in the city that never sleeps when you realize your chances at stardom rank right up there with the odds you'll hit the lottery. There is no street named 'Easy' anywhere in this country; at least, not for a poor man with a tenth-grade education who can only boast a doctorate from 'Thug University.' I remembered the last words my father spoke to me as I left for the bus station. *"Ya ain't worth a damn now, and ya ain't nev'r gone be worth a damn 'til da day dem folk throws dirt in ya face."* I guess that's the real reason I hadn't been in touch with my family since about two weeks after my arrival in the City.

It was almost as though the Lord knew of my need for the connection that had been all but severed with my biological family. One Saturday, while in Harlem conducting business for Oz, I had encountered a spirited old lady who so much reminded me of my mother. We ran into one another periodically over the course of the next few months, which allowed ample opportunity for us to become somewhat acquainted. That was because neither of us enlisted enough trust in the other to allow anything more for quite some time. Once, while passing near the apartment building, I witnessed a group of young undergraduate hoodlums giving her a hard time in the courtyard. Immediately, I'd popped out the Impala Oz had gifted me, because, "....man ain't a man if he walkin," he'd said.

I had hurried over, grabbed the groceries from her arms and asked aloud, "Hey, Moms, what's for dinner?"

I think later that evening was the first time since my moving to New York that I'd tasted cooking anywhere close to my mom's. Eunice and Sam; or Moms and Poppy, as I grew to affectionately refer to them, lived in a huge horseshoe-shaped brick building at 133rd St. and Broadway. The window in the front room of their quaint fourth-floor apartment provided a nice view of the Hudson River and a bit of serenity any time I was occasioned to need it.

Sam proudly began the brief "view-from-the-window" guided tour of Spanish Harlem, "Dat dere, right on da other side o' da river, be New Jersey," he declared. "If'n ya goes up 'at-a-way a li'l piece, dey's a bridge dat takes ya ova da Hudson. Dat used ta be da only way ya cross over years ago, 'fore dem folks gets smart 'an fixed up dem tunnels 'n shit downtown. Nev'r figured out why dey calls it da Holland Tun'el. Dat shit in New York, America…ain't gotta damn thang ta do wit no freakin Holland." By then, Sam was more engaged in conversation with himself than he was with either of us in the room, until he finally asked, "Eunice, what da name o' dat damn bridge?"

"What F-ing bridge Sam? I aint no damn tour guide!" Moms said, "And how you know he wanna hear 'bout this shit anyways. Could be, he been livin in New York all his damn life."

In an elevated tone, Sam stated, "Like hell... He ain't done lived in no damn New York City all his life!"

Eunice was already annoyed. "How the hell you knows where he done lived?"

"I aint never heard no damn New York talk like dat. Da words is like folk 'round dese parts but dat boy sound like he from down our way; somewheres in da South. Ain't dat right, Billy Boy?" Sam asked.

"His name William, Sam. You always tryin to change somebody damn name," Eunice argued.

"Dammit woman, don't ya knows nothin? Billy short fo Wil'am."

"That don't makes no kinda sense," she protested. "Them two names don't even sound nutin like each other...like Tom short for Tommy. Who come up wit some shit like that anyways?"

"Woman, I don't know...dat's just how thangs is," Sam said.

I honestly couldn't tell whether the two of them were fighting or joking. "You're right, Poppy...straight out the peanut patch." I tried to remind them of the original topic of conversation. "I was born in a small town in South Georgia."

"You for real Willie? I gots peoples in Georgia...place called Fitzgerald," Eunice said.

I tried to explain, "Well, I'm originally from a place not too far from a city by the name of Valdosta. I was sent to live with my aunt for a while outside Atlanta when my mom was sick," I said. "All those years of private school resulted with me *talking white*, as a lot of people accuse me. They seem to have a problem with the fact I learned what's called proper English. Everybody back home thinks that I think I'm better than them."

Eunice commented with an air of pride."Sam, you heared Willie; he come from 'round parts wheres I growed up. We's prob'ly kin."

"Now dere *ya* go messin up da boy name, Eunice. Did ya not jest tell me his name William? Why ya gone jest git dumb wit shit like dat?" Sam argued.

I cut in, to keep them from going at each other again, "I've been called some of most anything."

"Well anyways," Sam had just remembered where he was going with the whole conversation from the beginning. "Like I's tryin ta say; place used ta be real nice when we moved in 'bout twenty or so years a'go. 'Course dats 'fore all dem freakin Domiticans started comin in 'n takin ova da damn buildin."

Eunice spoke up to remind Sam they had company, "A'ight Sam, that's 'nough. Don't start your shit today…always got somethin to say 'bout some damn body. Them peoples don't be botherin you."

Again, Sam took the liberty of mounting a proverbial soapbox as he saddled his political thoroughbred, "Naaawwww, I jest gits tired of 'em wit all dat freakin conga music 'n throwin dey garb'ge outta da damn winders. Building man'gement can't do nothin 'bout 'em trashin da joint, but Whitey ain't gots no problem findin a reason ta keep tryin ta raise da rent in dis shit hole. Dis buildin s'posed to be rent control. Seem like e'ry other month dem folk tryin ta sneak a rent hike past us. Shhhiiittt! Dey don't know who da hell dey's dealin wit. I goes down ta dat city hall 'n gives dem somebitches a piece o' my mind…," Sam began.

"That's why you ain't got shit left for a brain now…a'ways givin someb'dy piece o' it," Eunice said.

His wife's comment didn't faze him, "…And if dat don't light fire under 'em," Sam continued. "I tells ya what I does; I goes to dat lawyer friend o' mine…well, we ain't really friends like dat. I ain't gots no need o' too many muthas callin me 'friend'…dat make me kinda nervous."

Eunice let out a sigh of frustration at the fact her husband wanted all focus on him when he had a purpose, "Sam, can you jest get to the damn point?"

"Anyways, 'dis lawyer fella, he Porta Rican. Dat son of a gun do most o' what I wants him ta do fo a six pack o' dat damn horse piss dey be drinkin and some smokes."

"Jeeefff!!!" screamed Eunice.

I sensed another fight brewing and launched a peaceful plea, "Moms, just give him a second."

Sam continued, "Dis last time, I had 'em ta fix up me one o' dem fancy, smart-soundin letters wit all dat 'in-so-much as' and 'afore-mentioned' shit dey be talkin. I ain't understand a damn thang dat piece o' paper was sayin, but it show got dem suits downtown jumpin all over theyselfs. B'fore twas all over wit, dem somebitches was 'pologizin ta me 'an offerin ta fix all kinda shit in dis 'partment. Hell, dey even give us a new winder air condition." He sort of chuckled to himself, "Give us a damn air-condition machine in Febrary; ain't dat some shit fo yo ass." Pausing for a minute, Sam then continued, "I gots da letter back dere in my sock drawer, if'n ya wanna see it."

"He ain't wanna see no damn letter. You done told him what the freakin thing say," Eunice commented. "'Sides, y'all come on 'way from dat window and get to the table; dinner ready."

I spoke up before realizing it, "Dang, Moms; that has to be the quickest meal I ever knew anybody to put together. McDonald's doesn't have anything on you."

I could tell Poppy was a little annoyed at the insinuation, "What 'n hell ya mean, McDonald's? No freakin burgers 'n shit comin up in here; dis McSammy's Home Cookin," he said. "She ain't touched da damn stove since 'fore we git hitched."

Eunice leaned over and whispered in my ear, "He takes his cookin real ser'ous...don't ev'n lets me mess 'round in that kitchen...won't eat fast food and won't go to no restorant neither. Alls I done is fix the cornbread."

He could be heard continuing his verbal assault on the entire fast-food industry as I started toward the bathroom.

"I's a cook in da damn army foe-teen freakin ye-ars. I used ta fix…" The more thought he gave the idea; the more pissed Sam seemed to get, "Why da hell I'ma go ta some fancy joint 'n pay dem folk too much 'o my hard-earned money ta have 'em gimme food on a pretty freakin plate dat don't taste good as da shit I can cook right here on my own damn stove?" He then directed me, "Man, go'on down da hall ta da bat'room 'n wash ya damn hands. Talk ta me 'bout some freakin shitburgers in my house. I knows ya done bumped yo head 'n lost yo damn mind."

The fact that I had left the front of the apartment, gone into the bathroom, and closed the door was of little consequence to Sam. He just kept right on babbling about his military experiences. Though I couldn't quite make out what was being said, I could tell he had no intention of stopping until his tale had been completed. I purposely delayed in the bathroom just to see if it would make any difference when he realized I wasn't there.

After finishing my business and washing up, I started up the hallway, posing a question to stop his rant, "We eating yet?"

"Damn, thought I's gone have ta jump in da mutha ta save yo poe ass."

Sarcasm laced my comment, "Naw, I was able to climb out without too much trouble," I said.

With a look of concern, "Could ya manage dat to'let a'ight?" he asked. "Dat's somthin else in dis shithole dem damn folks s'posed ta been fixed."

The three of us sat down to what looked like a miniature feast. There was a huge platter of pork chops, a bowl each of collard greens, potato salad, corn on the cob, and Moms' mouth-watering buttered cornbread. I reached for the empty plate in front of the chair to which I'd been directed.

Sam playfully swatted my hand to make me let go of the porcelain dish, "Gimme that damn plate; get over there and sit yo skinny ass down.

You a guest. Ain't ya gots no home trainin?" Eunice said.

Sam instructed in a fatherly tone, "Ya gits o'er dere 'n cop a squat," he said. "What ya drinkin? I'll fix it whiles I's at da icebox."

Placing my order, "I'll take a glass of lemonade, if you have any," I said.

Eunice spoke up to confirm, "Made some fresh this morning. Yep, I can tell you's from Georgia. Jest like Sam; the kids don't too much care fo it none-a'tall. They ain't gots a taste fo nothin but them freakin sodas, or pop, as they calls it. Youngins can drank a case of them things in a day."

"Yep, dats why I ain't puttin my stuff out here, so dey can't come in 'n eat up e'rythang," Poppy said.

Moms explained, "That's why he don't let none of 'em back there in that damn room…where he keep all his shit. Betcha he got most anythin you can think of back there in that closet; or b'low that damn bed."

"Dat's a'ight, don't ya worry 'bout what I gots in dere," he said, before asking, "Ya want me ta fix a glass fo ya, Eunice?"

"No, I gots a cup 'round here somewheres wit the rest o' my coffee in it."

Sam commented, half scolding her. "A wonder da damn stuff ain't done turned ta ice. I can't figure how da hell ya pours hot coffee in a cup—'cause it s'posed ta be hot—den jerk 'round doin e'rythang but drankin it 'til da shit gits cold…'much as dis stuff cost."

"How many do you guys have?" I interrupted.

From behind a look of confusion, "How many is we got o' what…cups?" Sam asked.

"Kids, how many kids do the two of you have," I repeated.

"Well, me 'n Eunice gets two," he said. "But wit dem other six, all total dey's eight. Eunice had a whole clan o' dem li'l crumb-snatchers when I met her." He smiled with his crooked grin and symbolically blew her a kiss across the table. "But I takes 'em all fo mine. 'Cause she my queen 'n I loves her like dat."

His wife commented in a somewhat authoritative tone, "Sitch yo ass down so we can eat 'fore all da damn food get cold...and stop being fresh; your old ass."

Sam glared at her, rolled his eyes toward the ceiling while doing what looked like a slow-motion samba, and affectionately whispered, "Who luvs ya baby?" as he gyrated his hips to symbolize sexual activity.

Moms lowered her head in embarrassment. "Sam, cut that shit out and eat yo damn food 'fore da shit git cold!"

Nearly doubled over laughing at the two of them to the point I had to catch the table to avoid falling out the chair, I tried to compose myself the best I could when the doorbell rang. Eunice looked to Sam. I couldn't quite make out the message behind his eyes when he stared at her from across the table. He quickly glanced over at the clock on the stove and let out an exasperated sigh that sounded like a whale surfacing for much needed air. The doorbell continued impatiently. *Ding...Ding...Ding...DING! DING! DING!*

"What da hell ya wants!" Sam yelled at the unsuspecting door. "Ya standin on the somebitch like ya got bidness up in dis piece!"

As soon as Poppy could twist the knob a good half-turn, the door flung open and knocked him off balance when their son barged into the apartment, "I do got bidness up in dis joint. Dis where my ma be restin her head, ain't it?"

I had instinctively sprung to my feet before realizing it and positioned myself between Poppy and the intruder. I wasn't sure what was going on, but I'm not the type to just stand back and watch shit happen. "I got this, Poppy!"

About the time I reached for my Smith & Wesson, I heard Moms yell, "Junior! What da hell yo problem, comin up in here like that?!" She made her way over to where I was, trying to help Sam get his feet back under him.

Poppy was in a rage. "Who da hell ya thank ya is? Ya don't come breakin down no damn doors up here! Ya can takes yo ass back out dere on dem damn streets where ya been hangin out! When ya can a'ford ta pay fo a freakin door, den ya can tear up yo own shit!"

Junior ignored Sam, as if he'd never opened his mouth, "Who dis?" looked at me as if *I had broken into the apartment.* "Who is you, fool?" He paused. "Oh mom, so dis the punk ass you and Sam been squawking so much 'bout?" Then, he turned again to me. "What cause you got being up in my ma's joint?"

Before I had a chance to stomp on his tongue, Moms came to Junior's rescue. "It ain't nunna yo damn bidness who this is; he in our house. What 'n hell you want anyway? You ain't come all the way up here jest to see who in our freakin house."

Sam slammed his fist on the corner of the table, as would a judge his gavel in the courtroom, "Why ya playin stupid, Eunice? Ya knows damn well why he showed his ass up here, 'cause da bastid hungry. E'ry time da somebitch git hongry, he be brangin his tired, good-for-nutin ass 'round when he thank I ain't home." Sam cut his eyes at Eunice. "And he keep comin 'round 'cause ya be throwin his ass a damn bone. Ya thanks I don't be knowin."

Heading toward the door, "What the hell you know, you old gray-head bastid? You don't know shit 'bout what you talkin," Junior argued. "Can't even throw no meat to yo flesh 'n blood, but got dis punk ass up in yo joint callin y'alls moms and pops 'n shit."

I could hear Junior as he stomped to the elevator half-way down the hall, still cursing that stranger, me, for all I was worth. Suddenly, it dawned on me where he had inherited that character flaw which had him carrying on intense conversation when no one was within earshot. Confirmation came shortly after when Eunice took it upon herself to point out the unwelcome visitor was Sam, Jr., the youngest of their litter. She explained that Junior was a nickname assigned to him when he was younger, but they had no idea how true it would prove to be. He had tried his hand at anything he could do to keep from having to get an actual job. When hustling didn't work out, he'd explored the benefits of burglary. After being caught and convicted five times in five attempts, it was determined that, as well, wasn't the most rewarding career choice.

It had taken a few informal visits to Harlem before Sam began treating me as part of the family instead of like a visitor, or, worse than that; like a tourist. I enjoyed their company so much until the place soon became like a second home. As I spent more time with Sam and Eunice, my affection started to grow. Honestly, more than I first realized or would have ever wanted to admit. It wasn't long before the both of them treated me like one of their own and often introduced me as their other son. Needless to say, that didn't go over very well with most of the biological kids. None of whom were kids anymore, but most found it rather difficult to sever the umbilical cord that had them bound to Eunice for all of life.

Sam commented to shake me back to the moment, "Ya better gits back ta ya grub 'fore it git cold. If'n it do, ain't gone be no mo good."

While proceeding back to the table, "I'm coming, Poppy," but my mind was on the elevator with Junior.

A little while passed without a word from anybody. All of us were preoccupied with thoughts of activities that had occurred during the past several minutes. Everyone had their own opinion of the events; and interpretation of the cause was as different as each of our understanding.

"You always this quiet when you's eatin?" Eunice asked.

I intentionally avoided the real subject. "I don't know if it's because I'm so hungry, or because the vittles so good."

Sam, not so discreetly, solicited a compliment, "Ain't ne'er had no cookin like dat, huh?"

"I guess it's all right, but I'll need another plateful to be certain," I answered. "Poppy, I haven't had pork chops like these since I left my mom's house."

He was chuckling to himself, "Well, I'll be sho ta send her da recipe," he said.

Eunice intruded on the moment, "Now, you knows damn well you ain't never wrote nothin down." Looking over at me, she said, "You never did git 'round to tellin us 'xactly where you's from."

I responded with what had, over the years, become the typical evasive reply, "It's a small town in Georgia. I think the city recently voted to install a second traffic light to handle the increased horse-and-buggy traffic," I joked.

Sam cut in, before I could elaborate, "Now, Eunice, don't ya be doin dat."

"Doin what?" she asked.

Sam was instinctively being somewhat protective, "There ya go 'in tryin ta git all up in da man bidness. Maybe he don't wont ya ta know all dat," he said. "One thang I don't likes, fo folk ta start throwin a bunch o' questions at me 'fore I had a chance ta decide if'n I ev'n likes 'em."

Sam had an insight that seemed more like a sixth sense. Truth be told, I'd never been at all particular about giving up too many specifics concerning the road I traveled. "She's all right, Poppy. I guess the both of you are all right." I was trying to be somewhat understanding. After all, they really didn't know a great deal about me at that point. Of course, people who had known me all my adult life didn't really know too much about me.

I pushed back from the table a short time later. "Well, I hate to eat and run, but I'm done eating, and I really do have to run; got kind of an early start tomorrow."

"More a'ditions 'n stuff?" Moms asked.

I had, for a second, forgotten the lie I'd been living, "Excuse me?" The words escaped before I could cage them, "Oh yeah, I mean, yes, ma'am," I said, upon realization of which tale I had spun them.

The entire thing wasn't totally untrue. I did originally come to New York to pursue a career in the entertainment industry. And still went on auditions and interviews, on occasion, when time permitted between my other activities.

Moms tried to prolong the conversation, "We gots some black cherry ice cream, Will, if'n you wonts."

I said, in the process of standing, "Thanks anyway, but I better get back to my neck of the woods before it gets too late."

"How's ya likin it, livin down dere wit all dem artist folk?" Sam asked. "What dey calls it, da settlement...or camp, or somethin like dat?" He was tickled at himself.

I said, in reference to his platinum-colored locks, "It's the Village, Frosty."

He cut his eyes at me with an impish grin while humped over in a position similar to that of a football quarterback while gyrating his hips, "Might be snow on da roof, but dat don't mean ain't no fire in da damn chimney."

Moms had to get in on a piece of the action, "Damit Sam, fire be in da freakin fireplace. Smoke go up da damn chimney."

Before they could get started again, "Okay kids," I cut in. "I'm out of here."

Eunice logged a formal complaint. "But you jest got here."

I playfully grabbed her arm, and pretended to be eyeing a wristwatch, "Moms, did your watch stop?" I gave her a big affectionate hug, and then extended my hand to Sam, "Catch you later, Frosty."

He winked his eye. "Be careful out dere. See ya."

They'd both watched me from the doorway of their apartment until I disappeared onto the elevator. I had always felt a little guilty about not telling them the entire truth. In certain situations, the less people know, the better they sleep at night. That was my first experience with Sam and Eunice; seems like just last week. And to think it has been a little more than three years since then. I've done a decent job keeping them from being exposed to my true art of living.

Amp's screaming like he was trying to wake the dead startled me to the moment, "Hey! Sleepin Booty! Get yo punk ass up, we still got bidness!"

I didn't even realize I had nodded off on the way back from Charlie's joint. The comfort of the ride from St. Nicholas Ave. coupled with fatigue resulting from a full ten hours of body blocking ole girl from last night had finally taken its toll. Or maybe it was just the life I was living. Whatever the case, I was one worn-out soul by the time we pulled up at 108th St. and Lennox Ave.

Amp questioned, "Ya comin, sweetheart?"

The grossly over-exaggerated sarcasm in his voice didn't much faze me but prompted a firm response. "No."

While remotely opening the Navigator's rear hatch, "What's the matter?" he prodded. "Ain't ya got no taste for the true money-makin side of the business."

As the seat reclined to a more comfortable position, "You know I don't do the pharmaceutical thing. Never have, never will," I mumbled. "…And leave the damn keys."

Displaying much attitude, "What the hell you gone do, drive off and leave my ass?" he asked.

I dryly responded, "I might," reaching to catch the ignition keys Amp had flung at me from behind. "Your aim is way off, silly bitch. I know you were trying to hit me in my damn head."

"You always thinking somebody out to get yo stupid ass," he stated.

I was always careful to never take my eyes off Amp, especially when he was behind me. "It's just that I know you would if you could… If you could."

As he passed the passenger's door where I was seated, "Why don't you move the truck to that parking spot where those fools pullin out?" he ordered.

I wasn't in the mood for the performance. "Why don't you just carry your sorry ass in there and give Harold his stuff? That's all you need to be worried about right now."

Oz and I had an understanding from very early in our relationship. I had let him know if there was anything he needed done I'd take care of it; anything except handling drugs or drug money. That's something I never wanted a part of, because I'd seen somebody close to me shot in a deal gone bad shortly before connecting with Oz. I had no fear of guns, but the control I've seen the drugs have over people is simply frightening. I too much liked being in charge of my body than to venture off into an area where I'd voluntarily give up all control and any semblance of rational thought. That was part of the reason Amp thought I was soft, but little did he know.

As Amp walked into the building, I noticed two thugs in the rearview mirror, easing their way up to the Navigator. I was thinking to myself, there's no way in hell those fools would try anything in broad daylight. Sitting perfectly still, I watched them from behind the 'Gator's blacked-out tinted windows. They crept up on either side of the truck and attempted to peer through the windshield. With me wearing my trademark all black and reclined in the black leather seat, I was easily unnoticed. Within a few seconds, the two desperate Jesse James impersonators had positioned themselves on either side of the building's entrance, waiting for Amp to appear. I carefully moved from the passenger's side to take a position behind the wheel and timed his exit perfectly. When the two amateur thugs stopped him in the doorway and went for the briefcase, I started the truck and sped toward the three of them, slamming on the brakes at the very last second. The two thugs were pinned between the truck and the building, while Amp had been simultaneously knocked back into the still unlatched door.

He was pounding on the hood of the truck, pulling himself up using the bumper guard, "What the hell you tryin to do, kill my ass, you dizzy bitch!"

I let the driver's window down about halfway. "No, stupid, I'm trying to save your ungrateful, silly ass. If I wanted to kill you, you'd already be dead," I said before questioning, "These friends of yours?"

In a rather dry tone, he asked, "What the hell make you think they my friends?"

I couldn't resist the insult, "Well, they seem to know you well enough to pull some stupid O.K. Corral shit like this in broad daylight, with no backup and no cover. Sounds like you all limbs on the same dumb-ass family tree."

He argued while motioning with his arms like a skycap guiding a plane, "How the hell you gone trip on me like that; I ain't see nobody comin at yo ass, all laid back in the seat like sleepin damn beauty." And then insisting, "Move this ship and let me outta this place."

About that time, Harold and a couple heavies finally eased up behind Amp to investigate all the commotion. They found the two would-be robbers lying face down next to the entrance of the building, bruised and bleeding.

The huge blue-black brother asked, "You want me ta call da po-leese boss?"

Harold just rolled his eyes at the lump and shook his head. "And what exactly you gone tell them, Gus? Two assholes just tried to jump the delivery driver and take his *bitchin drug money*! Have you lost your damn mind? The last thing the heat gone do is come up here and try to sort out a problem they blame us for startin!" Harold stressed.

He cautiously approached the skinny kid on the ground closest to the doorway, kicked ole dude to turn him over, and then crossed to the other side of the walkway to flip the other. He paused, took a second look, and then reached into a pocket for his cell phone. Harold could be heard dialing as he went just inside the door shaking his head in disbelief.

He answered sounding as though all the air had been depleted from his lungs, "Hello. Hello. Yeah, sis, I need you at the shop. No, I just need you to stop by down here soon as you can; there's a little pro'lem. And you might wanna call Oz to let him know. Just tell him his nephew up to the same dumb shit again…tryin to steal from the cookie jar."

Although I couldn't make out what was being said, the person on the other end of the phone could be heard screaming at Harold from where I stood outside the doorway. He returned from hiding with a look on his face that spoke of the embarrassment.

Harold directed the husky light-complexioned heavy standing in front of Gus, "Pick them fellas up and take 'em inside 'fore somebody complains 'bout the garbage in front of my place," he said. "And take it easy with the dread head."

The big dude looked confused. "What up wit dat, Boss? You done got a thang for little long-haired boys?"

The look in Harold's eyes kept me from laughing. As he started back inside, he said over his shoulder, "No, I got a thing for my little brother's baby boy. That fool is me and Oz's dumb-ass nephew. Barbra, his stepmom, don't want him to have nothin to do wit the family bidness since his daddy got killed couple years ago… She act like nobody hurt but her. Hell, Marcus daddy was my little brother… Barbra just Marcus stepmom and she tryin to keep him from what s'posed ta be his. That's our legacy," he said in a solemn tone while allowing the others inside and closing the door behind him.

Amp approached from the passenger's side of the truck and extended his arms to pass the briefcase to me, "Put this in the back."

I walked past him as though he wasn't there, climbed in, and repositioned my seat, "Put it in your damn self."

"I gotta drive," Amp insisted.

In the process of reclining my seat, "And you said that to say what?" I asked. "So drive." Moments passed before I had a clear understanding of what had just transpired. I said, more to myself than anybody in particular, "I didn't know Oz and Harold are brothers."

"They ain't…but the shit too hard for people to figure out," Amp commented. "Marcus stepmom married to this dude, I think his last name…Benton, brother of Oz's real brother, who was adopted by Harold's folks…I think. But it don't much make no difference. All the folk that knows is dead so don't nobody ask 'cause the shit too hard to figure out… He just call everybody his nephew."

"Who Oz?" I asked.

"No, his brother," Amp replied.

"You mean, Harold?" I questioned.

"No, the one that died," Amp stated.

"What?" I quizzed.

"Exactly," he concluded.

2

Irregular Bonds

BUUZZZZ, BBUUZZZZZ. I grabbed my cell phone from the car's console right about the time the light changed. Fumbling with the receiver, I proceeded through the intersection to the tune of frustrated motorists' horns blaring. All because I'd taken longer than the allocated zero point five seconds to stand on the accelerator the very moment the traffic light turned green. I even had a silver BMW attempt to go around at the passenger side of my car, but he was surprised by an unaware driver exiting his SUV double-parked on the side of the street.

I remember mumbling under my breath, "Damned tourist."

One of the few things I'd grown accustomed to was Sunday dinner with my adopted parents, and I looked forward to the conversation, "Hello, hello… Hey Moms. No ma'am, I didn't forget. In fact, I'm on my way up there right now.

I have to make a stop real quick, and then drop by the market on the corner from you. I'll be up to see you and Poppy in a just a few minutes. How's he doing anyway? Ask him if he needs anything from the store. Okay, see you guys shortly."

As soon as the conversation with Moms concluded, I was somewhat startled by a loud *THUMP* on my ride. Oz was, again, playfully protesting the fact I often chose to park blocking the fire hydrant in front of his store. He'd slammed his fist on top of the car, causing the obvious knee-jerk reaction as I palmed one of my 9mm handguns. Anybody else would've had to duck and run.

While climbing out and greeting him with as warm an embrace as two ballers could manage, "You bend it, you buy it," I joked.

"If I remember correctly..." he left the thought hanging.

The Impala was the first thing he'd given me sometime after we became acquainted but Oz wasn't one to continuously point out what he felt was readily obvious, "I know, I know, old man. You just want me to be sure and remember the fact that you did buy it."

Remembering our first meeting; it was several months after I'd arrived in New York. I frequented a barber shop located a few blocks from Oz's store. One evening, after stopping by to let Omar tighten up my do, some suspicious suits were seen coming from behind Oz's building as I walked past. I didn't know much about where I was or what I was doing, but I've played the thug game since before I knew what 'game' was. A simple matter of hanging out and watching to see exactly what was going down made it possible for me to inform Oz when he eventually showed up. It was just a matter of me telling him what had happened. He received a very detailed account of what I'd witnessed, including physical descriptions of every person who'd been there. Their identities were obviously known to the entrepreneur, right down to the high-yellow self-appointed chief with the dirty-blond hair who seemed to be in charge. It wasn't very hard for Oz to figure out who the guys were, and what they were up to.

I had stayed out front across the street where he told me to wait while searching the alley. Like most storefronts in that area of Harlem, Oz's store was nothing more than a pretty canvas covering all the dirt secretly being shoveled out the back. About twenty minutes had passed before I saw his husky, grizzly-like silhouette emerge from the darkness. Walking around the corner and part way up the side of the concrete-block building, the disappointment on Oz's chiseled face was unmistakable, even through the darkness. We slowly moved into the soft-white glow of the light that hung over a side door allowing access to the street. In his left hand was what appeared to be some sort of make-shift explosive device Oz had located at the private exit from his office. The thing that was most hurtful to him was something I discovered shortly after that night. The lead dog was a fellow Oz had taken under his arm some time ago. A half-assed punk named Jerome. I'd heard about how ole boy hung out with Oz, stayed at his house, drove his rides, and all but slept with the boss' old lady. Since that day, Oz has dubbed me his watch dog.

I began hanging out, running errands and shit like that to start. It damn sure made me a hell of a lot more money than hanging outside some director's office, waiting half the day just to be told I was too ethnic, too tall, not ethnic enough, too short, or any of the other bullshit excuses they'd come up with to keep a brother's ass off their payroll. The acting industry is far more openly racial than any Alabama redneck I'd ever run across on a country road in the middle of the night. The more comfortable Oz became, the more knowledge he shared, and the more responsibility he assigned me. I've been taking care of things for him a while now.

That's where the problem with Amp started, because he feels he was next in line to be kingpin and I unseated him. We've got that classic love/hate-relationship thing going. I don't have any love for him and he seriously hates the hell out of my ass.

I suddenly remembered what I'd stopped by his place to do. Playfully, I slapped Oz on the back of his neck, "What's up, fool?"

He spoke, pretending to be upset, "Hey boy! Ain't you got no respect for yo elders? And that's Mr. to you."

I was trying to lighten the mood as we walked into the building, "My apolodgies…Mr. Fool," I said. "Hey, you got a sec?"

As we entered the building, he closed the door behind me, "For you…if I don't, I'll steal one from somewhere. What's up?" he asked.

Knowing Amp had already logged his report, I was concerned about how bad he'd screwed up the info on delivery, "Well, I just wanted to drop the latest on that bum, Charlie… Paid him a little visit earlier today."

I could see the reaction on Oz's face, as he replayed the tragedy of that whole Jerome situation from years back in his mind, "Yeah, I heard," he said. "You didn't get done what I sent you to do. That concerns me…for obvious reasons." It was an unspoken warning. There are times that certain things simply don't have to be said. "You know, I treats you like you's my own. But boy…If I's to find out you tryin to screw me…"

It didn't take a split second for me to realize who was shoveling the shit into the flower bed, "Now, Oz, you know damn well there's no point even going there," I interrupted. "Where the hell would you get it in your head that I'd ever even think about rolling on you? All that I am in this cesspool of a town, I owe to you. I've never so much as considered disrespecting you, man." I already knew the answer to my question. "There's only one place you could've gotten that nonsense!"

About then, Amp strolled through the front door, grooving to whatever imaginary tune was playing in his thick-ass head. Before realizing it, I'd leveled off with one of the twin 9mm handguns and, fortunately for him, he eyed my reflection in the full-length mirror on the opposite wall. Before I could throw a nasty thought in his direction, Amp dove to the floor on his belly like the evil snake he was.

CRACK!!! It sounded like a firecracker exploded in one ear as Oz rocked my block with a quick right jab to the temple.

I was rattled, shaking my head, trying to clear the cobwebs, as Oz's voice roared like a lion, chastising me. "Now, you know damn well I don't put up wit that gunplay shit in my house! Don't care who you is, boy…I'll plant yo green country ass!"

I still hadn't regained my composure. Amp was so busy trying to slide his little sleazy hole back out the way he'd crawled in that he hadn't noticed the barn fire Oz had just ignited under me. I managed to steady myself well enough to find a chair at the table I'd rolled across. It felt as though I had gotten hit by the number two express subway train. I didn't even bother to turn and look for him. The back of my neck smoldered as Oz beamed from the same position where he had swatted me like an annoying gnat intruding on a summer picnic.

I could barely manage to speak above a whisper, "I'm sorry, Oz…sorry." Without ever raising my head, I said, "This is the point I offer to extend an explanation, if you trying to hear one." The tension was thick like a big-booty Georgia peach named Katrina I used to roll with back in the day. "I'm just saying…" I felt the sweat fall from my nose as an attempt was made at offering justification, "I mean you're a bad muthafu… You the heaviest hitter in Harlem, but you don't want to be just knocking folk off over a little misunderstanding. The streets aren't what they used to be, Oz."

The words erupted from deep in his gut like a grizzly bear, "That's all you see in this shit…a damn misunderstandin? How a fool misunderstand what it mean to pay me my damn money?' And what the hell you know 'bout how the streets used to be? These streets is mine; ev'ry bitchin one of 'em;

have been since b'fore you found Greyhound 'n stumbled yo hillbilly ass off up in my spot!"

I was a little hurt, a little agitated, and a lot pissed off, but not at Oz. He was only swallowing what had been served. The son of a bitch at the top of my list was that little black snake that had just slimed out the front door. That was the first time I'd ever seen Oz so pissed. Maybe it just seemed he was more pissed than usual because that's the first time his anger had ever been directed at me. It wasn't a welcomed feeling.

"What you tryin to explain? You screwed up. I can see that for my damn self."

I didn't say anything until Oz finally relaxed enough to take a seat across the table from where I now sat. The main reason being that, if he suddenly decided I was due for more thug guidance, my chair was positioned closer to the door. Then came the realization that no matter how close we'd become, beneath all the care and concern, to him I was only half a step from being just another fool on the street.

I summoned enough courage, "All I was doing...trying to look out for your...for you."

He didn't even try to mask his anger, "Boy, I been in da game longer than you been livin. Hell, it was me that brung you in!" he reminded. "What the hell make you think I need lookin out for?"

"Ok, Oz," I said. "That bum Charlie owes you. If you axe his ass, where's your money going to come from? If you knock off everybody that owes you, sooner or later there won't be anybody left to pay you your shit."

"But if they know they gone get visited, that won't be a problem no way," Oz said. "Who the hell is you to talk 'bout schoolin me on my shit anyhow? You must done forgot who the hell I am."

"No Oz, how could..." Just then, Oz's cell phone chimed. As he answered, I was playing through my mind the encounter with Charlie this morning and figuring on stopping by his place after I left Oz...to wish him good night.

I heard Oz say as he turned his back, "That'll be fine. No, I don't got a problem wit that. My only problem is when I'm made out to look like a fool and feelin like I been taken," he said. "Just leave it with the fella out front." He gingerly pressed end on the cell phone and whispered while walking away without turning to look in my direction, "You got angels…and a whole lot of 'em."

I wasn't able to breathe normally for at least three minutes after Oz had left the room. It was another moment before the thought entered my head of just how dangerous a situation I'd just escaped. That realization brought me even closer to the conclusion that, before too much longer, a certain fellow and I would occupy the same space. At this point, however, I just needed to get to a place where the atmosphere was a little more pleasant. Where I could empty my head and fill my gut.

As I passed from the rear of the building into the lobby on my way out, I paused for a word with Tony, Oz's general-purpose jack of all trades. Tony wore a number of hats, depending on the disposition of our employer.

I quickly scanned the room for any signs of Oz, "What's up, Tone?"

Without breaking his rhythm while opening cartons of cigarettes to fill one of the two machines in the lobby, "What's kickin young blood?" he asked.

I questioned, as if I didn't already know, "Did the old man pass through this way?"

"I thought you boys was done talkin," Tony said. "He came through couple seconds ago, asked me which way Amp went. I told him when I's comin in the door, Amp shot past me like a rat wit his tail on fire."

I mumbled, more to myself, "Interesting choice of words."

"What's that?"

Dismissing the comment, I replied, "Oh, nothing."

Tony walked over and leaned against the other machine. Looking at me, his face appeared as though it turned to granite. "That was a damn gutsy thang you done."

Not thinking, I asked, "What did I do?"

He wore a smirk that I couldn't quite interpret, "That shit wit Charlie today." Tony leaned closer and whispered as if trying to keep a secret from the walls. "That was him called while Oz 'n you was in the back, him 'n couple o' his boys."

I asked, "How'd you know? I mean, he called Oz's cell phone."

"Yeah, I know. He was up here when he called. Left a envelop Oz picked up on his way out. You know, ain't much go on 'round here don't find its way past me 'fore too long," he said.

Trying to make light of the situation, I said, "It wasn't all that serious."

He passed to get another box of cigarettes from the buggy, "Like I said, damn gutsy thang," Tony repeated.

I wondered what Oz had shared with Tony, but wouldn't dare question him. Knowing Tony, he wouldn't tell me anyway. Probably say something like that ain't a question you need to be asking, "Well, I'm out of here, Tone."

As the door swung closed behind me, "Take it easy, young blood," Tony said.

I was dialing the number as I started the car "Hello, Moms. Yeah, I was calling to let you guys know I'm on my way up. Is Poppy there? No ma'am. That's okay. Just tell him I'll be by in a few minutes. Anything you need me to bring? Sure, not a problem. I'll pick some up at the store on the corner. See you in a bit." Pulling out into traffic, the side of Amp's truck could be seen in my rearview mirror, "Damned weasel."

Before realizing it, I was cursing aloud and almost jammed the brake but I thought about Moms and Poppy waiting for me to bring the potatoes she'd asked me to pick up. I really needed some tranquility.

I mumbled at the mirror while accelerating into the flow of traffic, "There will be time for us to dance soon enough, mister man."

Thoughts of a much anticipated run-in with Amp had me seeing red as I cruised up Frederick Douglass Blvd. on the way to see Moms and Poppy for our dinner appointment. Needing a little extra time to calm myself, I elected to take the scenic route to Broadway by crossing over at 125th. It always interested me to see the vendors peddling goods from their portable storefronts on the sidewalks at either side of the street. I reasoned with my inner self as to why I'd never seen more than the marquee from the street when passing the famous Apollo Theater.

I was having a debate with myself, "That's a true piece of Black American history not many of us get a chance to see, and you pass the place at least three or four times a week without so much as getting out your damn car." My conscience scolded me, "Come to think of it, where in the City have you been?"

"I'm not a damn tourist," I said aloud, to no one in particular.

Minutes later, I found myself in a full-on debate with nobody, "There's the Empire State Building…the Statue of Liberty…Central Park…let's see…"

Before I realized it, I was in a full-fledged argument with me. "I told you, I'm not a damn tourist!" I yelled.

The entire situation was honestly a little unsettling. As if I expected to find someone, I looked over in the passenger seat, and turned to check the rear when my cell phone's ring startled me. *BBBRRRIIINNNNGGG, BBBRRRIIINNNGGG!*

"Yeah! I mean, what's up Moms? No ma'am, I thought you were somebody else. I was expecting a call. No ma'am, I don't have an agent yet."

An extensive period of time passed with Moms quizzing me about life's happenings for more than forty-seven minutes while I made my way up toward their apartment building. The feeling of being a bit annoyed crept up my spine and smacked me in the back of my head.

I interrupted the battery of questions, "Have you guys started dinner? Oh yeah, what was it that Poppy asked me to bring? Never mind, I just remembered. No, that's not a problem; I'm pulling up at the store on the corner now. All right, I'll be up in a sec."

I double-parked and ran inside the store to pick up a couple cans of those biscuits Poppy had grown so fond of since I'd introduced him to them, and a small bag of Irish potatoes.

The clerk and I had become buddies, of sorts, because I was constantly in and out picking up knickknacks for Moms and Poppy, "What's up Julio, you got what I need?"

"Hey Willie, ya look ova in da cooler? Let me know if it ain't none in there, 'cause I keeps some extras fo ya in back," he said.

"I appreciate that, because you know how Poppy gets when he hasn't had his Butter-Me-Nots," I joked.

"But I thought I be seein his wife buyin corn-muffin mix all da time?" Julio asked.

I explained to the exceptionally curious store attendant, "Well, I like Moms' cornbread and Poppy has taken a liking to these biscuits, so they cook both when I'm over."

"Fo e'ry meal?" he asked.

"Almost every meal," I confirmed.

"Not my wife," Julio stated.

I was playfully giving him grief about being almost sixty years old and already divorced six times, "Could be the reason you don't have a wife, you think?" I asked.

"I can cook fo my damn self." He said.

I decided it better to end our little verbal sparring session, "All right you old cuss, I'm out," I concluded.

Something in his tone told me more than the words he'd just spoken, and I had learned to listen to the things people don't say but only wished they had the nerve to. Julio was a decent fellow, but nobody to play around with. A hard life has a tendency to do that to a guy.

When I exited the store, there was a traffic officer walking away from the Impala. I immediately noticed a slip of paper beneath the wiper blade on the driver's side. Just what I need; to spend a whole day downtown in a damn courtroom with a bunch of folks agitated at the fact they have to take off work to be there. People who only become more agitated when dealing with the complacent attitudes of the assholes benefiting from the wasted use of our tax dollars.

There was a little bitterness in my voice, "Excuse me, officer." My attitude changed immediately upon noticing it was a female. A damn good-looking female officer from where I stood. "Excuse me, miss."

She slowly turned in the direction of the sound of my voice. "Yes, may I help you, sir?"

Damn, I thought to myself. The view from the front was almost as stirring as the landscape from the rear. "Now those are tax dollars well spent," I commented.

She took a step in my direction before asking, "Excuse me?"

Realizing I'd mistakenly spoken the thought aloud, I quickly corrected. "I said, I've only been here for a minute."

"Well, the sign says *NO PARKING*. Not even for a minute," she said.

I then playfully questioned, "Why so hostile?"

She retorted, "Because, it's a hostile-ass world. Is there a point you want to make?"

I was a little put off. "Damn lady, who done put you through...?"

"That's Officer Lady to you, sir," she said. "And *who done put me through* isn't any of your business."

I was somewhat shaken at her comment. But, tuning in to what she wasn't saying, I thought to myself; *what she's voicing is, back off. Keep your distance, and don't get any ideas. What she means is that she's been hurt and is having a difficult time dealing with some unresolved issues.*

I went out on a limb; "It may not be my business, but I am willing to listen, if you want to talk about it."

With a little less of an edge in her voice, "What? I mean, what are you talking about?" she asked.

With the expression of a concerned therapist, "I'm talking about whatever it is *you need to talk about*," I commented. "At least, that is, I am willing to listen."

She questioned, from behind something that could've almost been misconstrued as a smile. By now, all abrasiveness was gone from her voice. The tone of the conversation had changed to one of compassion. "And just how do you know there's anything I *need* to talk about?"

With the certainty of a long-time personal acquaintance, I said, "Because you just told me."

Trying to reconstruct the defenses she'd unknowingly allowed to be demolished, the officer said, "Maybe I did; and maybe I didn't."

"How long did you guys date?" I asked.

She stiffened a little. "What?"

Becoming much more relaxed, I repeated myself. "How long did the two of you date?"

She took a step to my right. "How you know we not married?"

While removing the citation from beneath the wiper blade as I opened my car door, "No ring; no mark where a ring once was," I replied before factually stating, "Listen, I'd love to stay and chat but I've already gotten a ticket for being double-parked."

The officer walked over and took the citation from my hand. "Don't worry about this one," she said. Writing her number on the back of the slip of paper with *AT 116th STREET NEAR CITY COLLEGE* in parentheses and passing it to me again, "Keep an eye out for the signs."

As I glanced at the phone number, I remarked, "You never did tell me your name."

"Yes, I did." Looking me up and down with the most beautiful hazel eyes, she simply tapped her name tag, which read: *OFFICER E. LADY*, before gracefully turning and walking to her patrol car.

I stood with one foot on the ground and the other inside the floorboard of the car while looking back over my shoulder, watching as she proceeded down the hill, turned left on 125th Street, and drove out of sight.

I climbed in the car, crossed over Broadway, and parked in the rear of Sam and Eunice's huge horseshoe-shaped apartment building that consumed about ninety percent of the block, "Damn." What else could I say? "Damn, damn, damn."

3

Getting Acquainted

When I passed the rear guard station, there was a security officer I didn't recognize so I acknowledged him while hurrying to catch the security door before it closed behind the last person who'd entered.

"What's going on, man?"

He interrupted my dash to the door, "Who ya comin to see?"

I remarked without realizing the scowl on my face at having missed the opportunity to enter, "Do what? My Moms and Poppy," I said. "Can you buzz me in?"

With his voice full of sarcasm, he asked, "Don't ya got a key?"

"No. I don't."

The make-believe police officer smarted back, "Well, I don't know ya. Ne'er seen ya b'fore."

A bit annoyed, I remarked, "Hell, I don't know you either!"

The guy sitting next to him was on the phone with his back to the entrance. "Hold the line a minute," I heard him say. He rolled the chair back a few feet to get a good look. "Hey, what's up Willie?" Tapping the new guy on the shoulder, he said, "John, you can let him through, he's cool."

John looked straight at me and said, "I don't know him, and he ain't got no key. All residents o' the buildin s'pose to have a key."

Fortunately for him, I still had that big-booty badge-wearing beauty from a few minutes earlier on my mind, "Can you just call up...?"

About that time, dude on the phone wheeled his rolling chair across behind John and pressed the door buzzer, "Have a good one, Will."

As I pulled on the door and proceeded to stroll through, I was beaming straight at John, "Thanks Kenny, take it easy." I said.

The new guy called after me, as I made my way down the corridor, "Next time, ya better have yo key or ya gotta sign in like the rest o' the visitors."

I yelled back at him without breaking stride, "I've been in and out of this place without a problem since before you thought about working that bitching desk. Take a hint: *I'm not a damn visitor.*"

With the complex constructed into the side of a small hill, entering the building from the back actually put you in what was recognized as the basement, given that it was below ground level when entering from the front. Approaching the elevator, I was startled by the echo of my cell phone. *BBBRRRIIINNNGGG, BBBRRRIIINNNGGG.*

I was immediately concerned because Sam never used the phone unless he had business or there was something wrong. Says he prefers to see a person's eyes when he talks to them. That way he can tell when they lying, "Yeah, uh, hello... Is everything all right Poppy?"

"I's callin ta find out if ya need help or somethin. We ain't know if somebody done jumped yo li'l skinny ass," he laughed.

"No Poppy," I assured. "Matter o' fact, I'm getting on the elevator right now. I'll be up before you can hang up the phone."

"Well, when ya gits here, me and Mommy, we's got a s'prise fo ya." he said.

"What's up Poppy? Now you guys know how I feel about surprises." I said.

Sam tried to play it off. "Oh, it ain't nothin ta git bent outta shape 'bout."

The elevator stopped on the fourth floor and I stepped into the hallway a few feet from their apartment door while asking, "What's the surprise Poppy? Give up the goods, or else I'm just going to get back on the elevator and take your biscuits…"

Once off the elevator, I looked up at the epitome of beauty standing in the doorway of Sam and Eunice's apartment. I stood a few feet from the door, speechless, entranced by the most attractive creature on who you'd ever want to lay eyes.

Trying to not display a total lack of composure, I asked, "And…you are?"

"I'm Cherish…Sam and Eunice's oldest; born year before Junior. You met him already." She extended her hand, "I'm in from L.A.… Mom and Sam told me so much 'bout you."

Disregarding the small bag in my right hand containing Poppy's biscuits, I reached to greet her, "Well they didn't tell me enough about you," causing the bag to fall to the floor.

"Hey! Ya bet'er watch dat," Poppy yelled from inside. "Don't let her make ya miss out on dinner."

His comment brought me back to their apartment.

"Speaking of dinner, what's in the pots?" I asked.

Cherish suggested, "I can take up yo plate, if you like?"

I questioned her while thinking that would be the icing on the cake if she could dirty the pots half as good as Poppy, "You cooked?"

"Ha!" Sam yelled, "Only thang dat girl cookin come wit micr'wave d'rections on da damn box."

Moms finally spoke up to chastise him, "All right Sam; she jest gettin here. Don't make her not wanna stay."

I replied, before turning to face Cherish without thinking of the implication, "Well, when you find everything in one package Poppy, most of the time you can't afford the product," I said prior to asking their daughter, "How long are you staying?"

"I don't know yet," she said. "Just taking a break from Cali."

Trying to prolong conversation, "What is it you do out there?" I asked.

She displayed an expression that stated her preference would be to find another subject. "Oh, I work in the entertainment industry."

Moms chimed in. "William, ain't that the same thang you does?"

Now, I really wanted to change the subject, "Yeah, something like that Moms. But there are a number of different jobs in the entertainment industry."

"I know you been in town a few years, but mom said you work all the time with the acting and stuff. Did you at least take time to see the sights?" Cherish offered. "Maybe I can show you 'round."

I was glad at the opportunity to explore another topic of discussion, "Actually, I haven't; I don't do the tourist thing."

"If you into acting, why you end up in New York? This city geared more for modeling, it seems," she commented.

Now she's going way too deep, I thought to myself. More direct than I realized, I said, "At the time I left home, I could only afford a bus ticket to New York."

Eunice spoke up, to keep from feeling left out, "But he sho done good fo his self," she said, "...doin bet'er 'n a lotta folk born 'n raised right here in the city."

Poppy input his contribution for what it was worth, "Willie doin a damn sight bet'er 'n yo no-good li'l brother ass."

Eunice spoke up, coming to her baby boy's defense in his absence, "All right, Sam. Don't start yo shit agin."

"Yeah Willie, what's stoppin you from hoppin on out to Cali now?" Cherish pressed. "I done met a few people; might help you to have some connections."

I thought we were beyond this subject. "I've got plenty good reason to stake my claim here in the Apple," I said. "Besides, I'm not too crazy about being someplace where as soon as you get your feet on solid ground it falls from under you."

"Watcha mean?" Cherish asked.

Without elaborating, "Earthquakes," I said.

Cherish's defenses automatically went up. "Oh get real. How many folk you ever known killed by a earthquake?"

"I've never known anybody killed by a lion either, but that doesn't mean I want to take my little happy ass over to Africa and run around the jungle trying to make friends with one," I said.

Sam spoke up, muffling his laughter, "Well, he gotta damn good point dere."

Cherish snapped, "Oh Sam, you just shut up. You old gray-haired fool!"

Sam cut his eyes at her, "Don't lets da gray fool ya, sista!"

As she walked around the table from where she'd been standing, "And just what the hell you gone do?" Cherish questioned, "What the fuc…"

I cut in over the two of them yelling at each other, "All right, Moms, I'll call you tomorrow," when silence suddenly filled the previously noisy apartment.

In an almost pleading tone, "But I thought you's stayin fo dinner?" Eunice asked.

I uttered the first thing that came to mind in order to allow reason to excuse myself. "No ma'am, I just remembered an appointment."

One thing I always had a problem with, even as a kid, was people arguing. I could remember how my parents would constantly go at each other like two pit-bulls. Before I was old enough to run out the house into the nearby fields, I'd hide in the closet with a blanket covering my head, which is where my mom would find me asleep after all the commotion had subsided.

I walked out Sam and Eunice's apartment to the sound of more yelling. Now, the three of them were arguing about whose fault it was that I had abruptly left. It didn't matter. I was still at the point of trying to shake the thought, or should I say, the sight of Cherish. She was definitely a looker, but I have a serious problem with anybody who disrespects their parents the way she did Sam. I guess it's a southern thing. But she sure was a looker.

Just about the time the elevator door opened in the basement, my cell phone brought me back to reality. *BBBRRRIIINNNGGG, BBBRRRIIINNNGGG.* I reached for the phone clipped to my hip, already prepared to defend myself against the onslaught of questions from Moms and Poppy so I wasn't my normal bright self.

"Yeah, what's up?" I answered.

"Hey Bill, its Cherish. I was just calling to apologize for running you off," she said.

"You must have the wrong number," I responded.

"This is Bill that just left Eunice's?" she asked.

Through my annoyance I questioned, "Who the hell is Bill? You know my damn name; it's Willie, and what you want? I told you I have an appointment. Don't give yourself so much credit."

"Why you trippin?" she asked.

"I'm not the one who's tripping. That seems to be your area of expertise with all your West Coast know-it-all bull-shit." I snapped. "I don't know what you do or how you go about it, but that doesn't give you the right to be up in your dad's house breaking him down the way you were."

"This my mama house," Cherish stated.

I snapped back, "The hell it is! It took both of them to bring your ass about, and it takes both of them to run that damn house. And they do just fine until one of their kids bring you all's asses around stirring shit up."

Noticeably bothered, she asked, "Hold on, now. You don't know a damn thing 'bout me. How you gonna cut me up like that?"

In the process of trying to calm myself as I passed the guard's station, I stated, "I've just got a problem with seeing anybody disrespect their parents the way you just did. That man deserves a damn sight more respect than you give him."

The freshman guard posed from behind a veil of sarcasm, "Ya leavin a'ready?"

Though it was unlike me to do so, I viscously remarked as I'd not realized the degree of irritation being harnessed, "No, I'm going to pick up your mama from the soup kitchen."

I had forgotten Cherish was even on the phone, "What you say 'bout Eunice?" she asked. "How you gone jump all over me 'bout disrespectin my dad and then come outta your face with some shit like that 'bout Eunice?" she demanded.

"I wasn't talking about your mom. Fact is, I wasn't talking to you at all," I said.

Suddenly, she was a little more pleasant. "Look, I don't even know how we got off on the wrong foot. Can't you just come back upstairs and have dinner? I know from talkin to mom you come and have Sunday dinner every week, so I know you ain't scheduled nothin else for today."

"You know, I don't think I like you very much. We've known each other less than half an hour and you've already disrespected your dad, insulted me, and now you're calling me a liar," I said.

Now, she was playing along. It was obvious Cherish knew I had made up the whole appointment story to get out the apartment. "No, I ain't callin you a lie. I just figure you can reschedule the appointment for later or another day. Tell 'em it's a family emergency or somethin.'"

"All right," I conceded. "Tell Moms and Poppy I'll be back up in a few minutes, but you'll probably have to buzz me in. The new guard and I didn't get off to as good a start as you and me... *He doesn't look as good.* See you in a sec."

I had barely passed the guard station on my way out when I concluded the phone conversation and immediately turned to re-enter through the security door. As I approached, John turned away pretending he was preoccupied so he'd have an excuse to not buzz me through. Knowing he had seen me, I simply walked past the counter at the guard station and took a position in front of the door. I stood there, percolating like a fresh batch of coffee until I caught a glimpse of him snickering from the corner of my eye.

Calmly, I approached the counter and asked, "Could you please buzz me in?" He ignored me without so much as even turning to acknowledge my presence. "Excuse me," I repeated. "Can you buzz me in?"

With a condescending smirk on his face, "My bad man, did ya say something?" he asked.

Just as I was about to leap over the counter and pounce on his little wormy ass, an elderly tenant came through with two small bags while fumbling with her keys.

Reaching for them, "Let me get that door for you, ma'am," I said.

She was somewhat reluctant at first, but then handed over her key ring after looking me over from head to toe, "That's such a sweet thing. Thank you, young man."

I cut my eyes at John while opening the door and offering to carry the woman's bags; glaring at him as I passed through the doorway, I said. "Not a problem, ma'am." And whispered at John while entering, "Naaawww, punk bitch, I didn't say a damn thing,"

The woman asked, "What was dat, son?"

"Oh, I was just asking if you'd like me to carry these bags to your apartment for you, ma'am," I said.

She was still not eager to trust a stranger, "Oh no, thank you; I can manage from here," and asked to confirm, "You must not be from New York?"

I answered, stepping onto the elevator as I pressed the button for the fourth floor, "No ma'am, not originally." Then I asked, "What floor ma'am?"

As the doors closed, "The sec...um, the seventeenth," she replied.

I stood to the front of the elevator for the short ride up to the fourth floor thinking to myself how this woman was going so far out of her way because a hard life had taught her not to trust anybody. She was in the opposite corner behind me with a death grip on her handbag that would put an eagle to shame. Neither of us spoke a word until the elevator came to a stop and the door opened.

As I stepped off, I commented without turning back, "Ma'am, the most difficult place to be in life is when you don't know where you are."

I was honestly not sure if what I'd said was intended more for the old lady or for myself. Before I could take the few steps from the elevator to their apartment, Moms' and Poppy's door swung open with Cherish standing in the way.

"Thought I was gone have to come down and rescue you," she said.

Without considering the fact Sam and Eunice could've been within earshot, my voice was filled with insinuation when I asked, "Then who would rescue me from you?"

In the short time between me leaving and coming back, Cherish had changed into a pink tube-type blouse and a sexy denim miniskirt. Before I realized it, a quick innocent peek had matured into a full-blown stare.

Sashaying back to the table a few feet from the door, "You drop somethin?" Cherish asked.

Scanning the front of the apartment for Moms and Poppy, "It's an old player's injury," I commented. "In the presence of a body like yours my jaw has a tendency to drop without warning."

I guessed there was something to how she'd looked at me and seemed to go out of her way to come into contact on occasion throughout my visit. It goes back to hearing the things people don't say.

Cherish stood up and stepped closer, "And, what exactly is the remedy for a condition like that?"

I answered with our lips nearly touching while her breathing grew deeper and heavier as our faces moved even closer, "Well, there's no documented cure, but it seems to help when I find a way to simply keep the jaw occupied."

Poppy's timing proved good for all the wrong reasons, "Billy Boy! Dat you dat come in? Cherish, who it twas dat opened da doe? I ain't heared nobody knock."

Cherish retreated before Sam made it up the hallway from their bedroom. "I got the door dad. It's Willie. He changed his mind and decided to stay for dinner," she replied.

Still unaware of his intrusion, "Well I's sho glad ya changed yo mind. Now all dis grub don't gotta be throwed out." Sam said. "Eunice, Willie back. Come on outch here so we can git back ta grubbin."

Cherish walked past me on the way to the stove. "I got your plate," she said. "I'm gone fix you up somethin real special."

While taking a seat in my usual place, "Not too much; I'm not all that hungry," I said.

Sam shouted toward their bedroom, "Eunice, is ya eatin?"

Moms yelled, "Be dere in jest a second!"

Moments later, Cherish returned and placed my plate on the table in front of me. She leaned over so far that I thought cleavage was on the menu. Hers were the only biscuits I could think about at the moment. It was a game to her, but if she knew how worked up I had become her butt would have been hiding under that table instead of prancing around it.

She took a seat directly across from me before stating, "Maybe after dinner we can go out for dessert."

I tried to compose myself as Moms approached the table and Poppy stood to offer the blessing, "Our Father, we grac'ously thanks ya," he began.

In the middle of Poppy's saying grace, I felt Cherish's foot slide into the chair between my legs. About the time Sam finished his prayer, her foot found my manhood at full attention.

"Oh, yes!" she blurted out. "So thankful for the abundant supply!"

Looking at his daughter, "Damn, dat's first time I e'er heard somethin from ya durin da blessin," Sam commented.

She responded, peering at me with eyes of invitation. *"It's just that there's so much to be thankful for."*

Eunice stood next to Sam, "That's right, don't ne'er fo'get ta be thankful fo all dere is baby," she reminded. "Good Lord sho is still in da blessin bidness, ain't He?"

When they turned toward the stove to take up their plates, I playfully mouthed to Cherish, "You know you going straight to hell for that."

The four of us sat making small talk for a little more than an hour while we ate before Cherish mentioned a traffic citation she'd received on the way to the airport before leaving Los Angeles. Immediately, I remembered the officer from earlier and tried to recall where I had put the ticket with her phone number on the back.

"So, what, were you speeding?" I asked.

"Naw, badge gave me some bullsh..." She paused; looking at Moms and Poppy, and then glancing over at me, "Dude gave me some crap about a improper lane change." she said.

I pretended to be interested, but my mind had wandered off past City College down at 116th Street, "Well, how much did it set you back?"

Rolling her eyes toward the ceiling, "It ain't cost me nothin. Not yet, but I'm gone take care of it when I get back to L.A.," she said.

Sam spoke up, "Be sho ya don't furgit ta go fix thangs right when ya gits back 'cause it be bet'er if'n ya don't wait fo da cote date."

Cherish made eye contact with me, and I commented before realizing it, "For some reason, I don't think the date to take care of that ticket will have anything to do with a court."

"Yep, I thank I knows what ya talkin 'bout," Sam said.

Both Cherish and I were a bit surprised and replied simultaneously, "You do?"

Sam explained with confidence, but was clueless as to what Cherish meant, "Yep, somma dem whitties I use ta works 'round be all da time talkin 'bout dat Pre-paid Legal stuff. Cherish, I ain't knowed ya done gone 'n joined up wit dat bunch. Dey says if 'n ya gits a tickit or most any kinda trouble wit da man, ya jest call dem Legal folks 'n dey takes care o' da whole thang. Ya ain't eben gotta go 'fore no judge."

I knew he had totally missed the mark, but I was feeling mischievous, "So Cherish, do you have to call or go see them about the citation?"

She cut her eyes at me and frowned, "I prob'ly have to drop in for a minute or two, ain't nothin serious."

"It a'ways ser'ous when it come ta da law," Poppy remarked. "Jest be sho 'n git it took care of soon as ya can."

"Yeah Cherish, soon as you can," I sneered. "Might require you to *go down* and do a *little lip service*...you know, explain yourself."

She ignored my comment and changed the subject, "How long b'fore you pull up to go back to The Village?"

"I don't know, a few minutes. What you need?" I asked.

"A ride," she stated.

I commented, hoping she was going in another direction given the fact I still needed to make that phone call and stop in the area of City College, which was only about fifteen blocks away, "Are you going anywhere in particular? I'm taking the West Side Highway."

Moms asked, to remind Cherish and me of the fact she was still at the table, "You done finish eatin?"

"I got the dishes mom," Cherish said. "Willie, you can help me."

"How you know I don't have something to do?" I asked.

Moms handed me her plate as she walked past, "Imma git me a shower 'cause I's tired. Good night Will; sees you later."

Reaching to give her a big hug, "Good night, Moms. I'll see you later, much love," I said.

Cherish dried her hands and walked over to hug her mom, "Good night, mom. Where Sam sneak off to?"

Eunice grunted, "He been in the room fo ten minutes ar'eady. Y'all too busy flirtin wit each other to notice."

"Moms, where'd you get that?" I asked.

She just looked at me and smiled, "I's jest old, I ain't dead. I's y'alls age b'fore too ya knows."

Cherish pretended to swat Eunice on the butt with the dish towel, "Just get your little grown self in there and take a shower."

As she headed into their bedroom, "You stayin here t'night?" Moms asked.

Cherish stood speechless for a moment, "Now, mom, where else would I be stayin?"

Eunice reappeared in the doorway of their room, "This the key to the secur'ty doe to git in the buildin and these two silver ones opens the doe to the 'partment. This big one's fo the dead bolt. I'll leave off the safety chain."

"What you sayin ma?" Cherish asked, "You puttin me on the street my first night back?"

Moms smirked, "Oh, I's sho you ain't gonna be left on da street. But I gives you the keys jest in case you figure on goin out. Likes I said, Imma git a shower 'n goes to bed."

Cherish teased, "There was more to that look than gettin a shower and goin to bed. I saw you."

Eunice chuckled, as she disappeared into the bathroom, "Well, likes I says, I's old; I ain't dead."

I called to her, as she was coming up the hall from near the bathroom, "I'm done with the dishes Cherish. You want me to put them away?"

While not-so-innocently brushing my butt as she reached for the dish towel, "No, I got it. You done plenty for a guest. I'll dry 'em an take care 'o the rest," Cherish said.

"So, you never said to where you needed a ride," I reminded.

She had an unmistakable look in her eyes, "I don't know, maybe to the Village."

I was leaning against the counter, playing stupid, "You know somebody down there?"

Cherish backed up until her butt rubbed against my zipper. Looking over her shoulder, she said with a devilish grin, "Well, there is somebody down in the Village I'm thinkin I might wanna get to know."

Trying not to laugh, "Is somebody expecting you? Did you call to let them know you were coming?" I asked.

From behind a pretentious frown, "Oh, stop play'in! What I gotta do, beg, to get you to take me to your place?" she asked.

"Never actually considered that," I said. "Begging might be rather interesting."

She ran her index finger down my zipper and whispered, "I'll beg, if that's what it takes. But you gotta promise to tie me up first."

I felt a chill run down my spine, "Damn girl! You're kind of freaky, aren't you?" The comment registered louder than intended.

She took a step in the opposite direction, turned, and said in a stern, but still erotic voice, "Why is it that when a woman see somethin she want and ain't afraid to go after it, that make her a freak or a ho? But when a man see somethin he want, if he go for it, that just mean he gettin his mack on."

It was obvious my comment bothered her more than she was willing to display. Normally, she would have tongue lashed a brother and straight verbally cut him to shreds. Then I realized the only thing that turned her on more than a good stiff argument was a good *stiff one* between her legs.

4

Filling the Void

This was the break for which I'd been waiting and I moved toward the door of Mom's and Poppy's apartment, "I guess I've overstayed my welcome."

Her voice fell like a feather on cotton, "No! I mean, you fine," Cherish said.

"Look, I didn't mean that comment the way it sounded. I've just got a lot on my mind right now. Tomorrow's going to be a long day," I explained. "It's getting late. I better be going."

By the time she could make it around the table to where I stood, the door was unlocked and already partially open. I gave her a peck on the cheek and said good night before starting over to the elevator. After pressing the button to go downstairs, my mind had moved ahead and was already in the Impala traveling down Broadway to 116th Street. Still trying to remember where I had put the parking ticket with Officer Lady's number on the back, I stepped onto the elevator and pushed the button for the basement. As the door began to close, I was thinking how I'd just dodged a serious bullet at dinner when an arm was thrust through the opening.

Cherish stepped in as the door retracted. "Thought the least I could do was walk you to the car."

"That's okay. You really don't have to do that," I told her. What I really wanted to say was, *Can't you take a hint? I've got business that doesn't include your fine ass.*

As the elevator started down, she asked, "You on your way home?"

Knowing I had already told her before leaving Sam and Eunice's apartment, I played along. "Yeah, I've got to get started pretty early in the morning."

As we stopped on the second floor, she asked, "Where you live in the Village?"

The door opened and four Hispanic teenagers came in with a small radio playing music to which neither Cherish nor I could understand the words. We were both quietly watching the new passengers as the two females seemed to recklessly throw themselves at their boyfriends. The couple closest to us was oblivious to our presence as they quickly engaged in a tongue-wrestling match. That rather uncomfortable display lasted until the door opened for us to get off in the basement.

As we let the kids pass out the elevator first, "Near Bleeker and Houston," I said.

Cherish seemed a bit confused, "Excuse me?"

"Where I live in the Village; you asked on the elevator," I reminded.

Approaching the Impala just outside the exit as I remotely unlocked the driver's door from a few feet away, she continued, walking around to the passenger's side of the car, "That's supposed to be a nice area, I hear. Lotta artists and them types down there. Some real nice buildings too. Mind if I sit for a minute?" she asked.

I was so ready to be gone but kept my cool with as sincere a smile as I could fake, "No. Not at all," I said.

The remote was pressed twice to unlock the passenger's door. Just then, the interior light came on and my curiosity was put to rest. There was the parking ticket with Officer Lady's number on the back about which I'd been wondering most of the evening.

Unfortunately, Cherish saw the citation in the console as she opened the door to sit down. Having recognized the legal form, "You ain't tell me you got one too," she said.

I dismissed her comment, "Well, like yours, it's not a big deal."

She cut her eyes at me, "Like mine, huh?"

I pretended it was a non-issue, "You know what I mean." I said. "I'd forgotten all about it."

Cherish picked the ticket up to take a closer look, "Why, you just got this earlier today, right about the same time you came over."

I commented, gently removing the paper with my thumb and index finger while hoping she hadn't noticed the writing on the back illuminated in the dome light, "Yeah, on the corner in front of the building."

Mimicking her father, she said, "Be sho 'n takes care o' it soon as ya can 'fore it goes ta cote."

Displaying my disinterest in her feeble attempt at humor after having located the phone number, now, I was more eager than ever to get away from the good badness I couldn't seem to shake, "Yeah right, sure thing," I said.

The citation was placed back into the console when I turned to Cherish, about the time my cell phone rang. *BBBRRRIIINNNGGG, BBBRRRIIINNNGGG.* When I answered, I was a bit surprised to hear Moms' on the line.

She said, "Tell Cherish she left and ain't latch da doe. She need to git her mind back 'nside her head. This ain't the place to be doin no shit like that."

"Yes ma'am," I responded.

Moms eventually asked, "She wit you?"

As I suddenly felt a slight tug at my zipper, "Yes ma'am," I answered.

Before I could intervene, the fly of my boxers was open and I felt the warmth of Cherish's hand searching until it discovered the fleshy treasure she was seeking. There came an involuntary cough.

"You a'ight?" Eunice asked.

I was caught totally off guard. Cherish just looked at me and smiled while holding the index finger of her free hand up to pursed lips, signifying I should keep quiet. Part of me wanted to stop her. The part of me in which she was most interested at that moment had no thoughts of doing so.

"YYeess, uh-hum, yes ma'am," I responded.

Eunice spoke from a place of motherly concern, "Hopes you ain't comin down wit nothin."

I said, in agreement while wishing she would just get off the phone, "Yes, ma'am. I hope so too. I mean, I hope I'm not coming down with anything either."

"You know, to catch cold this time o' year, the worst thang. Seem they's worse 'n colds you catch durin death o' winter," she said.

I was trying to keep my composure. "Yes ma'am. I take the vitamins and stuff you gave me."

Just before conceding to the thought of the unthinkable things I'd began thinking, it dawned on me where I was, and who I was with. This is my godmother's baby girl. We're in the parking area behind the building where the people live who've taken me as one of their own.

"Stop, no…no, stop," I mumbled.

Cherish continued pawing at my zipper as if I hadn't said anything, "Tell me you're not thinking what I think you're thinking and I'll leave you alone."

I softly yelled, "Stop…stop… Dammit, stop! I can't do this!"

She was a little shaken. "What the hell's your damn problem?"

"Nothing," I said abruptly. "There's not a problem."

Leaning over with her hand on my shoulder she whispered, "But, I thought that's what you wanted."

My head was laid back on the headrest. "Yes; that is... No! That's not!" I sprang up like a soldier snapping to attention.

"What the hell goin on wit you? One minute you into me and getting all worked up, the next, you bouncin off the damn walls tryin to get away from me like I'm a disease or somethin," she said.

"It's not you," I assured. "Well, it is you; but not the way you think." I know she was confused because I was confusing the hell out of my damn self. I was pressed against the door like a nervous puppy. "I keep trying to get past the thought of you being my sister. I mean, you're not my sister like blood and shit, but your mama is my Moms. That's how close we've gotten...and your dad."

"You mean Sam," she said.

I was already agitated, "No, I mean your damn dad!" I said. "Give the man some bitching credit, why don't you?"

"How you gone crawl all up in my shit 'bout somethin you don't even know?" she snapped. There was a long pause. "Wait, don't get it mixed up. The situation with me and Sam...well, my dad...it is what it always have been and it ain't just gone be different 'cause you showed up. But it don't got nothin to do with what's goin on right now...at least, not far as I'm concerned. It ain't like we no kin for real."

"I'm feeling you on that, but you have to understand when I say; commitment is a really big deal to me," I said.

Looking like I had just punched her in the neck, Cherish held her hand up to stop me from talking, "Now wait a minute; you got it going on and all that but I ain't said nothin about no commitment. You musta took me wrong when I told you to come out to L.A. and all. I just got things workin good for me out there. I'm down for some fun and good times, maybe even a *good hard time* when the mood hit me, but I ain't wit that livin together like no husband and wife shit."

"Where the hell did you get that?" I asked. *I'm not trying to be anybody's damned husband.* You never heard me spit some stupid shit like that out my damn mouth."

She sat back in the seat and sighed, "So what you saying?"

Feeling I was no longer in any immediate danger, I relaxed a bit, "Well, I'm going to be straight with you."

"I would hope so," she said. "Wouldn't expect you to give it to me no other way…straight and hard."

I was trying to figure out the best way to approach the subject, "Now, I know you've heard a lot about me from Moms and Poppy."

"I done heard enough," she said.

"This is already hard as it is. Can't you just bite your tongue and let me finish what I have to say?" I asked.

She grunted, "Uuugh, just like a damn man. Always want to get his first."

I ignored the sexual connotation, "They told me about you, but not very much. All I really knew was that you're the youngest girl and live somewhere in California."

"Hell, they didn't tell you nothing," she stated. "What, you mean they didn't give you no dirt on they wild, rebellious daughter? The one child that can't decide what she want in life and always moving from place to place trying to find herself. Shit, 'least I ain't gonna settle for being stuck in one place depending on no damn man to take care of my ass. Hell, a little privacy, some batteries, and I can take care of my damn self just fine if I need to."

I was trying to get a word in over her continued bantering, "Cherish, are you going to stop long enough to breathe or not?" I asked. "You posed a question. If you let me, I'm trying to give you the damn answer."

Noticeably annoyed, she huffed, rolled her eyes, and said nothing. Her hand went to the keys, switched the ignition to the "aux" position, and she began surfing the radio stations, "So what you trying to say?" she asked.

I began trying to explain again, "What I'm saying is, when I walked in that apartment upstairs and took a good look at you, everything that was rational and made sense, suddenly, didn't make sense."

She intruded on the moment, "Man, just say what you trying to say? Damn all that mumbo-jumbo bullshit. Just spit it the hell out."

"Okay, look; I've got much love for your folks, but when I saw you...when I look at you...Damn." I closed my eyes and dropped my head. "I'm not trying to disrespect them in their house."

"I told you, we can go over by your place," she offered.

"No, we can't," I said. "I'm not just talking about the apartment. I'm talking about the family...the family into which they've invited me and of which I've now become a part. Something I've honestly never really had before. Maybe you just can't wrap your mind around the whole thing."

In a most sincere tone, "Naaaaw, I gotcha," she answered. "I ain't dumb as I pretend to be; but there is sometimes certain advantages to being blonde. Guess that means I done got myself another brother."

I glanced at her and apprehensively stated, "That could be one way of looking at it; in a weird kind of Old Testament sort of way."

She looked me over with those enticing bedroom eyes, "So that mean we can't be getting together and hanging out 'n shit."

"Well"—I adjusted myself in the seat— "I don't see a problem with us getting together and hanging out when we're both in town. It's the *'n shit* that would sooner or later stir up some trouble."

"You know," she said, "This the most decent I ever been rejected. Don't feel nothing like usual."

I had a surprised look, "It's not that you're being rejected, just a matter of unfortunate circumstances. Besides, I don't imagine you have to deal too much with rejection."

Pushing the door open and climbing out the car, she said, "If only you know'd what I go through." Cherish looked up and made note, "Starting to rain. Roads can be kinda slick when they get wet."

I looked over and winked, "Be sure I'll keep that in mind." I said. "Thanks for the concern."

She turned, climbed back in the car, putting her left knee in the seat, reached into the console, handed me the parking ticket and flipped it over, "Maybe it ain't too late to call the police," as she stood up, gently closed the passenger door, and sashayed back inside the building.

I watched through the drizzling rain as she gracefully strolled through the entrance. It wasn't until after the doors closed behind her that what she had said registered. All I could do was shake my head while whispering, "Damn... Damn, damn, damn."

5

A Strange Encounter

I sat near the rear entrance of Moms' building for several minutes thinking after I watched Cherish's tempting waltz before finally dialing the number on the back of the traffic ticket. Hoping it hadn't gotten too late, I anxiously waited as the phone rang the fourth, fifth, and sixth time before a voice came on the answering machine.

I was mesmerized when I heard, *"Hello, this is Ms. Lady. You're not talking to me because I can't talk to you right now. You know what to do...Beep!"*

When the message first began, I was thinking how much I hate answering machines and would normally have just hung up as soon as the recording started. The tone caught me off guard because I was holding the phone listening to Ernestina's captivating voice when I began thinking of our encounter earlier this evening.

I was trying to organize my thoughts, "Uuugggghhhh, yes Officer...umm Miss Lady... It's Willie from this afternoon at the corner of 133rd Street and Broadway."

Suddenly, the recording was interrupted by what sounded like someone fumbling with the receiver, "Hello...hello. Wait one second." There was a momentary silence, then a series of short beeps. I started to hang up. "Hey Willie, I'm glad you called," Ernestina said.

I felt the need to explain, "Sorry it's so late. I'm just now leaving my godparents at 133rd Street. I didn't want to not call you."

"That's okay," she said. "I really wasn't expecting your call today anyway. When I ran into you this afternoon, it was obvious you already had plans. Meeting me was an unexpected thing."

I laughed, "That's one hell...uh...heck of an explanation for it. So, do you often give your number to guys you just happen to 'run' into?"

"No, actually, I don't. But you're different," She said.

"That's not exactly safe; giving your info to a total stranger," I warned.

"But, like I said, you're different," she stated again.

"Still...I am a total stranger."

"Not a *total* stranger. You forget, I'm a police officer," she reminded.

"You know what...you're not right," I commented. "Is that why you screen your calls?"

She paused. "I'm not right only if you're not right. And I wasn't screening the call. I actually just got out the shower."

It was already getting late, so I planted a seed, "Well, we can get together whenever you want to discuss who's right and who isn't. I could stop by in a few minutes on my way home, if you want."

"Well, it is on your way to the Village," she said.

Optimistically, I started the engine and put the car in gear, "I'm leaving from 133rd and Broadway right now. Be over by you in less than ten minutes."

"On second thought," She strategically dismantled my hopes. "Maybe we could get together another time. It is a little late in the evening and I have roll call at five forty-five."

"Five forty-five A.M.!" I exclaimed.

She giggled, "Yes, A.M… When you think?"

I was doing the math in my head, "So, you have to be up and out the house…"

She interjected, "No later than four-thirty."

"If you leave home by four-thirty, then you have to be getting up about what, half an hour before?" I asked.

She was laughing. "You forget, I have to do more than just pee and put on my pants. I *am* a female. Or did you not notice?"

I thought to myself, *Daaammmmnnn, how could I not notice?* As I accelerated onto the West Side Highway, I posed a question, "So, while we're on the subject of waking up, what do I call you first thing in the morning? Unless you're going to be okay with me calling you *baby*?"

Clearing her throat, she asked, "And just what makes you think you'll be waking up with me first thing in the morning…on any morning?"

"Natural progression," I replied.

She instinctively began reconstructing that wall of security, "That's assuming a whole lot of progression isn't it? We just met. In fact, we haven't really met; we just ran into each other."

"Well, that's the part I'm trying to get to; meeting you," I suggested.

"It's not my fault you waited until nearly ten-thirty at night to see if the number I gave you was really mine," she said.

"You're right," I conceded. "Guilty as charged."

"Speaking of guilt—what exactly is it that you do?" she asked.

Given my choice of careers, her word selection was a little unsettling, "Uh…a…What do you mean, guilt? I haven't done anything."

"Dang! Calm your nerves, why don't you?" she said. "I didn't mean to suggest that you've done anything wrong. That's just a little cop lingo. What is it you do that can be verified? A simple play on words."

"Well, where I'm from you don't point your finger unless there's something to be seen," I explained.

"All right, fair enough; I can respect that," she apologized.

My mind had begun to wander off in the direction of a number of possibilities the distant future might hold. I imagined her, a lieutenant or detective heading an investigation in which I had become the prime suspect; or an incident that had us on opposing sides during a shootout. All manner of crazy thoughts ran through my head. It's difficult to know how long I was daydreaming because, when I woke from the daze, I was sitting in the car parked on the street in front of my building.

The melodious sound of Ms. Lady's voice beckoned me back to reality, "Did you even hear what I've been saying? Are you ignoring me or have you changed your mind about coming over?"

"Um…no…I haven't changed my mind. Uh, pardon me, but changed my mind about what?" I truly had no idea what she was talking about, what I had said, or how I'd managed to get to my apartment building in the Village. "Baby, I'm sorry," I apologized.

"I guess your day has been a lot longer than you realize," She reasoned. "Maybe the best thing for you to do is try getting a good night's sleep. We'll talk more about you visiting me another time."

I only half listened to what she said because I was still trying to piece together the past forty-five minutes to an hour, "Okay, perhaps I'll speak to you tomorrow. Good night."

She offered before the call disconnected, "Ernestina."

"Excuse me?" I asked.

"Ernestina Lady; my name…it's Ernestina Lady. You can't call me 'baby.' At least, not yet. Good night," she whispered.

Still a little baffled about how I'd gotten from where I last remembered driving to where I realized finally ending up, I slowly unfastened the seatbelt and pushed the car door open. I made my way to the second floor with the door key in my right hand, and a much deserved forty-year-old bottle of cognac picked up at Julio's earlier when I'd stopped in to snatch up Poppy's Butter-Me-Nots, unlatched the deadbolt and then the bottom lock. Turning the door knob, I suddenly became aware of the husky but feminine Polish accent of my neighbor, who lived directly across the hall. No matter what time of the day or night I came in, she always seemed to be there with a warm greeting to welcome me.

Wearing a silk teddy, standing in the always partially opened door, she asked, "Vaas for chu come in dis earlvy?"

While checking the time on my signature Movado time-piece, "Hi Natasha," I returned the greeting. "It's after eleven o'clock; that's not early."

Pointing at the bottle in my hand "For chu, dat be bery earlvy," she said. "Vaast dat?"

"Company," I replied.

Looking at me with eyes I had seen too often today, she was more direct than usual, "Vaas for chu needs dat botle zu kept chu compaanee vven I vvright heer?"

Her English was sometimes difficult to understand, but I understood enough. I replayed the events of my incredibly long day and immediately began craving female compan-ionship. The female I would have preferred be here had just kept me company on the ride from Harlem to the Village but she couldn't come upstairs. The one who would have liked to come to the Village with me, I had to leave uptown. That series of events brings me to the door of my apartment where I find *temptation* in black lingerie.

Opening my door, I asked, "So where is Uri?"

She seemed surprised, "Vvere ist who?"

"Your man. You know, the guy who lives with you," I said.

I couldn't tell if she was searching for the right words to tell me the truth, or just searching for the right words. She pieced together a viable explanation, as well as her broken English would allow, "He go avaay. I means, out. Him hab olde friend fvrom ouver kuntry stop zu zee he. Dey goes ouvt."

What the hell ever! I thought to myself. In the process of uncorking the bottle, "I guess one drink won't hurt," I said before informing, "I'll have to get some glasses."

I turned to enter my apartment and intentionally left the door cracked just enough that Natasha could see inside. On the way to the kitchen, I hit the remote to summon some smooth jazz and turned the dimmer on the lights to one notch above the lowest setting. I removed two crystal glasses from the cabinet over the sink and turned for some ice cubes from the refrigerator-freezer. There she was in the soft light from the street lamp that had found its way through the blinds covering the kitchen window. She stood next to the dining room table wearing nothing but a black satin lace bra and matching thong panties. I almost dropped the ice pale but quickly covered my blunder by appearing to allow it to tilt just far enough that a few cubes found their way to the table-top. Gently, I sat the pail upright and put one of them into my mouth as I moved closer. Natasha never uttered a word; her body was quietly screaming for my desire to be unleashed and allowed to tame the inferno that now raged within her.

She moaned, feeling the chilled moisture from my tongue on her neck. "Oooooh, zat veels zo gute."

Her body tensed...then relaxed at the realization that she was no longer wearing a bra, when I allowed the lace restriction to fall softly at her feet. With each hand resting on either shoulder, she guided me until the flesh of her 36B's was captured by the contrasting coolness of the ice and my warm lips. The floral centerpiece fell to the floor, as she reclined and laid the full length of the cherry table.

I whispered to her navel, "Natasha."

She responded, "Jes?"

I asked softly, "What do you like."

While raising her legs to rest both feet on the corners of the table, "Me zinks chu allveddy knows," she answered.

I was thinking to myself, *Yeah, I know, but I've never been too interested in the gourmet dish unless I know a little something about the chef.* Nonetheless, I proceeded to test the boundaries of her erotic anticipation, passionately kissing the area below her navel and allowing my tongue to peruse the upper-most part of her inner thighs. The gyration of her hips became more intense as swells of anxiety rose and fell like the surf on the shores of the Pacific.

"I vaant chu," she whispered. "I vaant chu."

I retreated and gingerly kissed my way the length of her body to the vicinity of her ear, "Come," I simply whispered, while helping my neighbor from the table. I took her by the hand and slowly led her to the bedroom.

Natasha stopped in the doorway, pulling back as I entered. She peered into the darkness, "How chu zee?" she asked.

"This *is* my apartment," I said. "I just know my way around."

Reluctantly, she followed my lead until we ended up beside the raised queen-size bed and half laughed, "I's too szort," she commented.

Turning to lift her onto the bed, "Let me help you," I replied before stating, "I'll be right back."

Already on edge, she questioned, "Veere chu go?"

I reached for the small lamp on the nightstand at the head of the bed. The shaded, already dim twenty-five-watt bulb cast barely enough of a glow to make out shadows and large pieces of furniture.

"Just right here." I opened the drawer of the nightstand before asking, "Do you mind, safety first?"

"Vvy no, of koorse not," She smiled through the inadequate light. "Dis is gute ting."

In the process of undressing, "Glad you think so," I said. "Do you prefer the light on or off?"

"Es ist gute," she responded. "I vaant luuke szee chu." She began to kiss me on the chest and ushered me beneath the comforter to join her, "Es ist bery gute." She quietly repeated, "I vaant chu."

My neighbor and I spent more than half an hour composing a sweet song of seduction alongside one of the all-time musical greats. When the tribute to Miles Davis on the jazz station finally ended Natasha callapsed into the plush king-sized pillow and lay face down on the bed beside me.

I rolled over onto my back, searching for much needed oxygen to avoid passing out from exhaustion. The thirst now quenched, I lay there feeling the heat radiating from Natasha's body while secretly wishing hers was a body that belonged to someone else. At that moment, she was in my bed but my mind had never left Harlem.

With much concern, "Chu okvaay?" Natasha asked.

While still staring at the ceiling, I replied, "Yeah, just tired."

Panting to catch her breath, "Vvy vee vait zo long?" she asked.

I remembered having lounged on the bed for quite some time sipping cognac with the neighbor but, the nature of the conversation, I could only vaguely recall. Suddenly, I was awakened by the intrusion of my cell phone. *BBBRRRIIINNNGGG, BBBRRRIIINNNGGG*... I searched the night stand in the darkness with no luck, *BBBRRRIIINNNGGG, BBBRRRIIINNNGGG*, before eventually locating the phone at the foot of the bed still clipped onto the belt of the Levi's I'd worn until a few hours ago.

Glancing over at the digital clock, I answered, "Yeah, what?"

Still half asleep, I could barely make out Cherish's voice, "Damn, that's how you answer your phone?" she asked.

With a serious display of attitude, "That's the way I answer my damn phone at two-thirty in the bitching morning," I said.

Seemingly unaware of my intentionally nasty disposition, she said, "Oh, I was just checkin to see if you made it home a'ight."

I wasn't in the mood for friendly conversation and snapped, "If something had happened, my body would be at the damn morgue by now...Do you know what the hell time it is?"

"Well, after I left you out in the car, I ran into somebody I ain't seen for a while..." Cherish said.

I was still trying to go back to sleep, "I don't care."

She either didn't hear me, or disregarded my comment altogether, "...And we got to talkin 'bout all the shit done happened since I left..."

I tried to stop her gums from flapping but she wouldn't take a breath, "Cherish...Cherish." Finally, I said in a very stern but quiet whisper to shut her up, "...*I don't give a broken damn!*"

"What's your problem?" she asked. "A sista just tryin to check up on your ass. The way muther..."

I was too sleepy to argue my point and really couldn't care any less about the point she was trying to make. The *end* button on the phone was gently pressed before I tried to find my way back off into dreamland. Moments later, I sprung straight up in the bed, looking around to see whether I was by myself. Exiting the bedroom, I slowly walked through the apartment skinny-creeping while looking for anything that was out of order. I checked to verify the refrigerator was closed, there was no ice container on the table, my centerpiece was in place, and the stereo was off. After giving the apartment a good once over, the only thing I discovered to be a little unusual were the ice chest and two glasses upside down on a dish towel spread across the counter. That, and the fact I'd forgotten to latch the chain lock on the front door. Since the bottom lock latched automatically, and it wasn't the first time I'd been so tired when getting home that I'd forgotten, it was no big deal.

"Natasha? No! That was one hell of a dream," I reasoned aloud, while scratching my head. "Damn, it seemed so real."

6

The First, Second Job

I woke Thursday morning to the sound of my previously happy-on-the-surface neighbors arguing again. Maybe it had just seemed they were happy because I never paid them much attention. That was, before the premonition of last night's dream which didn't do much to help relieve me of the, sometimes indecent, thoughts either. It was still unclear as to whether the whole thing concerning last night was just a dream or if it actually happened the way I saw it. There obviously hasn't been an occasion for us to speak on the matter since last evening. If opportunity did present itself, I honestly wouldn't know exactly how to approach the subject. It's funny how you never see things that are right in your face until they affect you. I'd made a good life for myself not getting involved in other people's business and wanted to keep it that way.

Once dressed, I started out to my car and ran into Uri and Natasha in the breezeway; greeting them both, as I normally would, "What's up?"

Uri spoke flatly, without ever taking his eyes off Natasha, "Hello."

Still looking at her man, "Havoe," Natasha answered.

When I had passed and started down the stairs, I heard him tell her to go inside and help with his things. Undoubtedly, he was preparing for one of his frequent three or four day excursions. At any rate, I was already running late for my nine fifteen appointment at the office of the casting director for an upcoming film. I'd gotten wind of the opportunity through the usual sources that spread unofficial information about official events that seemed to somehow unofficially get out.

I was on the phone with the auditions coordinator as I pulled out onto Bleeker, "Yeah, this is Willie. Is Gary there? Can you just give him a message that I'm on my way to his office for my nine fifteen appointment?"

Some female by the name of Christie had answered the phone and was giving me a hard time, "Well, if your appointment is at nine fifteen, you should already be here. The nine-fifteen is second to go in, and Mr. Monroe don't like to be kept waiting. He'll probably just scratch you and move on to the next candidate."

"I understand that, Ms. Christie," I said, trying to be respectful. "If the third person to read is already there, can you simply let them go on in ahead of me? I should arrive by the time they're done with the audition?"

She started to whine, "Well, I don't know, Mr. Monroe don't like things outta order. He gets real mad when that happens."

For some reason, the thought of what Cherish would say about blondes popped into my head. Having decided to take a different approach, I laughed to myself before inquiring, "Ms. Christie, who schedules the order of candidates that show up for the audition?" I asked.

She replied, somewhat apprehensively, "Umm, I do."

"And who has the list of people scheduled to read for the various parts?" I inquired again.

Looking for clarification, "Uh, various?" she questioned.

I forced the respectful obvious explanation, "That means different."

Sounding impressed with herself, "Oh. Well, I do," she said.

Playing on her intelligence, I then established, "So that means you're in charge of who gets to try out and who will eventually be cast in the different roles."

Sounding proud of her newly discovered status, "You know what?" she asked before concluding, "I am in charge." She pondered the realization for a moment. "I tell you what... if you can, be here to read by nine forty-five," she said.

I tried to help her fully grasp the significance of the role she played, "Are you sure that won't cause a problem with Mr. Monroe's schedule?"

Reflecting the added boost of confidence, she replied, "Honey, don't you worry yourself with them details. I'm the one who decides how and when things will happen around here. I'm in charge of this."

To psychologically confirm her status, "All right *Miss Thang*. Then, I'll see you around nine forty-five," I said.

Demonstrating a newfound confidence, "Okay, But you do need to be here a few minutes before the scheduled appointment to make sure we have all your information, like phone numbers and stuff," she said.

Just as we concluded rescheduling the appointment, I moved to replace my cell phone in its clip holder and became aware of the blue lights flashing in the rearview mirror. I proceeded through the intersection and pulled over at a construction site where I waited for the officer to approach. When the patrol car pulled up behind me, I heard someone announce aloud over what sounded like a bullhorn, making me aware that I needed to relocate my car.

"You'll have to move your vehicle, sir," the patrolman directed. "You're not allowed to park in a construction zone."

Moving the car forward to double-park beside a Toyota Camry, I took the license from the wallet in my right hip pocket and got the insurance card from over the sun visor where it was always clipped for easy access. The policeman sat for a few minutes before climbing out the patrol car as I watched in the mirror. *Running my plates, no doubt,* I thought to myself. I remember glancing over at the car next to me and thinking how much I disliked the color green, "Nice car," I said, "Ugly color."

The officer captured my attention as he stood outside the driver's door, "Can I see your license and registration please?"

I had to correct my initial statement as I passed the information to the manly sounding female, "Yes sir...Uh...ma'am."

"What your name?" she asked.

I was annoyed at the question, "Isn't it on the...?" but clearly understood the situation, "Um, LeBeaux... Willie LeBeaux, ma'am," I said quietly.

From the time that I'd first started legally driving down in Georgia, my old man always told me, "Don't never do nothin ta give dem badges no reason. Alls dey needs is a good lie, or good 'nough reason ta make up one." I remembered the story pop would tell me about the reason he had no love for police, or 'badges,' as he called them. He'd told of his younger days coming up in rural Georgia and how 'white folk' used to mistreat Blacks just because they knew the law wouldn't do nothin'. Dad often made mention of the day a white woman spit on him outside a store. He said, when they finally did beat him off 'dat lady,' she was hardly able to be recognized. "Boy, you talk 'bout some po-lice whuppin a brotha ass"—he would lower his head and grin—"Best day o' my life."

Her deep voice jarred me back to the moment, "Where's your insurance card?" Handing the card back, "This one's outdated on yesterday," she said.

I attempted to explain, "The new one must be at the house."

"It's s'pose to be in the car." She looked at me for a moment, then asked, "Any idea why I stopped you?"

Sarcastically, I replied, "Figured you'd eventually tell me."

Displaying a little attitude, "Well, sir, I been in behind you for more than three blocks 'cause you run a stop sign li'l ways back," she explained.

Somewhat humbled at the realization I was at fault, I replied, "Don't recall a stop sign. I come through here on the regular, because I live in the area."

She responded condescendingly, "I know, I saw the address on your identification. Could be 'cause you is tryin to drive and talk on the phone all at the same time. Wasn't paying much a'tention to what you doing, I guess."

"But I was tryin to schedule my..." I wasn't even aware of my attempt to explain—as if it would make a difference, which was confirmed as soon as she opened her mouth.

The officer spoke, "It don't make no difference why you run the stop sign; like it won't make no difference if you was to get in a accident and kill somebody...dead is dead. Wait here."

I could only agree, "Yes ma'am."

The officer returned several minutes later to hand my driver's license back with what appeared to be a citation. She-man warned, "You just need to be real careful out here," returned to her car without any further comment and proceeded to drive away.

I was a bit puzzled as to why she hadn't given the usual instructions on how to deal with the ticket as far as disputing or paying the citation before the court date to avoid the additional fees charged. I mean, I'd had enough experience with cops to know a little about the routine. I sat in my car, fastened my seatbelt, and started the engine before looking at the ticket. Opening the fold, I saw in quotation marks "WHY HAVEN'T YOU CALLED?" and a phone number. Not knowing who the officer was, and trying to figure why she would want any man calling her, I dialed the number.

I heard a familiar voice, "Hello, Officer Lady speaking, may I ask who's calling," after the second or third ring.

The phone nearly fell from my hand, "Uh, yes…uh, so what's goin on? This is Willie."

"I know," Ernestina said snickering. "I was expecting your call. Actually, I've been expecting your call for a few days now. Did I make that bad of an impression?"

"No. Not at all," I replied still trying to recover from the unexpected surprise of hearing her voice on the other end of the line. "How did you…?"

"I keep telling you, don't ever underestimate the long arm of the law," she joked. "It extends much farther than most people realize."

Never having been one to like the idea of being under anybody's thumb, I was somewhat troubled by the expression of control Ernestina's actions represented. "How did you know…how did she know…what the hell is going on here?"

After realizing my level of displeasure, "Damn Will, relax a little," she said. "I heard Jamie—that was the officer who stopped you," she explained. "I heard her when she called in the traffic stop and requested identification on the vehicle. When everything came up clean, I radioed back to let her know you were a friend. No big deal, nothing to get all bent out of shape over."

"I just don't like…well, I don't like being controlled like that," I complained.

"Nobody's trying to control you," she retorted. "You know, you really need to lighten up. The world isn't such a bad place."

"Yeah, maybe you see it that way because you've never had to live in the world I came through," I said.

Ernestina's question came across at though she was engaged in the interrogation of a suspect, "And just exactly what world is that?" she asked.

Knowing this wasn't a conversation I wanted to have, especially with a cop of all people, I dismissed the comment. "Never mind," I responded.

Ernestina politely threatened, "You know, you might as well answer me because if you don't, I do have ways of finding out, whether you want me to know or not," she said. "I mean, you act as if there's some deep dark secret from your distant past that you don't want the rest of the world to know about." Half-jokingly, she asked, "Is there something you want to disclose? Don't worry; your secret will be safe with me. In this country, a wife can't testify against her husband. But be careful, if you tell me anything incriminating, that means you can never file for divorce," she said.

I changed the subject. "There you go talking that marriage nonsense again. I'm telling you, I don't talk about it because talking about it will have you doing it before you know what happened…Lay down one day with a girlfriend and wake up five years later struggling to make ends meet for your old lady, three crumb snatchers named Junior, Bobby, and Sally…with a damn poodle to boot."

Rather defensively, "And what's wrong with kids?" she asked.

"Oh, nothing's wrong with them," I answered, "As long as they belong to somebody else."

A little more serious, she questioned, "You mean to tell me you really don't want any kids? Children are a blessing from God."

I was beginning to think the conversation about my past would have been less nerve-racking, "Well, that's one blessing the Man upstairs can hold on to for somebody else, because I'm not trying to be anybody's daddy," I stated.

Sounding somewhat disappointed, "Are you serious?" she asked.

I remarked with an air of sarcasm, "Look, we better put a stop to this. I've got to get going to my appointment and you're supposed to be at work," I told her. "Besides, we haven't even had our first date and you already talking about marriage and kids. Let's take this thing one step at a time, baby."

"All right," Ernestina agreed. "...And I done told you my name. The reason we haven't had our first date is because you didn't call like you said you would," she replied. "I guess I better let you go so there'll be enough time for you to get to your appointment without speeding. I might not be able to pull any strings for you the next time."

"Oh, I'm sure you can," I commented.

"Point is," she said, "I might not want to. At least, not until after you take me out...If that's ever going to happen."

"Okay, I'm going to let you get away with that one. I've got to get going...I'll call you...Serious," I insisted.

"I'm holding my breath," she answered. "Bye."

When I pressed the button to end the call, I noticed the LED time display on the cell phone, "Damn!" I shouted to myself. "I have to be at the place in less than ten minutes and still have more than twelve blocks to go."

I sped out onto the street to the sound of aggravated horns and pissed off New Yorkers yelling all sorts of *unpleasantries* while volunteering to donate their middle fingers to me. I hurried through two or three stop signs while on the lookout for Ms. Mister with the badge and sped down a street with a posted thirty-mile-per-hour speed limit at about twice the recommended rate of travel. It wasn't hard to find a parking space in the rear of the building that housed the office of the infamous Mr. Gary Monroe. If there was anything happening in the field of entertainment on the East Coast, he was involved, or knew how to get you involved.

"That space is reserved for the disabled," I heard the security officer yell from behind me, as I entered the building.

I commented without looking back while entering the exit door leading from Mr. Monroe's office, "I'll be long gone by the time anybody you call shows up anyhow."

As I rounded the corner, I heard someone call, "MR. LeBEAUX...MR. LeBEAUX, is there a Mr. LeBeaux here to audition?"

"YES!!" I screamed in mid-stride, "I mean...yes," as I came to a sliding halt at a small folding table outside a door with a paper sign taped to it that read "AUDITIONS."

The woman seated at the table asked, snarling about the minor disruption I had caused, "Mr. LeBeaux?"

"Yes ma'am. Miss Christie, I presume?" I asked.

She barked at me without so much as lifting her eyes from the list in front of her, "You're late."

Argumentatively, I explained, "My appointment time is for nine forty-five. It's just now nine forty-five. I'm here just in time."

"Have you ever been here before?" Miss Christie asked.

"No ma'am," I answered.

"Ever read for Mr. Monroe before," she posed.

"No ma'am," I said.

Her voice rumbled like a volcano ready to erupt, "And are you affiliated with Mr. Monroe in any way within or outside the industry except for today's appointment?"

Somewhat confused as to the point of her line of questioning, I responded, "Uh...well, no ma'am."

She stopped marking on the notepad in front of her, rolled eyes resembling an owl up to look at me above the thin black frames of her glasses and scoffed, "Then, you are late!"

I was remembering the timid, spineless jellyfish who was scheduling appointments earlier when my phone interrupted, *BBBRRRIIINNNGGG...BBBRRRIIINNNGGG.*

Christie snarled as she stood up from behind the table, "You can't have that on in here." Passing by me, she commented, "I'll see if Gary, uh, Mr. Monroe, is ready."

Something about the comment she made had me pondering the meaning of things people don't say as I turned my attention to the caller. "Hello," I answered.

I heard Oz's raspy voice, "Planning on stopping by Uptown sometime soon? Got some things I need you to check on."

I was trying to delay at least long enough to have time to finish at the audition and drive up to Harlem, which could take a good forty-five minutes to an hour, depending on traffic. I didn't want to reveal too much. Oz was supportive of me in most anything I chose, except my ambition to become an actor. His opinion held that actors were unrealistic people who lived an unrealistic existence with unrealistic expectations from an unrealistic world.

"Yes sir, I can be there in about an hour to an hour and a half."

I heard Christie, as she passed to perch in her chair, "You can go in, but you need to leave that phone on the table."

"Who's that?" asked Oz.

As the call ended and Christie reached for my phone, "Nobody...I'll be in touch. Sorry, but I have to run... See you in a bit," I said.

She growled, "Thank you."

Handing over the umbilical chord that sustained my very existence, I said, "Yeah whatever." I instructed her while entering the door to the room for the audition, "...And don't be out here talking up all my minutes either."

I heard Mr. Monroe's assistant before I was completely in the room, "What part you reading for?"

Prior to my responding, the heavyset guy in the chair next to him spoke up, "Why don't you read the part of Bo?"

"Well I was honestly leaning more toward the part of Terrence," I said.

Looking at the skinny guy next to him, "Naw, I don't think so. You look more like the Bo type to me," he said. "I mean, I know of a few Black guys named Terrence, but that's more of a Caucasian man's name. Ain't that right?" he asked.

For a split second, I found myself back down in Georgia late at night out on one of those country roads in the middle of nowhere, where the type things happen to Black folk that few people believe happen anymore. There was a serious attitude churning deep inside my gut by the time I realized where I was. This is New York's acting industry, where they can be openly racist with little consequence.

The skinny assistant spoke up, "Yes sir, Mr. Monroe," he said. "I think he'd do a lot better to read the part of Bo, the sharecropper."

By this point, my blood was starting to boil. "You know what, I think the agency sent me to the wrong audition. Sorry about the mix-up Mr. Monroe," I mumbled, with as much respect as I could muster while starting for the door, "Why I think I'll just be gettin outta your way."

"But you look the part," the skinny assistant called out. "You sure you don't want to read anyway...since you here?" he asked.

I don't know why I was feeling so insulted when I responded, "Nawsa massa Charlie; I ain't gots no bidness bein hure. Why, I's done fogot, I cain't eeben reed."

Mr. Monroe asked, shrugging his shoulders with hands turned palms up in front of him, "What the hell is his problem?"

Casually, I approached the table where the two men sat, leaned over in their faces with both fists on the notes they'd been taking, "My problem is greasy asses like you perpetuating some foolishness that should've been put to death a long time ago." I stood up and turned to leave.

Walking out the room, I heard the skinny assistant, "You don't know who I...uh, who he is. You'll regret this."

"I already do," I chimed back, while approaching the table where Christie was now standing with my cell. I growled, snatching the phone in the process of passing her station, "And give me my shit."

When I made it out to my car, I noticed a tow-truck driver over at the guard station. I quickly got in, started the engine, and proceeded to back out. The young attendant ran after me halfway across the parking lot shouting obscenities he didn't look old enough to have ever heard, not to mention, repeat.

Back out on Bleeker, I found myself looking for the male/female officer from earlier while dialing Oz's cell.

7

Truth Revealed

I was still debating with myself aloud about what had happened last night while in the process of dialing Oz. "Did what happened, that I know shouldn't have happened, actually happen, or had I only dreamed it happened, because that's what I really wanted to happen but know it couldn't?"

"Hello." I took the initiative of informing him, "Yeah Oz, I was just calling to let you know I'm on my way up by you."

He somberly stated, "I thought you's gone be a while."

Not wanting to get into a long drawn-out discussion. "Stuff happens...plans change," I told him. "I'm on my way."

"On yo way here; need you to stop by Charlie's Place," he requested.

"What's up with Charlie now?" I asked. "Has he gone and messed up again, already?"

"No, it's cool. He got somethin for me...need you to stop and pick it up on yo way here," Oz explained.

"Where's Amp? Why can't you have him run over an' get it? He's the one who likes playing in the dirt," I protested. "You know I don't mess around with that…"

"Just get over there and do what I told you!" Oz demanded. "I don't remember askin you a damn thang. Somethin need doin, and I told you to do it. Now that's all the talk there gone be 'bout it!"

I was honestly more concerned than I was upset; trying to figure out what was eating at the old man. *Regardless of what's going on, he knows this is not the music I dance to,* I thought as I continued up the Westside Highway on the way to Harlem.

While thinking how it was so unlike Oz to ever raise his voice…especially at me, "All right," I conceded.

Since Oz had me going without backup, I was a little on edge; not knowing what to expect. I exited on 86th Street to try a different approach. The thought bounced back and forth between my ears: *Would he hang me out like that? Why would he hang me out like that? BBBRRRIIINNNGGG. BBBRRRIIINNNGGG.* I was so deep in thought the sound of the cell phone startled me. My reaction nearly resulted with a young lady pushing a stroller in the crosswalk getting run down.

She yelled, giving me a look that nearly peeled the paint off my car, "You might wanna pay attention to the damn street instead of watchin what's on the freakin sidewalk!"

I answered my cell phone. "What! I mean, yeah, what's up?"

The sweetest voice imaginable asked, "My, are we having a bad morning or what? Who kicked you in the butt?" Before eventually identifying, "This is your favorite police officer. What's going on?"

"Nothing Ernestina," I cut. "Look, this really isn't a good time. You mind if I ring you back in a few?"

"I called to see if you had made any plans for lunch," she said. "But if you have something more important to do…"

"Oh no," I spoke up. "I wasn't trying to put you off. I'm just dealing with something at the moment. Lunch sounds like a good idea. What time do you break?"

"My schedule is a little flexible," she advised. "I can go as early as eleven thirty, or, if I want to go later, around twelve or twelve thirty. It's up to you."

This was no time for a debate, "I'll call you as soon as I'm done," I said.

"Speaking of being done; how was your appointment that you were in such a hurry to get to when we spoke earlier?" she questioned.

There was an awkward moment of silence before the line went dead after my response came across a little more brash than I'd intended, "I said I'll call you when I'm done."

In a tone absent any emotion, "I'm holding my breath," she'd replied in the process of disconnecting.

Instinct had me start to dial her back. *A situation like this is the wrong time to have your body show up without inviting your mind along for the ride.* I rationalized within. It occurred to me how dangerous things could potentially become when pulling off the street about a block from Charlie's. I'd recognized several vehicles I knew belonged to people who weren't interested in becoming Oz's pen pals. Motionless, I sat in my car trying to figure on the best way out of the spot in which I'd found myself. Going to Oz without doing what he'd sent me to do would be like drinking gasoline, striking a match and swallowing it. But walking inside Charlie's with all that heat up in there would have the same effect as crawling into a lion's den with a steak hanging around my neck. I remember thinking to myself, *This would have been a good day to sleep in.* I braced for the anticipated reaction while dialing Oz's cell phone. *BBBRRRIIINNNGGG, BBBRRRIIINNNGGG, BBBRRRIIINNNGGG,* and *BBBRRRIIINNNGGG.* I was more nervous than I could remember being since before leaving Georgia and was at the point of hanging up.

"Yeah," Oz sounded as though somebody had their hand over his mouth. "What's goin on Willie?" he finally asked. "You stop by Charlie's?"

My tongue kept getting in the way. I couldn't bring myself to tell him what I knew he had to know, "Yeah...well, no. I mean I did, but I haven't..."

Oz was noticeably frustrated, "All right, I ain't got no time for this bull...ain't halfway in the damn mood. Spit out what ya got on yo mind."

I started to explain, "Now Oz, you know I've never crossed you." I detailed. "And anytime you ever needed me, I've been there."

"What is this, some *Days of Our Lives* bullshit?" he asked. "Get to the damn point, William. Did you get the shit done that I sent you out there for? Right about now, that's all the hell I wanna know!"

Before realizing it, I blew up at him. "Well, the question I can't find an answer to is why the hell you sent me out here in the first place? This is no damn place for me to be by myself... and at lunch too? You know every snake in Harlem is posted up in that joint around this time of day...every snake in Harlem that doesn't like your ass. And it's not like these bastards don't know who signs my check."

He waited patiently for me to take a breath. "You musta done lost yo damn mind. Did you forget who the hell I am? I'm the fool that watch yo back when nobody else look out for yo skinny ass. I put you up to keep other muthers from knockin yo country ass down," he refuted. "What the hell, you think I'd roll over and put you out there like that?"

Feeling as though the weight of the world had been lifted off my shoulders, "I didn't know man," I answered. "I mean, you haven't really been trying to talk to a brother; got me out here on some kamikaze suicide shit. For a minute, I'm thinking you the one tripping."

He answered in a more solemn tone, "For a minute, I was. Got a call this mornin from that fool Charlie...said he had

some info he knowed I'd 'preciate...somethin 'bout somebody close to me," Oz explained. "First person come to mind
was you, 'cause you 'bout the only one can get to me like that.
Then he told me somethin 'bout the evidence...some pictures, he say. That's what you s'pose to be pickin up."

"How you know it's not me in the pictures?" I asked.

"Well, 'cause the pictures is from couple weeks ago...on a
Sunday. And I know you be up by yo folks ev'ry Sunday," he
said. "Couldn't been you 'cause you wasn't no where 'round."

"So, who the hell's in the pictures?" I questioned.

Oz spoke while trying to control his anger, "That part,
Charlie wouldn't spell out on the phone; told me he don't
wanna get up in the middle 'o no family bullshit," Oz said.
"Just go get the shit he got and explain for me I owe him."

"Funny," I said. "For some reason it's hard for me to believe
he's doing this because he wants to be your new best friend."

"We two lions in the same part o' the bitchin jungle;
ain't much chance for us being friends," Oz said. "This 'bout
respect." He paused, and then reminded, "Bring me what
he got."

Still somewhat leery of Charlie and his friends, I elected
not to move the car any closer to the entrance. Instead,
I climbed out and walked in the direction opposite where
Charlie's was located to the next street over. From there, I
circled around, walked three blocks back and came up on the
side of the building opposite of where I'd parked.

I was nearly in the doorway before the two heavies noticed
me. The smaller of the two asked, "What can I do for you?"

Without making eye contact, "Yeah, I got business with
Charlie," I responded, "He in?"

The big dude wearing the baseball cap answered, "He
might be. But don't nobody go through witout being checked.
I gotta walk you in."

Knowing the routine, I had disarmed prior to leaving the
car and asked, while being frisked for weapons, "What's with
the added security?"

The guy checking me for weapons responded, "This ain't added security," he said. "Clean," he confirmed before directing, "Come wit me through here."

The heavyweight had me follow him through the entrance, around the pool tables, and back to Charlie's private office. I paid particular attention to the door that had been installed to replace the one I'd crashed through last week. Again, stained glass inside a wood frame, but this one had bars; I assumed to keep people like me out. I was surprised that nobody seemed to recognize me from my previous visit.

When the door opened, I could hear Charlie, "I'm on the phone," he said. "I'll be done in just a minute. Tell him to have a seat out front."

The heavy led the way back out past the pool tables and directed me to a bar stool near the jukebox. Ironically, it sounded a lot like the same jazz cut that was playing the last time I happened through. This time though, I could appreciate the music a lot more without all the screaming. My agenda wasn't quite the same today as when I'd passed this way before. That day, I was too focused on doing what I was here to do, and getting my ass out as quick as possible.

The sound of the music prompted me to raise my voice. "Tell Charlie I got things to do," I yelled. "I didn't come by to hang out for the rest of the damn day."

The heavyweight sounded back, "He said he'll be out in a minute."

I wasn't in the mood, "Yeah, I know, but that was like, fifteen minutes ago."

Out of the corner of my eye, I saw Charlie appear from the area leading back to his office and approaching the end of the bar where I waited, "I'm impressed," he said.

With it obvious I was a little puzzled, "What's that?" I asked.

The owner wore a look I couldn't quite figure out, "You been here more than five minutes and ain't none of my shit broke," he said. "I'm impressed."

Suddenly, nearly every person in the place was eyeing me like I was in a police lineup. *So much for not being recognized,* I thought to myself.

"Well, I was here on a different sort of business the last time," I remarked. "Don't take it too personal."

"Speaking of business: We might as well get to it," Charlie said.

"That works for me," I answered. "The sooner we get this thing done, the sooner I can get back to Oz with what he needs to know. By the way, he told me to let you know he appreciates you looking out for him."

Charlie nodded, "Tell Oz I ain't so much looking out for him as I am the network."

I commented, while taking the brown envelope Charlie passed me, "All the same, he appreciates it." Without opening it, I took the envelope and started for the door, "Thanks, you know he'll do what needs doing."

As I passed near the register, the bartender called out, "You tell the old man what goes 'round oughtta come back 'round."

Without breaking stride, "...And what comes back around should go around again," I replied.

I'd gotten what I came for, and all I could think about was the fastest way out. Hurrying to my car, I dialed Oz, pulling out onto the street.

BBBRRRIIINNNGGG, BBBRRRI... The way he snatched the phone up, you'd think the old man was sitting on it. "Yeah, Willie?" he asked.

I questioned, before considering the seriousness of the situation, "Were you expecting somebody else?"

Without the least bit of understanding in his voice, "Don't play," he said. "This ain't no time for playin. You get it?"

"Yeah," I said. "On the way over to you now...be there in a few minutes."

Apprehensively, he asked, "You look to see what it is?"

"Nope, sure didn't," I responded. "That would be your job. I don't make it a habit to look under another man's bed. If there's something to be found, best he be the one to find it." Checking the time, I said, "I'm going to have to leave this one with you. I've got a run to make. I'll drop this off but I have to be out; need to make it on over to Spanish Harlem in less than an hour."

Trying to conceal his disappointment, "What's so damn important you ain't gone stay 'round to help me wit this?" he asked.

"I'll be back," I assured. "It'll only take a couple hours at the most. Besides, what could be so bad that you can't handle it?"

"Well, we'll talk 'bout you leavin when you get here," he said.

My drive over to Oz's spot seemed to take twice as long as it normally did. The more I considered getting back to Ernestina, the faster I drove. Leaving Oz in a bad spot is something I would normally not even consider. The rationalization continued until it began to sound almost logical to me. Besides, if anybody could take care of themselves—Oz had helped make the streets what they'd become. I pulled up outside his place, taking my usual spot blocking the fire hydrant on the street out front and hurried in with the envelope for which he'd been impatiently waiting all morning.

Oz met me at the door, "That it?" and took the envelope before I had a chance to hand it over.

Opening the clasp and removing a photo to closely examine it. "Damn," he said, flopping down in one of the lounge chairs. "Damn, and after all I done." He relaxed his grip and allowed the picture, envelope, and all to fall to the tabletop without any further comment.

I was headed back out the door when I heard Oz's pride hit the floor like a sack of bricks.

I turned and asked with a puzzled look, "What's up old man?"

"Shoulda buried that bastard when I had the chance," he mumbled.

Eyeballing the picture, "What bastard?" I asked.

"Who you see?" Oz questioned.

I explained, "All I see is a brother standing outside a black 'Gator…looks like the one your boy Amp be wheeling. But I don't recognize the dude."

Oz took another look at the photo. "The one you don't know; Jerome…witout the blond hair. He sportin a shaved head…And that *is* Amp's Navigator. He sittin inside the truck."

I asked, without thinking, "Why would Jerome be standing outside Amp's ride?"

"The question of all questions," Oz remarked. "Yeah, why would he? I tell you man, somethin don't smell right. I need you to check this out for me. Make sure our boys ain't up ta no good." He stood for a minute staring into nothingness, then said, "The way I remember, if Jerome involved, ain't nothin 'bout it good."

The thought of leaving him at a time like this didn't even cross my mind. I excused myself and walked outside the building to call Ernestina. Oz had been there for me more times and in more ways than I could remember. Other than Eunice and Poppy, he was the closest thing to family I had in New York. On the other hand, this was the chance for which I had been waiting with the woman for whom I'd been waiting, it seemed like, my whole life. On the day we'd met, there was a feeling like we connected and I knew it was destined for us to be together. The problem we kept having was with trying to actually get together. About the time I started dialing Ernestina's number, my cell phone rang. *BBBRRRIIINNNGGG.* I picked up on the first ring trying to sound enthused, "Hey baby."

"I done told you, it hasn't been established that you have the right to call me baby, at least not yet," Ernestina joked. "I was calling you because you were supposed to call me about making plans for lunch and, well, that didn't look like it was going to happen…again. So, I guess this phone call makes me guilty of putting myself out there."

"Well, to be honest, I was dialing your number when my phone rang," I explained. "I was calling you to let you know…"

Ernestina cut me off with her attitude front and center, "Yeah, I know, you can't make it. There's something you forgot you were supposed to take care of," she replied. "No problem, I'll just grab a sandwich at the deli around the corner."

"Now wait," I interrupted. "You don't understand…"

She interjected, "If you really want to know the truth, I'm tired of being the one who has to understand. Several days passed after we talked the evening we met…and I understood. Maybe you already had plans. I contacted you earlier today and you got a little pissed because you saw that as my attempt to control you; again…I understood. I like a good, strong man who can handle things on his own." The anger became even more pronounced, "And now, what you're going to tell me is that something came up and you have to back out on the lunch date that I…well, I was actually looking forward to; that you want me to understand. Well I don't! How much more understanding do I have to be?"

"Look baby…" I said.

She let out a muffled yell, "And I done told you about that baby shit!"

I was on the verge of being done. If it had been most anybody else, I probably would gladly have been finished at that point, but I knew there was something about this woman that just wouldn't let me go…something about her that wouldn't allow me to let her go. Not before ever having the opportunity to know her. "I know you're kind of pissed off right now," I started.

"Kind of…" she cut. "Huh, you don't know the half."

"Okay now, I can understand you being a little aggravated," I said. "But there has been a lot going on today. My day isn't even half over yet and all I've been doing is wishing it hadn't started. To begin with, you're wrong. There's nothing I remembered that hadn't been taken care of. But something has come up since I talked to you this morning. It's an issue that has to be dealt with right now and I don't know what I'll have to do or how long it's going to take," I explained. "I was honestly looking forward to getting together with you for lunch as well. Hell, I've been looking forward to getting together with you since we spoke this past Sunday, if you want to know the *whole* truth."

Her comment came from a more pleasant place but was still laced with an air of bitterness, "I wouldn't know that you've been looking forward to doing anything with me," she said. "What could have come up in the past hour and a half that is so important you have to deal with it right now anyway?"

I was trying to smooth the situation over when I walked back inside where Oz was still waiting. "Listen, it's not a big deal but I have to do something for my old man."

Sounding more sympathetic, "Oh," she said. "I didn't realize it was something concerning your father. Is everything all right with him? I mean, he's not sick or anything like that is he?" she asked.

"No," I answered. "Just something that needs to be taken care of before it becomes worse than it already is."

Ernestina started what she believed was a related example, "I remember when my dad had gone in for a checkup about four years ago and they found a polyp in his colon. It's always best if you can catch things like that early; the earlier the better, for sure."

"Baby," I uttered. "I really need to go take care of this."

"Okay sweetheart…I mean, okay Willie…call me when you have a chance. I hope everything checks out all right," she said.

I walked over to the table where Oz had taken a seat waiting for me to finish the phone conversation, "You all right?" I asked.

"I'm straight," he replied. "Just tryin to figure out how to deal with them asses...wonderin what they up to, you know?"

I commented, trying to put him more at ease, "It can't be bad as you're thinking. Both of them learned all they know from you, and I wouldn't stake my life on what Amp knows because he's not exactly the sharpest knife in the drawer."

"Don't take 'em for fools," Oz cautioned. "They kids to the game, but they hungry. And ain't much tougher to deal wit than a hungry animal. You just be sho and watch yoself."

My response was laced with sarcasm, "Oh, I didn't know you cared so much," I said.

Reminding me of the reference I had made during the conversation with Ernestina, "What kind of a *old man* would I be if I ain't care 'bout you?" he asked.

"Well old man, I got business," I said. "I'm going to run and see some people who might be able to help us with our little pest problem. If I'm thinking right, that warehouse where they were out front in the picture is up in the Bronx. I need to borrow that if you don't mind."

He passed the evidence to me, "Keep it long as you need," Oz replied. "I knows what them snakes look like."

With an old-brother-from-the-block handshake, "I'm out," I said before asking, "Is that fool due to come back around here today? Wouldn't want him to get stupid and try you if he catches you by yourself, especially if he's not coming alone."

He chuckled at the comment, "It takes more 'n them two moles to make me go hide. 'Sides, my man Tony 'round here somewhere."

"You just need to be careful," I cautioned. "There's no way of knowing how long those two have been sneaking around together. I wouldn't put it past them to try creeping up on you."

Oz commented out of the blue, "She make you talk different."

With a genuine look of confusion, "What, who...What are you talking about, old man?" I asked. "It's called proper grammar. One of the few benefits realized from years of private schools and tutors."

"Ole girl you was talkin wit on the phone," he answered. "I might be old, but I ain't that old. I still knows what it mean when a brother walk out the room 'cause he talkin on the phone. The way you talkin all nice wit the right words 'n shit an' callin her baby."

"How you know it was a female?" I questioned.

"Hope like hell that ain't no brotha you callin baby," he laughed, before questioning in a serious tone. "That where you s'pose to been goin ain't it?"

"Yeah, but she understands," I said.

He half grinned, "Didn't sound too understandin to me."

I was somewhat defensive in my answer, "Understanding or not, business comes first. I mean, we just met a few days ago. It's not like we've known each other so long that the two of us have to be together like that."

Oz remarked, with a devilish smirk, "Sound to me like you wanna be knowin her so y'all *can* be gettin t'gether like that," he said. "Like I say, I'm just old, I ain't stupid."

In a tone that more-or-less spoke to the degree of my feelings on the matter, "Okay, enough of this Oprah Winfrey moment crap. I've got things to do," I replied. "I've got to get up to the Bronx and check on something."

Oz spoke up as I turned to leave, "You know, I think I wanna handle this a li'l bit dif'rent," he said. "You go'on 'bout yo plans. I got a few calls to make."

I turned back. "Now, you don't need to be concerning yourself with my plans. Like I said, business is business, and business always comes first. I'll deal with whatever plans I've got when the time comes. *Just know I've got this.*"

"No, for real," He stopped me. "If we start doin stuff different, them fools might get suspi...suspic...They might start thinkin somethin up."

"So how you plan on dealing with this?" I asked. "Something has to be done."

"Yeah, I know," he reassured. "And somethin gone get done real soon, just not by somebody they think. They's some peoples in the Bronx owe me a favor. You can call girl back 'n do what you gone do," he said.

"Not right now," I replied. "Sometime later, maybe. What I need now is to just bring the level down a notch. A big part of the day is already gone. I haven't *done* much of anything, but I feel like I've been on a post-hole digger since five o'clock this morning."

He had no idea what I was talking about, "On a what?"

Realizing the comment was a little too regional for him to grasp, "Never mind," I replied. "It's a Southern thing. You wouldn't know about anything like that."

"Don't think I wanna know," Oz stated.

"Well look, I'm going to get out of here. Maybe if I just go back to my apartment, take a nap, get up, shower, and start the day all over, things might work out a little better," I hoped. For the sake of clarification, I asked, "And you're sure you don't want me to go handle things up in the Bronx?"

His face looked as if it had been carved from stone, "Naw, you go'on," Oz said. Then, he grinned and commented while walking toward his office, "*Just know I got this.*"

I was on my way back to the Village replaying the whirl-wind of a day I'd already had and started thinking about the disappointment I'd heard in Ernestina's voice when we spoke on the phone earlier about lunch. It was quite flattering to find out that beneath the armor-plated exterior, she had some-thing of a vulnerable interior. The more I thought about her, the more I hoped for the opportunity to explore that interior. She wasn't like any other woman I'd encountered since arriv-ing in New York. Come to think of it, she didn't appear to be much like any woman I had come across anywhere.

The thought of her got to be too much. *BBBRRRIIINNNGGG,* *BBBRRRIIINNNGGG,* *BBBRRRIIINNN…* Her phone was ringing as I adjusted the volume of the jazz station.

"Hello," she answered. "This is Ernestina..."

"How are you doing, baby?" I asked.

"There's only one person I know who is allowed to call me that," she replied.

I let go a hearty laugh, "Oh, now I'm *allowed* to call you baby?" before jokingly asking, "What happened to not knowing you well enough?"

"It doesn't much matter what you call me, it seems we're never going to have the opportunity to get to know each other any better than an occasional chat on the phone between your appointments," she said.

"Well there might be a solution to that situation, if you would be receptive to dinner," I suggested.

Ernestina's question was posed from atop a mountain of optimism, "When and where?" she asked.

I commented, "I would imagine you have to have food tonight, and you can choose to eat wherever you'd like. You set the time and name whatever place you want. I've kept you waiting long enough that you should be allowed to choose."

"You sure a night out won't conflict with anything you've already got scheduled?" she asked. "Or maybe we should just plan a quiet evening in to allow you some flexibility in the event you get called out on emergency."

"Okay, I'll allow you that one," I said. "I guess I deserve a punch or two."

"You're serious?" she questioned.

"I think it was me who asked," I said.

"You also asked me to lunch today, and I ended up with a deli sandwich and a pickle accompanied by an oversized chocolate chip cookie for desert," she reminded.

I jovially warned, "Okay, okay, that's enough. It's beginning to feel a little more like abuse at this point." Then confirmed, "Seriously though, you make plans for whenever and wherever you want. It'll be my attempt to make up for the past week."

She hesitated for a moment. "There is this one place that I'm familiar with where the atmosphere is real nice, there's good music, and the food isn't half bad either."

"That sounds like a good spot. What time should I pick you up?" I asked. "Tell you what, I'm driving and my memory isn't all that great, so why don't I call you…say, around six and you can give me directions where to pick you up; or if you'd rather meet me at the restaurant, that'll be cool too," I said.

"How about this?" she started. "I sort of volunteered for a few hours overtime, so I won't actually be off work until seven. Then, by the time I make it home, shower, get dressed and finish, you know, all the girl stuff…can we say, have you pick me up around nine or nine-thirty?"

"Isn't that a bit late for dinner?" I asked. "What restaurant are you going to find open after ten o'clock at night?"

"Don't tell me you've forgotten where you are," she laughed. "*This is New York; the city that never sleeps.* You can find most anything you want at most anytime you want it."

"It's not the city's sleep about which I'm concerned; it's yours and mine," I commented. "Just because we live in the city that never sleeps, doesn't mean we don't have to."

"All right, all right, Cinderfella, I'll be sure to turn you loose before midnight," she joked. "Don't worry, there's plenty open at night in this city. I'll think of something by the time you get over by me."

"You know, I can still pick you up from work if you'd like," I said.

"Um, no that's all right. Call me later and I'll see you at my place. I don't too much like these cackling hens around here all up in my business," she commented.

"Okay then, guess it's a date," I confirmed. "See you in a little while."

"Where are you on your way to, now?" she questioned.

I thought to myself, there's that control thing again and playfully put my foot down, "Excuse me, but I think what I do doesn't become your business until around nine o'clock tonight." Little did she know, that controlling nature was the one problem I had with her up to that point. "How about I let you know what I'm up to when I call you later? That's when I'll be on my way over to pick you up for dinner," I said.

"Careful, I just might change my mind," she said.

I pretended it wouldn't make any difference, "You could," I replied.

"Just don't stand me up again," she protested.

"When did I stand you up?" I asked. "We've never had a confirmed date since the day we met, have we? I'm sure I would have remembered if there was something we were supposed to do together."

She repeated, "Like I said, just don't stand me up...again. Now, I have to go so I can pretend I'm doing something to give them a reason to pay me. Be careful on that phone while you're driving. Talk to you later."

The call was concluded as I turned onto Bleecker Street, "Later."

I had only left home a few hours ago but it seemed as if I was returning from a long trip. All I could think about was how good it would feel to get a much needed shower and wash away the city before reclining with Miles Jay or Nancy Wilson. Theirs was the only company I was in the mood for at the moment.

8

Unscripted Encounter

U nlike most any other time of the day or night, I was fortunate enough to find a vacant parking spot directly in front of my building.

"Go figure," I said.

The personal discussion persisted as I parallel parked and remotely locked the car on my way to the entrance. "Even still, there's a big difference between traffic on this street at one-thirty in the afternoon versus what it would be like in a few hours," I concluded.

Perched on the stoop atop the concrete steps was the unexpected sight of Natasha, my neighbor. Unexpected, because she normally remained inside their apartment peeping out the window or watching people come and go through the barely opened front door until after sundown.

"Howv vare chu?" she asked.

"I'm good, what's up?" I responded.

Her attempt at soliciting conversation couldn't have been more obvious, "Chu home earlvy," she said.

I stated, while passing through the double doors, "Yeah, for a minute, but I have to go back out later."

I hadn't noticed her walking into the foyer and up the stairs behind me until she spoke, "Me likes zat muzic chu flays."

I asked, in the process of unlocking the dead bolt on the front door of my place, "Do what?" I was somewhat caught off guard, and her poor English didn't help matters, "What was that you said?"

Apologizing for her poor English, "Sory, me szay me vlikes zat…May-be I no szay vright," she repeated.

"No, no, that's okay, I understand. I think," I responded while trying to be sure I'd heard her say she liked the jazz. I commented, under my breath without realizing I'd spoken loud enough for her to hear me, "The obvious question would be from where? My music is never so loud that it can be heard outside the apartment," I said. Instinctively, I covered my mouth with one hand while tossing the keys on the kitchen table, "Oh damn! That wasn't a dream."

Natasha moved closer, "Chu don't zemembver?"

"Yes." I extended my hands in front of my body to keep her at a safe distance, "No…wait! Wednesday night didn't happ…well, it can't happen again. I'm your neighbor. You're engaged…and…I'm your neighbor!" I immediately began replaying the events of the unforgettable, regrettable event a couple days before. As it turned out, I hadn't dreamed the whole thing. I yelled at the thought, "But my apartment was clean! The stereo was off. The ice pail…the centerpiece on the table…the condom! Oh, damn!"

Looking at me with those eyes I remembered from my dream which, as it turned out, actually wasn't a dream. "Me knows, me kleanz up," she said.

"Damn! Damn! Damn!" was my only response.

Lowering her head, "Chu not vwant?" she asked.

As the events of the experience flashed repeatedly in my mind; careful to position myself so that the table remained a constant divider, I realized the more I recalled of the last time we were in this situation, the distance was as much to keep me from her as it was to keep her from me, "No. I mean, yes I want…but no, I can't. We can't. Oh damn!" I replied.

She asked again, "Chu not vwant?"

"No… No, I'm sorry, I shouldn't… I can't. You can't be in here. You have to go. You're engaged, and I…well, I…I have somebody," I said, before realizing it.

Natasha tried to discount the remark, "Me never zsee zu vit…"

As I realized the meaning of my own words, "Well, it was just earlier today," I hesitated. It had only then occurred to me the reason for the feeling I had when talking to Ernestina; I dismissed it. "But the reason you don't see me with nobody… anybody, is because I work a lot. I don't have much time for things like that."

"Chu make time vor me udder dayz," she said.

"Yes, but no, not again," I said. "Haven't you ever heard; you don't get your meat…" It occurred to me as to whom I was talking. "Oh, never mind. We just can't do this anymore. Now, you have to go so I can get some things done."

My neighbor posed from a place of genuine concern, "Vwat chu hab do?" she asked. And again, moved, strategically trying to get at me from the opposite side of the table, "Vaant me helvp?"

"No! I mean, no; you can't help me," I responded. "Not like that. Not again. Now, I really need for you to go."

"Go vwhere?" she asked.

Being short, "Go home," I replied.

"Me vwaant szay here. Novody atz me home. Me not vwaant bee der," she said.

I was beginning to get a bit annoyed, "Okay look, you don't have to go home."

"Chu vwaants me sztay?" she interrupted.

"No," I demanded. "You don't have to go home if you don't want, but you've got to get the hell up out of here."

Natasha lowered her head sulking, as she rounded the table and hurried toward the door. "Chu no vwaant Natasha," she whined.

More instinctively than any other reason, I grasped her left wrist with my right hand and gently tugged to prevent my neighbor's escape, "Look, I don't want you to leave like…"

"Chu no wvaant Natasha vleeb?" she concluded.

With our bodies briefly coming into contact, I explained, "No. I mean, yes, you have to leave. I just don't want you to leave like this. You're pretty upset."

There was a distinctly pleasant aroma of mint as I felt her breath on my face when she responded, "I all vright. Chu not vwaant Natasha; me goes avaay."

I was mesmerized by her beautiful brown eyes that pulled me in like metal to a magnet. "No. I don't…want…"

Almost without warning, those succulent lips engulfed mine and she thrust her satin muscle deep into an unsuspecting mouth. My mind was adamantly protesting the unrestrained actions of an eager body as I submitted to the will of Natasha's passionate attack. It was as though I was having an out-of-body experience witnessing her rip the shirt open and devour the flesh of my neck, then, consume my broad chest with the fullness of her lips. I would like to think my reaction was involuntary, but it would have been a task within itself to prevent Mother Nature from taking her predestined course. My heart pounded like it was trying to tear its way out my chest as the two of us undertook a passionate session of, seemingly, attempting to swallow each other's face. Clothing somehow found its way from the position on our bodies onto the floor. We'd both stripped down to our underwear when the sound of reality summoned.

BBBRRRIIINNNGGG, *BBBRRRIIINNNGGG,* *BBBRRRIIINNNGGG.* The scream of the cell phone interrupted my trip to ecstasy.

I fumbled with the phone as Natasha, unfazed, continued kissing my neck and chest, "Um…Uh, hell-o…hello," I recovered.

The concern in her voice was unmistakeable, "Yes Willie, this Ernestina; you all right?" she asked.

"Yeah, baby…I'm good," I managed.

"I was just calling to give you directions to my place. It looks like I might be able to slide out of here a little earlier than originally scheduled. You are still coming aren't you?" she asked.

I was desperately trying to get Natasha to stop kissing me; at least for a moment until I finished the phone call, "Yes… uh, okay, baby. I'll be there to meet you after work." I quietly confirmed plans with the welcomed, unwelcome caller while attempting to ward off my neighbor with a free hand, "Ernestina, I need you to hold on a second."

"Me needs stop?" Natasha asked.

"Excuse me?" Ernestina questioned.

I cleaned up the comment, "Oh, I was saying hold on a minute while I turn down the volume on the television; get some paper, and something to write with."

Ernestina continued giving me the address to her apartment and detailed directions as to the quickest way to get there from the Village. "Uh-hmm," was the only audible response I could muster to each comment or question without incriminating myself. I tried to cut the conversation short.

"I ha-ve to go, so I c-a-n come…by. Uh, so I can come by and pick you up," I corrected.

Ernestina asked, in an insinuating tone, "What are you up to?"

"Get-ting rea-dy," I replied.

She whispered into the phone, "And just what are you getting ready to do? Sounds to me like you having a good time all by yourself. If I didn't know any better, I'd say…are you naked?"

"Uh…yeah," I responded. "That normally is a requirement when you're getting ready to shower."

Ernestina questioned, trying not to let me hear her giggle, "Sounds like you're getting ready to do more than shower. I caught you in the middle of something?" She asked. "You're not embarrassed?"

"Embarrassed at having to shower?" I questioned.

"Now, you know darned well that's not what I mean. I'm talking about what you're doing," she said.

I was concerned that maybe she could hear Natasha, "And just what do you think I'm doing? I wasn't expecting you to call so soon. But I do need to go…seri-ous-ly…so I can shower and get ready."

"I bet you do need to go," Ernestina smirked. "Normally, I think I'd be a little put off, but I'm rather impressed by your openness," she commented.

Not realizing Ernestina really didn't know what was going on, at least, not all that was going on, I asked, "Openess with what?"

She concluded, "Well, I always say a man can't please a woman unless he first knows what it takes to please hisself. I'm going to let you go so you can *go on and work that out.*"

It wasn't until then that I caught on to what she must have been thinking but knew there was no way I could offer any other logical explanation. The realization I'd just narrowly escaped a burning building prompted me to hold my peace.

"All right babe," I remarked.

Ernestina then informed, "Oh yeah, you know, I like when you call me baby while you caught up in the moment," she detailed. "That is such a turn-on."

Relieved to find out she was none the wiser, I reiterated, "Well, I re-ally have to go. I'll give you a call whe…when I'm on the way."

She commented through her own embarrassment, "You enjoy…bye."

"Later," I responded, almost simultaneously pressing the end button on my phone and dropping it to the floor. "Natasha...Natasha!" I yelled in a whisper. "You have to stop! I've got to go shower."

She interrupted her Lady Dracula impersonation long enough to say, "Me goes shover vwit chu."

"No," I said. "If that happens, I'll need to take a shower *after* the shower. I have an appointment."

"Chu haab deate," she responded.

"What?" I asked.

"Chu goes ouvt vwit vwoman," she clarified. "But ist o-kay, I be herve vwhen chu kome beaack."

I was somewhat shocked at the thought; a woman so understanding that she was actually *willing* to take back seat. The fact that she wasn't at all hard on the eyes was an added bonus. That was the ultimate dream of every Neanderthal of the male gender I'd ever encountered. For a split second, I actually entertained the idea of a purely sexual relationship with no strings, no expectations, but was shaken back to the realities of life with a Black woman when my phone rang again. *BBBRRRIIINNNGGG, BBBRRRIIINNNGGG.* Natasha had her arms wrapped around my torso and held me in position, refusing to allow the opportunity to retrieve my phone. The more I squirmed, the tighter her grip became until it appeared we'd engaged in a wrestling match.

I continued the protest, "Natasha, this isn't supposed to happen. Not again. The other night never should have happened and it definitely can't continue happening."

After what seemed like an hour long fight with a northwestern grizzly bear, Natasha suddenly stopped, reached over, picked up the phone, and gently placed it in my hand, "Chu haab go; no?"

For a second I considered calling Ernestina to cancel. Then I realized the consequences of such an action. "Yes, I *have* to go," I whispered.

Without so much as a single word, my assailant gathered her things, straightened her pony tail using the darkened television screen as a mirror, kissed me on the left nipple of my still bare chest, and simply walked out, leaving the door to my apartment partially open. I sat motionless for at least fifteen minutes before checking to verify the missed call on my cell.

It was one for which I'd been eagerly waiting, but now, wanted to avoid. I pressed "send" to dial the number. *BBBRRRIIINNNGGG.*

Ernestina answered on the first ring, "Hello." And didn't bother waiting for a response, "Please tell me you are on your way to my place," she said.

"I'll be leaving shortly," I answered. "Is there a problem? Was there something you needed?" I asked.

"No and yes," she stated. "There's no problem; at least there won't be when you get here, but there *is* something I need."

"Well, I'm not quite dressed yet but let me know and I'll stop by the store on the way up," I said.

"Oh, you won't find what I need at any store," she commented. "That phone call earlier got me so worked up I had to leave my job as soon as the conversation ended. I'm at the apartment taking a hot bubble bath." She was silent for a moment, then added, "Come to think of it, I could use some double-A batteries for later; maybe after you leave," she explained before politely stating, "I didn't realize how long... well, never mind...just get your ass over here."

"I must say, I'm a little surprised at your indiscretion," I said. "Those don't sound anything at all like the words of that sweet little innocent police officer I remember running across in Harlem several days ago."

She was a little more insistent, "Stop playing, get your fine self in that car, and come up here as soon as you can."

I assured her, while thinking; *what the hell have I gotten myself into?* "Okay, okay, I'm on my way."

"I keep remembering that phone call and visualizing you with no clothes on...," she reminded me. "Man, if you don't hurry up and find your way to Harlem, I'm gone have to start without you. You know all it takes for us is a good flex hose on the shower massager."

Reviewing events of the past hour, I was having a serious moral debate with myself when I commented half-jokingly. "Now, you know I don't have any business trying to push up on you after us only knowing each other for a few days. What ever happened to a gentleman wining and dining a beautiful young lady before trying to strip her naked and jump her bones?"

She questioned, "So, you're saying you don't want to *jump my bones?* What ever happened to a man throwing caution to the wind and being willing to do whatever it takes to satisfy the woman he loves?"

I then questioned through laughter, "Oh, so now it's all about love," I poked. "You've gone from meeting me on the street to being in love in a month. Have you no dignity?"

"Actually, it has only been about a week, give or take a couple days, and I honestly do like you enough to possibly take a chance with my heart. But, tonight doesn't have a damn thing to do with love, or my heart," she explained. "Tonight ain't hardly 'bout nothing but some good old-fashioned S-E-X. Something of which I've been in need for a lot longer than I like to be without it," she stressed. "Now get off the damn phone and make your way up here before I have to do this on my own. We've talked long enough for you to have made it here by now."

"All right," I conceded. "I'll be there within the hour," I confirmed. "But that means you can't start without me."

"Don't worry, if I do go ahead and get started, I'll be sure and save enough for you to have plenty to occupy yourself," she advised. "Now stop all the unnecessary chatter and bring your ass!"

I reassured her, "See you in a bit." Hanging up the phone, I cursed myself. "Damn you; the chance for which you've been waiting with the woman you wanted, and you've fucked yourself out of the opportunity…literally."

I slowly got up from the chair where Natasha had caused me to actually break a sweat fighting her off, thinking how most of the guys I knew would be feeling on top of the world if they were in my situation. But for some reason I felt like the world was on top of me. I remembered the comment Ernestina had made about a man doing whatever he could to satisfy the woman he loved. *Was that what this feeling was about…love?* I wondered to myself. The bigger question though: *Was that what I really wanted?*

To shower only took about fifteen or twenty minutes but it seemed like the hot water massaged my back and shoulders for hours; offering much needed relief from the tension building at the thought of my actions. A vivid reminder of the experience with Natasha only a short time before, the feeling of the soft terrycloth towel actually made drying off more of a task than normal. Often I found myself strategically going over specific areas of my body for a second and third time while day-dreaming about her velvety touch.

"Damn," I uttered to myself while shaking my head from side to side at the thought. "Damn!" Came the comment again while I draped the towel over the bar leading into the master bedroom as I passed from the bathroom.

As was normally the case after showering before I ventured out, my clothes were matched and neatly arranged on the bed. I noticed the reflection of my bare body in the mirror when moving to pick up the boxers. Looking at my reflection in the full-length mirror, I commented, "You's about a greedy bastard."

Imagining the response from my alter-ego, I mumbled in a squeaky tone. *"Yes, we most certainly are a greedy, selfish pair aren't we?"*

Once dressed, I left the apartment to discover Natasha sitting in her usual place on the stoop entering the building. As I descended the stairs it was noticed that her hair was still noticeably damp from the apparent recent shower she, herself, had taken.

I hesitated for a second and then passed out the doorway. "Natasha," I said, simply to acknowledge her presence.

She responded without ever turning her head, "Vwillie."

For the first time since moving into the building, I sort of regretted having found a parking space right at the bottom of the steps. Approaching the curb, I remotely disarmed the security alarm and reached for the door to climb in. I was secretly checking her out in the reflection from the car's window as she sat motionless like the carved statue of a goddess.

I heard her call out, as I closed the car door, "Haab gute time."

In the process of accelerating, I asked myself aloud, "Was she being sarcastic, or genuinely sincere in the comment?" *Oh well*, I thought. *It's not like she doesn't know what time it is.*

The clock on the CD player displayed "8:45 p.m." by the time I hit Broadway at Columbus Circle. Remembering that I never did write the directions down when Ernestina gave them to me earlier due to being distracted, I figured this would be about as good a time as any to call her and "verify" how to get to where she lived. That would also give her sufficient opportunity to get out of the tub and be dressed by the time I could make it up to Harlem. I spoke while dialing her number, "Cause you know how I hate for folk to make me wait." *BBBRRRIIINNNGGG, BBBRRRIIINNNGGG.*

"Hello, Willie?" she asked.

I tried to make light of the fact that it had taken a lot longer than I'd planned, "Yeah, did you miss me?"

She began explaining, "I was beginning to wonder if you had changed your mind about coming over or, even worse, if something had happened to you," she said. "I was in the bathtub so long that my hands started to wrinkle."

I asked, simply for the sake of making conversation, "Are you still in the tub?"

Sounding a bit agitated, "No. Didn't you hear me say I *was* in the tub? As in past tense," she said. "Where are you? Have you left the Village yet?"

"Yes, I have," I answered. "But time did get away from me when I was taking my shower." Not wanting to tell a complete lie, I said, "Funny, I just realized a few blocks back that I don't have the directions you gave me."

"Men," she replied. "I was honestly surprised you even wrote the directions down. I don't know what it is about most men that they just will not write down directions when somebody gives them…like all of you can just know how to get to where you're going after hearing somebody say it once."

Pretending to be disappointed, "Okay, so you don't want to give me the directions again?" I asked. "I mean, if you don't want to see me, I guess it won't be too much trouble to run on up to 133rd and Broadway to see Moms and Poppy."

Seemingly out of nowhere, she asked, "Why do you call them that?"

"Damn idiot!" I yelled, suddenly switching from the right lane to the left when someone pulled out from the curb in a gray Volvo without checking for traffic. I then questioned, "Call them what?"

Ernestina anxiously inquired, "What is it?"

"Some fuc…some doggone tourist," I corrected myself.

"You don't have to be so polite," she noted. "You forget, I am a New York City police officer. I imagine I've heard just about every profane word that was ever uttered."

"Well, with me, it's a respect thing," I explained. "Has a lot to do with the way I was brought up. If I was lying in bed and so much as dreamed about disrespecting anybody, my mom would slap me so hard in the dream I'd wake up on the damn floor. She'd knock me out of bed all the way from Georgia at the thought of it."

She questioned from behind a veil of confusion, "But, I thought Eunice and Sam up here in Harlem was your mom and dad? Any time you speak of them, you always say Mom and Pop. Well, actually, you call them Moms and Poppy. That's what I was just asking you: Why do you call them that if they're not your real parents?"

Thinking about my biological parents down South, "Truth is," I paused. "My real parents are back in Georgia, where I'm from originally."

The comment came all the way from the back of her mind. "Rea-lly, I thought you talked kind of funny, just couldn't place the accent. But you don't sound like anybody from the South that I ever met," she said.

Without elaborating, "I get that a lot," I said.

She went back to her original question, "So, this Sam and Eunice, exactly who are they? And I thought you were talking earlier about taking your dad to the doctor? Wasn't that Sam you were talking about?"

"No."

"But you said something was up with your old man. I thought you were talking about your dad...who would be your pop...who I figured was Sam," she deduced.

"No. You assumed the reference to my old man was about Sam because I refer to him as Poppy. Just like you assumed he was my dad," I explained. "Listen, the references to Poppy, old man, and dad all represent different people for different reasons," I said.

"So, how many dads, pops, or old men are there in your life, and which one is really the sperm donor?" she questioned.

"Look," I changed the subject. "I'm coming up on 110th Street; are you going to continue interviewing me until I get to New Jersey or are you going to give me directions to your apartment?" I asked.

She laughed before stating, "So, now you all anxious to get here. It's your own fault. You could have been here an hour ago...before I got waterlogged."

"All right then, six more blocks and I'll be past you. I'm not turning around and coming back," I said.

"You've got to come back past me to get down to your place in the Village anyway," she said.

"I don't *have* to," I replied.

She was fishing when she asked, "So what, you got some soft warm place you can stay uptown if you're out past your bedtime? Is that why it took you so long to want to get together, because you were preoccupied?"

"Yeah, you're right," I admitted. "If I get caught off uptown and just don't feel like driving all the way back down to the Village, I can just stop off at old girl's house and relax my cares away," I said. "There's always a good meal waiting, I don't have to lift a finger to do anything, and can hang out as long as I want without worrying about anybody bothering me."

Her tone turned serious. "Sounds to me, that's where you need to be on your way to then. I don't know why you bothering to stop by me at all. Now I'm beginning to see the picture a little clearer," she said. "Talking all sweet when you met me on the street, but taking a whole week to dial my damn number; what the hell was I thinking? That's probably where you were on your way to when I saw you that day!" She scolded.

I tried to interrupt, "Ernestina, it wasn't more than a couple days."

She continued the rant, disregarding what I'd said. "I don't know what the hell I was thinking: a fine, good-looking specimen of a man alone in this city! I must have been out of my damn mind...getting all sentimental and displaying feelings and shit you aren't even interested in."

"Baby," I interjected.

By this point, she was yelling, "You know what, I'm glad you left the damn directions at your place! And when you find them, just throw whatever paper they're written on in the damn trash!" Ernestina became angrier with every word. "And since you all the way up here in Harlem, why don't you just go on by..."

I yelled over her, "By my Moms!"

Timidly, she asked, "By...where?"

"Go by my Moms," I said, in a softer tone. "The comment I made about my old lady; I was talking about Moms... Eunice."

The sound of embarrassment in her voice was obvious, "Oh, I thought you were..."

Now I felt somewhat vindicated, "Yeah, I know what you were thinking."

"Why did you let me carry on so?" she asked.

"Well, I tried to stop you," I answered. "Now, you going to give me the directions or do you have something else to bitch me out about?"

Her comment originated from humility, "All right, I guess I should tell you how to get here so I can apologize in person," she said. "Where are you now?"

"I just crossed over 125th Street...a few blocks from the Apollo," I said.

Her tone was somewhat more subtle, "I am a cop. I've been living in this area as long as I can remember," she said. "I know which 125th Street you're talking about. But you've got to turn around."

"There's no place to turn around up here," I explained. "And I said if you let me drive past you, I *wasn't* turning around."

Ignoring my comment, she continued. "You'll have to go all the way up to 133rd Street by where your mom and pop live, and turn back."

"Moms and Poppy," I corrected. "Besides, the signs say *NO U-TURN* at that intersection. You trying to get me a ticket?"

"Anthony is working this area tonight," she noted. "If he stops you, tell him to call me. I'll take care of it."

I reminded her of the comment she'd made this afternoon, "I thought you told me earlier today that you weren't going to pull any more strings for me if I got into trouble."

"No," she volunteered. "What I said was, I wouldn't pull any more strings until you took me out on a date. Now, when you turn around, come back down to 115th Street and make a right. You go about half-way down the block and there will be a building on the left with a wrought-iron fence. The gate is usually unlocked because people got tired of going downstairs to open it for visitors," Officer Lady said.

Looking around to make sure there were no police on the prowl, I made the quick u-turn at 133rd and Broadway before starting back down toward 115th Street, but then decided to cross over to Riverside Avenue.

"All right, I'll see you in a minute; you can meet me downstairs," I said.

The abrasiveness in her voice became distinctly more apparent, "Do you not hear very well, or do you just not pay attention to what I say when I'm talking?"

"What are you talking about?" I questioned. "You just said take a right at 115th and your building is on the right, didn't you?"

Ernestina scolded, "Well, that definitely answers my dog-gone question, now doesn't it? I said the building will be on your left; and I'm not coming downstairs," she repeated. "The gate should be open. It usually is."

More to annoy her than anything else, I asked, "What's the building number?"

Being funny, "It's zero-zero Iron Gate," she said. "You won't be able to see the number on the building because the street lamp is out. That's why I told you to look for the Iron Gate. Or were you not listening then either?"

"Truth is," I replied. "You have such a sexy voice I just like to hear you say everything twice."

She joked, "And all this time I thought you were just hard of hearing."

"Nope, I simply enjoy hearing the sweet melodies you sing," I said. "I be hanging on your every word."

"Apparently not," she said. "I gave you my number nearly a week ago and still ended up having to call you to get a date. I guess you don't like hanging very much."

"Aw, come on, babe. Can't we get past that? I feel like I'm in front of the parole board every time you bring that mess up," I said.

"All right, I'll leave it alone...for now," she noted. "Speaking of alone, where are you?"

"Trying to find a place to park," I said.

"Dang that was pretty quick. How fast you driving?" she asked.

"Well I actually came back Riverside Ave. past Grant's Tomb to avoid all the traffic lights. Figured I've kept you waiting long enough," I explained.

"Why thank you for being so considerate," she commented.

"So, you still not coming downstairs?" I asked.

"There you go not listening again. How many times are you going to make me repeat myself? Come up the stairs and turn left...its number 2-0-6," she insisted.

9

Wrought-Iron Gate

parked and waited for a car to pass before crossing the street and walking through the Iron Gate leading to Ernestina's building. Two older gentlemen on the sidewalk simply paused and eyeballed me from the fence all the way to the entrance. I glanced over my shoulder as the solid wood door swung closed and caught a glimpse of them pointing over toward the Impala; motioning in the direction of where I'd gone. The concern lasted only about as long as it took the door to close behind me, as I couldn't understand a word of what they'd said anyway...sounded like Greek or some other foreign tongue. Topping the stairs while admiring the handy woodwork of the banister and railings, the thick wooden door tagged 2-0-6 gently opened as I raised a hand to sound the buzzer. I didn't see anybody so I stepped inside to the sounds of Luther Vandross crooning the paint off Ernestina's walls.

I pushed the door closed and turned to see beauty personified standing in royal purple lingerie, and my jaw damn near fell to the floor. Realizing my mouth was still hanging open, trying to keep my composure, "I...I hope you not wearing that to dinner," I said. "By the time you get dressed and we make it to the restaurant..."

"We're not going to any restaurant," Ernestina interrupted. "I decided that we should stay in...get to know each other a little better. Why, are you hungry?"

While trying not to appear too dumbfounded at the site of her thick legs and perfectly rounded ass, which was only accented by the silk drapery she wore, I stammered, "Well, I...uh, no...I mean, I'm okay."

Taking me by the hand and leading in the direction of the oversized butter-leather couch, "Good," she said. My host assured me with an inviting smile, while taking a seat on the middle cushion, "If you'd like, I can hook up some finger food."

Playing the devil's advocate, I teased while taking a seat beside her, "And just what type *finger food* did you have in mind?"

Without uttering a word, she took the index finger of my right hand into her mouth and proceeded to act as though it was a lollipop. My imagination ran wild and explored a gauntlet of possibilities which caused my libido to shift into high gear. However, constant thoughts of earlier events kept me subconsciously applying the brakes. I was both shocked and excited at the mere thought of the anticipated future.

With full lips, warm and inviting, I couldn't resist the urge to shower her with tender kisses. I gently slid one spaghetti strap off her soft shoulder to expose the most perfectly toned physical features while simultaneously massaging her upper arms and shoulders with my lips. A whisper came without restriction of thought.

"Are you sure?" I asked.

She moaned, "Is that a question you think really needs to be asked? Don't you realize the answer?"

While continuing to kiss her neck, I spoke softly in Ernestina's ear, "I just don't believe in going any place I'm not invited."

She advised in a soft whisper, "You have an open invitation to do whatever you want, however you want."

"Are you sure?" I insisted.

Placing both hands on my shoulders and gently pulling me forward for our faces to meet, Ernestina whispered, "You talk too much. Like I said, whatever...however you want."

Being there on the couch with the object of my desire wearing little more than a thought was where I had longed to be since first meeting her last week. My body was in the mood, but my mind was constantly scolding me for what had happened earlier with Natasha. Nevertheless, I definitely didn't want to disappoint Ernestina.

I continued caressing her softness and tasting her almond-scented flesh. The contrasting texture of her firm muscular frame in comparison to the satin-like skin became more apparent when I perused the full extent of her body. The scent of almond was particularly prevalent when my tongue encountered her naval.

Perceiving my reluctance, she asked, "Do you want to stop?"

I paused, "It's not what you think," and then answered, "Pleasing you pleases me."

"Well, its okay if you don't want to," she started. "I mean, you don't really know a whole lot about...!"

The next forty-five minutes were consumed with the two of us sharing the stage beside Luther Vandross as we made beautiful music together. I must have kissed every part of her gorgeous body to the point that my lips were numb as she'd tried climbing over the back of the couch. It was as though I was, for the first time, in the presence of what sensuality was designed to be like. We danced to a new song and found ourselves thoroughly enjoying every note while lifting our voices in unison at the finale to rest our heads on the over-sized pillows.

I whispered, again, "Pleasing you...pleases me."

"Daaammmnnn!" She said.

Obviously concerned, I asked, "Something wrong?"

"You...ain't no good. Not a bit of good at all." The officer's inhibitions were effectively dismantled and condemnation levied against me as she rolled to the end of the couch. She whispered again, "Damn," and positioned her head on the armrest.

A few minutes later, I moved to where she lay, placing my head on her stomach with my arms encircling the two most pleasant thighs I'd ever had the pleasure of knowing. "I'm feeling a case of the munchies," I said.

"Oh hell no!" she screamed, pushing me to the floor in front of the couch. "You've done got all the good from this one, baby!"

I volunteered, as I rolled up onto my side, "I meant food."

She said with an impish grin, "Oh."

I laughed, "What I need is some rice and beans."

"If you're really hungry I can cook something for you," she said. "It'll only take a minute."

Reminding her of what she had told me before, I pretended to argue. "Now when I got here you told me we weren't going out and that you'd prepared some finger food."

"But you told me that you were okay when I asked earlier," she said.

"That was earlier, before you caused me to work up an appetite," I admitted.

"You are so silly," she said.

"I'm so serious," I replied.

"You have to be kidding me!" she exclaimed. "I am spent. When I told you there isn't anything left, I wasn't joking. Remember now, it's been quite a while since I've had the pleasure of *being pleasured*."

"I bet you say that to all the guys," I joked.

Somewhat defensively, she commented, "Seriously, I don't get down like that. I mean, with all the crap that's going around these days and the fools you have to deal with who'll just give you crap if you're in a relationship, it's just not worth it."

"Not trying to raise the dead," I said. "But I thought when we met last week, you told me something about issues with a man. In fact, I'm positive you told me the trouble was with *your* man."

"I never said it's been a while since I had a man. What I said was, it has been quite a while since I've been pleasured," she explained. "Part of the problem with the man I had, when I wasn't sharing him with somebody else, was the fact that he didn't care too much about pleasing anybody other than himself."

"That's such a waste," I stated.

"The biggest waste was the amount of time I spent with him," Ernestina reasoned.

"How long were the two of you together?" I asked.

"Several years," she calculated. "Several years too damn long, truth be told."

"That's a long time," I confirmed. "I know there must have been something about it that was good enough to keep you interested for so long."

"Hope is a powerful thing," she said. "When you're fortunate enough to find somebody who's more into you than they are themselves, that's rare…like a diamond in the rough," Ernestina continued. "Take just now, for example. Usually a relationship starts out with the man; that would be you," she joked. "But, with the man being all considerate and concerned about what the woman; that would be me," she added. "Anyway, the man's interested in what the woman wants. At the point they become comfortable with each other, or when he becomes comfortable with her, all that kindness and consideration crap just goes out the damn window."

"That depends on where you've been shopping for your men," I said. "If you been out picking up strays or unwanted mutts, why are you so surprised when they prove to be the dogs you knew they were before taking them in?"

She adjusted her position on the couch to be certain we made direct eye contact. "Not to bring up the past either, but take the creep I was just involved with. We met in trade school, had a lot in common, even dated for a few years after I attended the police academy. Everything about him told me *he was the one*," she noted. "I mean, we were together a little more than three years…three wasted years," she assessed.

"Well, folk down South never consider time in any situation wasted unless you come out with no more wisdom than you went in," I rationalized. "If you consider yourself wiser now than when you guys got together, then, that wasn't wasted time…just an education."

"You bet your sweet ass I'm smarter. Smart enough not to fall for the bullshit and take his trifling butt back again," she concluded.

"Not smarter but wiser," I corrected. "Don't be so hard on yourself. You can't get a diploma unless you complete four years of college, which includes a lot of reports and exams. On some you do well and some you don't, but that's all part of the educational process…the experience."

She wore a puzzled expression, "What? Speak English, and cut out all that biscuit-and-gravy philosophy. Nobody understands that shit except you. If you're going to talk to yourself, I'll go take a shower; you coming?"

"Well, I was actually thinking of making that trek back down to the Village. I've got quite a few things to check on tomorrow," I said.

Motioning for me to let her off the couch, she asked, "Don't you have to be back in Harlem tomorrow morning?"

My response was a little more direct than intended, "Yeah, but it's not like I packed an overnight bag with a change of clothes."

Taking what I perceived as a stab at my heritage, she asked, "Now, you mean to tell me you're a true country boy and have never worn the same clothes two days in a row?"

"Yeah, I have, but that was a long time ago, when I only had two pairs of pants and three shirts," I said. "Times have improved. I've got a few more pieces of lint in my wardrobe now."

Moving toward the front door, she reasoned, "If you're going drive all the way back to the Village just to take a nap and come back to Harlem tomorrow morning, you might want to go ahead and take off. It's already close to midnight, and you've still got an hour or so to drive."

With a somber expression, I half-jokingly questioned, "So, is that the way it is? You get what you need and then show me the door? Suddenly I feel so used."

"Rest assured, I didn't exactly get what I needed, not *all that I needed* anyway. You're the one who keeps saying you have to go back home. I asked if you wanted to join me in the shower. It was you who declined my offer to lather you down," she explained.

"You dangerous," I joked.

She spoke from behind a slight giggle, "I'm serious…if you'll permit me to borrow your phrase," she said. "At any rate, you do need to get a move on if you're going to take that drive. The night's not getting any younger."

Checking the time on my wristwatch while opening the door, I responded, "Man, you're right, where did all the time get off to? Seems like I just got here a few minutes ago."

"Don't blame me," she defended. "You're the one who messed around and didn't show up until nearly eleven o'clock. In reality, you *have* only been here a few minutes. And man, what a few minutes they were!"

By now, Ernestina was literally crawling up my left leg which was still just inside her apartment door. While trying to escape, I said, "I think you *really* need that shower; a cold one, in fact."

She replied in a pleading tone, pretending to sulk, "What I *really* need is running out my door. You sure there's nothing I can do to convince you to stay over?" she asked.

"Naw, I have a thousand and one things to do tomorrow, which means an early start. If I stay here with you, I'll be lucky if I'm able to get started at all," I reasoned. "I really do need to go, but I'll ring you up some time tomorrow."

More instinctively than anything else, she directed, "Well, by the time you make it home, I should be done in the shower. Just give me a call to let me know you made it in okay."

I asked with a serious look, confusing concern for control, "Excuse me?" but immediately realized my error. "I'm sorry baby...uh, I mean Ernestina. It's that control thing; I guess old habits really do die hard."

She spoke with the sympathy of a life-long friend, "That's okay, I understand it has a lot to do with your life," she said. "Oh, and I think you have *earned* the right to call me baby at this point."

I assured her with a final kiss goodnight, "Well, baby, I'll give you a call when I make it home. Just so you won't worry your pretty little head."

"Thank you," she responded. "Good night."

I whispered, while exiting the apartment, "See you later," and then tiptoed down the stairs to avoid disturbing Ernestina's mostly elderly neighbors.

When I left the building and started across the courtyard, I noticed two guys passing near my car on the street. They were on the opposite side in the shadows close to the fence. I kept watching but never saw them come from where the car was parked. I crossed over at the point the street lamp was blown and crept up, keeping cover behind the other cars beside the curb. I determined they were just teenagers, probably looking for wheels to go joyriding or maybe as part of some gang's initiation.

I stood up and walked around the car in plain sight before calmly saying, "This one has a security system that disables the starter if you don't use the key to unlock it."

Noticeably startled, the skinny kid with the spiked Mohawk reluctantly asked, "How you know that...you done tried to lift this piece?"

Retrieving the keys from my pocket, "No, not exactly," I said, before disclosing as the alarm chirped to disarm, "I installed it."

The other youngster shouted in mid-stride, "Oh shit!" as they both turned to run. "That's the some-bitch owns this joint!"

Pulling my trusty Smith & Wesson from the belt holster, I couldn't resist popping off a couple shots: *CA-CLACK, CA-CLACK*, just to drive home the point as the two misdirected aspiring thugs rounded the corner of the building, "And neither of you have ever met my mama!" I exclaimed.

I sat and buckled in before pulling out while having a hearty laugh for most of the drive to the Village. The ride was a little more pleasurable as I couldn't help thinking about the expressions on those kids' faces when disarming the security system and they realized what had happened. *Just two punks doing what they think they have to in order to get ahead,* I thought to myself. I instantly replayed that journey down the road I'd traveled which started pretty much the same place theirs had.

Miles Davis' horn was screetching from the Bose speakers when I conceded to no one in particular, "Little do they know, it's just a dead end street."

10

Instant Replay

Unlike parking on my street in the early afternoon, finding a close place in the evening or at night was extremely difficult, to say the least. Locating a space at nearly one o'clock in the morning was absolutely out of the question unless you happened upon some visitor pulling out as you came through. Still, I was fortunate enough to find a space newly abandoned at the end of the block opposite the entrance to my building. I checked for traffic and crossed the street to notice Natasha in the same place she'd been when I'd left, perched at the top of the steps. When I passed her earlier, she was wearing jeans with a pullover NYC T-shirt, but now, looked particularly stunning in a floral-print blouse and a black fitted skirt, which hit her not quite halfway the thigh when seated. Even in the dim light, the turquoise underwear was unmistakable from the bottom step as she sat with her knees a few inches apart.

I spoke coming up the steps while holding the rail that stopped beside the stoop where she sat. "Natasha...what's up? How are you this evening?" I asked.

While standing and waiting for me to pass, she replied, "I gute, und howve ist chu?"

When I opened the door, she followed me into the building and started up the stairs behind me. Without turning around, I said, "Not tonight, Natasha. It has been a very long day and I have to get started again in just a few hours."

"Jes zu tzalk," she stated.

I unlocked the door, pushed it open, and said, "But only for a few minutes. I have to be out early."

Watching the skirt dance like it was intentionally teasing me as she passed and walked into my apartment, I suddenly began having flashbacks of the last time we were in similar positions. Immediately, I summoned the assistance of John Coltrane by pressing the power button on the stereo remote. Then, I remembered the comment from her that had come following the first incident about how she liked my jazz music. Almost in a panic, I killed the power on the stereo and turned on the seldom watched television for company. She took a seat on the couch and picked up a magazine from the small coffee table in front.

Sitting down at the opposite end, I asked, "So, what's on your mind."

"Vwhen I kome herve tzudaye, me likes spends tyme vwit chu," she explained. "Uri alvays ist go avaay..."

I considered the nature of the conversation and pretty much figured out the direction it was going. Recalling activities involving the two of us the last time we were on the couch, I became a bit uncomfortable and moved toward the kitchen.

I said, "Maybe talking to him would help. I mean, if you explain how you feel, perhaps he won't be gone as much, or maybe you can go with him sometime."

Natasha stood, and, approaching the table, said, "Me kant go vwit hime…alvready me aesk. He szay me, sztay homve."

The colors in the floral print of her blouse brought my focus to the centerpiece on the table and my mind was pulled back nearly a week in time to when it had been inadvertently pushed to the floor in the midst of our passionate exchange. It seemed that everywhere I looked there was a reminder of the incident that haunted me. What I'd begun to realize caused me to regret the dependency I was developing for the one woman I had discovered I wouldn't mind depending on… Ernestina.

I moved hurriedly toward the door, "Well, Natasha, I don't know what more can be done. The fix just doesn't appear to be in the cards," I said. "If I had the answers to everybody else's, I wouldn't have any problems of my own."

"In der kards?" she questioned.

"Oh, never mind," I said. "But I have to get ready to go. Like I told you before, I only had a few minutes."

"Chu goes beckt out?" she asked.

"Yes, I have to go somewhere other than here. I have to go *anywhere* other than here," I answered. "It was a mistake to come home…should have just stayed where I was."

In a tone that sounded more concerned than with which I was comfortable, she asked, "Butte vwhy chu goes beckt out?"

Trying not to show my frustration, I simply said while pushing the door closed behind her, "Because I have to."

After I thought she was gone, I went in to take a shower and get ready for bed. It seemed the water barely had time to get hot before I turned it off and reached for my towel. *THUMP, THUMP, THUMP!* I dismissed what sounded like a knock at the door as my imagination playing tricks on me due to being so tired. *THUMP, THUMP, THUMP. THUMP, THUMP, THUMP,* it came again.

From somewhere between being aggravated and frustrated, I grumbled when emerging from the bathroom, "What the hell?"

THUMP, THUMP... the noise continued.

After donning my robe, I checked the peephole to see who was kicking on the door and snatched it open to be face to face with Natasha. I yelled softly in consideration of the neighbors, "What the hell is it now?"

She just stood silently and looked at me for what felt like an hour before speaking. "If chu cheange mindst und vwaant I kome overe..." she started.

I interrupted before she could finish. "No Natasha, I won't change my mind about you coming over. I told you earlier, what happened before shouldn't have happened at all. Certainly shouldn't have happened the second time, but listen, it definitely can't happen again. You're engaged and I'm... well...sort of involved."

"Vwhat means szort of?" she asked.

"It doesn't matter. What matters is the fact that you have a fiancé," I offered, "Now, if you'd like, I can talk to Uri. Maybe see if there is anything we can come up with to help resolve the problem you two are obviously having with communication."

Frightened at such a ludicrous suggestion, Natasha was suddenly eager to go and, pulling my door closed between us, insisted, "No. Ist okay, I speak vwit Uri."

I walked away thinking how much trouble this situation could have turned out to be if I'd chosen to get involved in a sexual relationship with Natasha as she had first suggested. It was uncertain to me whether she'd be back, but I wasn't in the mood to take that chance. Without much consideration, I quickly dressed and threw a few pieces into an overnight bag. On the way out, I ran into Natasha again at the top of the stairs. I didn't even bother to make eye contact but hurried downstairs and out the door before there was an opportunity for her to start another conversation.

By the time I parked on the street outside Ernestina's building, it was nearing three thirty a.m. and I was still trying to make up my mind to call her. Getting out the car with the small duffle bag, "You're here now," I said.

There was an elderly lady out to give her dog a chance to relieve himself who stared at me like I was somebody from *America's Most Wanted* as I crossed the courtyard. "She'd probably shit her pants if I coughed hard," I humored myself in the process of climbing the stairs and standing outside the door at apartment 206. In the process of trying to build up enough nerve to ring the buzzer, I heard the lock disengage and the door swung open.

"Oh damn!" Ernestina was as surprised as I was. "What the...! How long have you been....Willie, what in the hell is it that has you outside my door after three in the damn morning?"

Looking her up and down suspiciously, "You obviously weren't expecting me. Did I catch you at a bad time?" I asked.

Understanding my train of thought, she answered before I could comment, "Just get that craziness out your big-ass head. I'm not one of your past encounters. Told you already; I don't get down like that."

I led, "Okay, I'm listening."

Intentionally avoiding the answer, she asked, "Listening to what?"

Trying not to show any annoyance, I said, "To whatever explanation you might want to offer."

She remarked with accentuated sarcasm, "And you are who?" she asked. "I'm Ernestina Lady...Ms. Ernestina Lady. Was I clear in stating *Ms*. Lady?" she repeated.

My expression confirmed I wasn't in the mood, "Okay, I got your point, now answer the damn question."

Realizing the significance of my issues with trust, she volunteered an explanation, "Well, shortly after you left earlier, there was a report of gunshots outside the building. I remember hearing something, but in New York City you always hearing something. My being a police officer, and the fact most of the residents in this building are elderly; they naturally count on me to unofficially keep an official eye on things. Since you left me in the condition you did"—she laughed— "I haven't been able to sleep much, so I just come outside occasionally to check on things."

"I see, so you're on duty, huh?" I teased.

"Well I'm never officially *off* duty; that's one of the consequences of being a police officer," she informed. "And what the hell you doing back here; you left my place a little after twelve?" she questioned. "You call yourself checking up on me or something?"

Trying to play off the seriousness of the matter, I questioned through an incincere laugh, "Do I have a reason to check up on you?"

With what appeared to be a smirk, she responded, "Only if you trying to see how boring my life *really* is." She then posed in a more stern tone, "But seriously, what brings you here? I know you didn't go all the way to the Village, and then turn around just to come back."

I responded while displaying the small duffle bag on my shoulder, "I needed to go get my overnight bag with a change of clothes."

"I think there's more to it than that; the way you were talking about getting home and going to bed because of the day you're facing tomorrow," she reminded. "But I'll let you get away with that lame explanation for now…since it's so late. You know there's a charge to stay overnight, don't you?"

"And just how much is it going to cost me?" I asked, before confessing, "You are aware, I don't have any money."

She took my bag and placed it just inside the apartment door, "That's okay; I'll think of something." Ernestina said. "Come on; let's check things out in the courtyard and along the street."

Following her down the stairs, I complained, "I don't work for the city; you're the damn cop."

"That's police officer, thank you, and it should only take a minute," she said. "I don't much expect to find anything wrong but it makes the rest of the tenants feel comfortable to see me out and about on the grounds every once in a while.

Besides, it validates the discount I get on my rent for being an officer and living in the building."

I joked while opening the door, "Yeah, I feel so much safer when you're around."

Ernestina playfully slapped me on my butt, "Don't be such an ass," she said, while passing out the door before continuing. "I'm surprised you didn't see something or, at least, hear the shots when you left earlier. I mean, seemed it happened just a few seconds after you walked out my apartment."

"Well, you know how sometimes a person can get off into what they're thinking and hours seem like a few minutes," I said.

"You can say that again, because I was some kind of caught up after you worked me over the way you did...Damn!" Ernestina shivered at the thought. "You can say that shit again a few times. From now on, I'll just call you my *lap* dog."

About the same time Ernestina made the comment, we both were surprised by the little old lady standing just outside the Iron Gate with her poodle. The woman coughed discretely so as to make us aware of her presence. We passed through the gate without looking in her direction, trying to conceal our embarrassment.

"Have you no respect for your elders?" I snickered.

Burying her face in my shoulder, "I didn't even see her," Ernestina said.

"Hell, hearing about it is probably the closest she's come to actually having sex in forty years," I mumbled. "If she'd been in the breezeway outside the apartment earlier tonight, the way you were carrying on would've short-circuited her damn pace maker."

Ernestina playfully scolded while punching me in the arm, "Stop that, you are so mean. That lady's not bothering you."

I whispered, "Looks like she has to be pushing at least a hundred and twenty. That dog is probably the only friend she's got. I wonder if it's male or female."

"Okay now." The police officer came out in Ernestina's voice. "That's just a little bit disgusting. To suggest the woman be making it with her damn poodle; shame on you!" Grabbing me by the wrist, she commanded, "Let's go back inside before you get me kicked out the building; talking about these old people."

I laughed. "You just want to get me back upstairs so you can take advantage of me...rob me of my innocence."

Guiding me back inside the courtyard, she asked, "Can you honestly remember the last time you actually were innocent?"

By the time we arrived at her apartment, it was on the upside of four a.m., and I was starting to feel the adverse effects of having been in *go* mode since early the previous morning.

Ernestina asked, picking up the small overnight bag, "You bathe or shower?"

I responded while tucking the bag under my arm, "Oh, that's okay, I'm straight. I jumped in the shower when I stopped by home a little while ago."

Passing through the front room, she said, "Then I guess we're ready to turn in." But then asked. "What's your preference, the bed or the couch?"

In the process of sitting to remove my shoes, I commented, "If you're going to make me choose, my preference is to be wherever you are."

"Just thought I'd ask because people have all sorts of strange habits," she explained. "Like this one girl I used to hang with. She dated a guy for more than six years, and the entire time they were together, I never knew him to sleep in the bed with her at night."

Her comment had me somewhat puzzled. "They lived together?" I asked.

Ernestina replied with a frown, "Yeah...well, after the second or third year they dated, she moved in with him. Even then, he wouldn't sleep in bed with her." Ernestina's eyes suddenly darkened. "Heard from some of his family he had been in the Army or Marines or something…some kind of Special Forces stuff. Say he had a real bad experience in one of the conflicts, but you couldn't get him to talk about it. I think they finally broke up and he went away to one of those government hospitals," she said. "I don't know; my girl and me sort of lost touch a while back." A few seconds passed as she pondered the thought. "Come to think of it…I wonder how René is doing these days."

Pointing at my shoes, "Where do you want me to leave these?" I asked.

"They're fine right there, unless you want to take them into the bedroom. I know how some people are funny like that. They don't want their shoes too far from them when in a strange place," she said.

I said, with a slight chuckle, "Well, it's just that when you're in an unfamiliar place, you don't ever know when you'll have to leave in a hurry," I explained. "A lot of strangers have been caught creeping and end up shot or dead because they couldn't find their damn shoes. It's never any fun running down the street or out across the woods barefoot."

"Sounds to me, you know a little too much about those situations. How many times were *you* the stranger?" she asked.

My comment was intentionally defensive as I picked up my boots, "Okay, take off the badge. You're off duty tonight, or this morning," I said. "I'll take them with me."

She exclaimed in a whisper, "So, what are you trying to say? You think somebody will be coming up in here this time of the morning!" At that point, she seemed almost offended, "If that was the case, you never would've gotten in the door. And I damn sure wouldn't be talking about you sleeping in my bed."

In an effort to defuse the mounting tension, I felt it better to simply abate the conversation altogether, "Speaking of your bed, you want to show me where it is—and possibly join me, if there's enough room?" I laughed.

"Keep it up with the comments and you'll find your smart ass on the couch for real," she responded while playfully grabbing me by the neck, "Now get up and bring your butt on… Mr. Man," Ernestina laughed. "Oh, you thought I forgot… told you it was going to cost to sleep over."

Following her into the bedroom, I suggested, "How about I write you an I-O-U and we talk about a payment plan."

She said with an inviting look, while stripping to her Victoria Secrets and climbing atop the massive oversized king bed, "Well, in a few short minutes, I was kind of hoping you'd be a little too busy to talk about anything."

I asked, placing my overnight bag on the floor at the foot, "You think this thing is big enough?" Feeling somewhat relieved at the sight of her in the Victoria's Secrets, I commented, "I was a bit nervous at first because I don't sleep in pajamas, but I see you don't either…guess the boxers will have to do," I said.

Reaching for the dimmer switch, "You want the lamp on or off?" she asked in the process of loosing her bra and thong underwear, "I actually don't like pajamas either. In fact, I prefer to sleep in nothing at all," Ernestina said. "Does that bother you? I hope not."

While trying not to let her see me straining to make out the remarkable physical features in the dim light, I said, "Well, what I was actually trying to tell you is that I'd usually sleep in my boxers, but if you're comfortable sleeping in skins, that's straight too."

"Which side of the bed you want? You not a wild sleeper are you?" she questioned.

I reasoned while sliding beneath the silk sheet, "When I'm home, I sleep by myself. So the middle is where I usually end up. Do you have a preference? I mean, it is your bed."

"That's weird, I like the middle too," she said.

"This big ass bed and we both want to be in the same place. I guess that means we just have to stack up. I'll gladly get on top if that's all right with you," I joked.

Reaching over and grabbing my shoulder to roll me on top of her, "In all seriousness," she said. "That'll be just fine with me."

There was an incredible heat that radiated from Ernestina's flesh and the remarkable feeling of her feather-soft lips had me entranced with every succulent kiss as she repeatedly thrust her tongue deep into my mouth. My willing hostess moved from orally massaging my tongue to nibbling an ear and imitating Dracula's bride, biting at my neck and chest.

I was caught up in the moment before I realized. "Baby," I whispered.

"Baby, we forgot..."

"Forgot what?" she asked.

"Protection," I said. "You didn't give me a chance to ..."

"I know," she said. "But its okay, we good."

Pointing out the obvious, I whispered, "We're taking a hell of a chance."

"You safe?" she asked, before confirming, "I'm...safe."

"Come on, one of us has to be the responsible adult. I'm not going anywhere. Let me stop long enough to get protection," I insisted.

She joked, as her hold was relaxed to permit my retrieving protection from the overnight bag, "Okay, but that's gonna cost you double."

I searched aimlessly in the dark only to come up empty-handed. "Damn, I just knew I put some in the bag," I said. "Maybe they're in the car."

Moving over to turn up the lamp beside the bed, Ernestina said, "That's all right Will, give me a second." Opening the bottom drawer of the nightstand, she located the vital shield and handed it to me. "Relax, as a cop, I'm taught to always be prepared for any situation. Handle your business."

With protection in place, I returned to continue where we had left off. Ernestina pulled and I pushed, rehearsing until our motions were synchronized and we appeared to perform an intimate waltz for at least a half hour before she reached the *point of no return*. On the eve of that moment, she let out an ear-piercing squeal that I thought would have the neighbors scrambling for the fire exits or dogs coming from miles around.

Gasping for air, she whispered while caressing my perspiration-soaked back, "Will...Willie...baby, you are incredible."

"What I am sweetheart, is whipped. Go to your side of the bed," I joked. "You are banished."

"Are you all right?" she asked.

"Yeah, I just need to breathe," I responded. "Thought you said it had been a while."

"Been a while since what?" she questioned.

"Since you did what you just did," I gasped.

"Seriously, it has," she said.

"If you weren't out of shape, I'd be in a damn coma," I replied. "Good night."

Snuggling closer to me, she whispered, "Good night, baby."

11

Rude Awakening

BBBRRRIIINNNGGG, BBBRRRIIINNNGGG, BBBRRRIIINNNGGG... The unmistakable screech of my cell startled me back to consciousness.

I sprang up wide-eyed in the middle of the bed, "What the hell!"

Ernestina was sitting, stark naked, with her back against the headboard and her knees drawn up to her still bare chest. "Your phone is ringing," she whispered.

Still trying to crawl from beneath sleep, "What time is it?" I asked.

BBBRRRIIINNNGGG, BBBRRRIIINNNGGG.

"A little after ten," she said.

I said to no one in particular, "Oh, damn! I overslept something serious. I should've been over by Oz no later than eight thirty." I complained, "Baby, why didn't you wake me?" I asked her.

BBBRRRIIINNNGGG,   BBBRRRIIINNNGGG,
BBBRRRIIINNNGGG…

"I figured you needed your sleep. You didn't close your eyes until it was almost daylight," she explained. "Are you going to answer that? It's been ringing off and on since around seven this morning."

"You could've answered it," I said.

Ernestina reached across, picked up my cell from the nightstand, and held it in front of me. "It's not my phone," she said.

BBBRRRIIINNNGGG, BBBRRRIIINNNGGG…

"Answer it," I insisted.

Placing the phone on the pillow beside my face, she simply replied, "Answer your damned phone already; both of you starting to get on my nerves, now."

BBBRRRIIINNNGGG,   BBBRRRIIINNNGGG,
BBBRRR….

I answered without taking my eyes off Ernestina, "Yeah, hello…what's up?"

"Well it's 'bout damn time." Oz's voice echoed. "Beginnin' to think the next time I saw you, be on a slab downtown."

"I don't think they still do that downtown any more," I mumbled. "…Been relocated somewhere out in one of the boroughs."

"Don't tell me you's still in the fuckin bed, not this time o' mornin…Mr. 'Wake the sun and remind him to start the day," he joked.

I finally mustered the strength to sit up beside Ernestina. "Well, to be honest, I didn't get to sleep until it was about time to greet daylight," I said.

Somewhat concerned, "Sound like somebody been playin *hide the meat* all night. She still there wit you?" he asked. "If this ain't a good time, I can talk to you in a li'l while."

Hanging my feet over the side of the huge bed, "Well, actually, I'm over by her," I explained. "Listen, I'm sorry I

overslept but I'm not too far from you. Give me a few minutes...less than an hour."

"What I wanted you to do this morning, I already been
downtown and done it," he informed. "They's one more thing,
but it can wait 'til you have time."

Making my best effort to reassure him, "I'm straight, I got
time. Like I said, see you under an hour."

With an offer of fatherly advice, he told me, "Look Will,
now, I know it ain't like you to fall over for e'ry ole girl, so
this gotta be somethin worth takin a chance wit. Don't mess
it up...I done got things under control up here. You need to
handle yo bidness."

"All right, one last time," I insisted. "What I've got with
you, old man, *is* my business. When it seems like things are
under control is the time they need to be checked out. Now,
I'll be there in a bit."

"Okay, you stubborn cuss; since I can't get nothin through
that thick-ass head, see you when you get here," he conceded.
"Watch your back."

As the call ended, "Later," I said.

Without raising her chin from its resting place on soft,
but firm forearms folded across her knees, "Everything all
right?" Ernestina asked.

Digging around in the bed for my boxers, I replied, "Yeah,
everything's good, or it will be. Just a couple things I have to
take care of for the old man."

Ernestina raised her head slightly and, with a quizzical
expression, she asked, "Now, which old man would this be? Is
it your father, as in the sperm donor, Sam the surrogate, or the
other dude you call pop?"

While pulling on my Levis, "If you must know," I said.
"It's the other fella, and I call him the *old man*. Sam, I call
Poppy."

She continued the line of questioning, "What is this guy's
name?"

"You know, I never thought to ask. I don't know if Oz is his real name or not, but that's what everybody on the block calls him. Nobody goes by their real name anymore," I said.

"Oz...seems like I should know that name for some reason. It sounds really familiar," she determined.

"Maybe from TV when you were little," I said.

"What does that have to do with anything?" She questioned. "Did he use to act or something?"

Trying to keep a straight face, "You mean you never saw that movie?" I asked. "I think his first name was something like, The Wizard, and he had a bunch of pet monkeys with wings 'n shit."

Somewhat embarrassed, she playfully tossed a pillow at me while pretending to shout, "You are such an ass." Then, she questioned, "What about your real dad?"

I was silent for a few minutes, sliding each foot into the Tony Lama cowboy boots and straightening the legs of my jeans; I said minus any expression, "Him, I don't call much at all. But, that's another story for another time." There was a brief pause prior to asking, "You do breakfast?"

"Normally, I just grab a bagel or some cereal, but today, I'm supposed to be meeting Sheila over on Broadway at this little bodega. It's someplace new that we both wanted to try," she explained. "It'll be a nice change because I'm usually by myself, and, since we haven't seen each other in a while."

"Sometimes being by yourself isn't so bad," I surmised. "At least that way you don't have to worry about anybody stabbing you in your back. But, I wouldn't have time even if I wanted to. I'm already running late. Maybe we can do breakfast another day," I suggested.

"Tomorrow sounds good, if you're not too busy," she said, which actually came across more as her thinking out loud. "I'm pretty certain I'll have the day off as well. At least, I had requested off and, as far as I know, the girl who I worked for yesterday is supposed to be back from Virginia."

I put on a shirt and brushed my hair before realizing I'd forgotten to pack a toothbrush. "I guess folk will just have to wrestle with the dragon today…no brush for the grill," I said.

"There should be an extra one in the second drawer on the left side of the sink," Ernestina directed.

Emerging from the bathroom moments later with the toothbrush in hand, I questioned, "What's this, one *he* left here?"

"Actually, it is, but it's new. I imagine he forgot it. It's been in there at least a couple months," She said.

"You sure it hasn't been used, or is this the one you have to clean under the rim of the toilet bowl?" I poked.

She confessed, "No, Randy used to play games like that when I first put him out. He'd intentionally leave things and use that as an excuse to stop by anytime he felt like there was another man at my house."

"Oh, that's his name. So how did you stop him from stalking you?" I questioned.

She stated in defense of her ex, "He wasn't stalking me."

"Sweetheart, if your man isn't your man anymore and he keep showing up uninvited…that's stalking," I explained. "Hell, you're the cop. That's one of those rules you guys made up."

Finally moving to get out of bed and take a shower, she responded, "I didn't want to make a big deal out of it…"

"Yeah," I cut. "A lot of graves in the cemetery because folk didn't want to make a big deal out of their problems. I've never been to a funeral in all my life that wasn't a big deal."

"Okay, you made your point," she answered rather brashly. "I thought you were in a hurry."

I determined, "Oh, I guess that's a nice way of telling me to mind my own business."

"No, what I'm telling you is that I don't want to have this discussion," she volunteered. "I've gotten over the nonsense. I had a good day yesterday, and a damn good time last night. I won't start what's supposed to be a much deserved day of relaxation reviewing the bullshit that'll just have me stressed out, and needing another day to recover," she stated.

I spoke through laughter, "I think that has to be the most polite way I have ever been told to shut the hell up."

Stepping into the shower, she said, "As long as you know."

I yelled over the noise of the running water, "Hold up, you have to come lock the front door!"

She shouted back, "There's an extra key in that glass container on the counter, to the left of the stove. Lock up on your way out."

I hurried to the bathroom sink to brush my teeth before the steam from the shower got the mirror all fogged up. After slaying the dragon and performing a final check in the now fogged over mirror, I picked up my overnight bag off the floor, phone, and keys from the nightstand. Peeping back into the bathroom, I shouted, "I'm gone. Give me a call later, if you're not too busy!"

"Don't forget the key in the dish," she shouted back. "If I don't call, just stop by after you get things situated for your dad or fath...your old man. I should be back around four o'clock."

Leaving the bathroom, I noticed Ernestina's home phone ringing as I entered the front room of her apartment. *BBBRRRIIINNNGGG, BBBRRRIIINNNGGG...*

Rather than interrupt her in the shower, I decided to simply let the answering machine catch the call. When I passed to the kitchen, I heard the machine: *"Hello. You have reached... Please leave a message at the sound of the tone...beep!"*

I had paused for a second to admire the sound of her sexy voice on the recording when I heard the caller, "Hey, this Randy. I ran into old lady Everett at the market buying produce and dog food for that little mutt she call a poodle. She was telling me she thought we got back together 'cause she saw us going in the building late last night." His tone changed, "I don't know what asshole you wit, but I'm on my way and when I get over there, I better not find that son of a bitch at my house." There were more inaudible profanities being mumbled as he disconnected.

I left the apartment without mentioning anything to Ernestina about having heard the message. Reasoning it a better option to stick to the practice of keeping my nose out of other folks' business, I simply made certain the door was locked and proceeded down the stairs, thinking of the conversation she and I had this morning about all my fathers. There were several older residents in the courtyard walking their dogs and conversing, which, for the majority of them, would be the most excitement they'd have all day. Not wanting to bring attention to myself, I walked off the concrete path to the gate and on across the street to my car.

As I strapped in and reached for the door to pull it closed, I heard one of the residents, "Hey...Ran-dy...what's been going on?"

I looked back toward the entrance of the building to see one of the elderly women picking up her poodle while speaking with a large dark-complexioned fella wearing fatigue pants and a black T-shirt.

I said to myself, while patiently waiting for the moment he'd turn so his face would be visible, "Well, hello Mr. Stalker; pleased to have almost met you."

It was obvious the call to Ernestina's apartment had been from his cell phone, unless he lived in the next building. I sat in the car watching him for a few minutes until her ex turned, so I'd be aware of who to expect on that fateful occasion, before deciding Ernestina could take care of herself. I concluded, before finally deciding there was a greater need for my presence at Oz's place, "Whatever was going on between them was going on before she met me, and it will continue to for as long as she allows it."

12

Coming to Terms

I drove up at Oz's and immediately noticed Amp's Navigator parked out front. Instinctively, I dialed the old man's cell phone. *BBBRRRIIINNNGGG, BBBRRRIIINNNGGG.*

Oz answered and I could tell by the sound of his voice, something had him on edge, "Yeah, what's up?"

"Oz, this Willie. Is everything all right in there?" I asked.

"Why wouldn't it be? Just givin some last minute n'structions on how to handle this fool up on 153rd that don't wanna pay his dues," he said, before inquiring, "Where you?"

Getting out my car, I was peering at the blacked-out windows of the Navigator. "I just pulled up out front," I confirmed, prior to suggesting, "Oz, something doesn't seem right."

He asked, trying to be discrete in Amp's presence, "What you got?"

I was still checking out the 'Gator when I informed him, "I don't know; something just doesn't feel right about this whole situation." I cautiously walked completely around the outside of the truck looking for any sign that things were the least bit out of the ordinary while headed for the front door. "I'm on my way in," I said. When I got inside, he was standing over near the cigarette machines opposite Amp, who stood closer to the bar but I paid no attention to him, "How's it hanging old man?"

"A li'l bit lower than I like," Oz replied.

Amp snarled, trying to get under my skin, "He da only one you see, punk?"

Still thinking about the last time we were in similar positions, I commented, "He just happens to be the only one I can bring myself to give a damn about."

Emphasizing the authority of his position Oz snapped, "All right, there ain't gone be no mo shit like last time you two was here! I ain't gonna have no mess in my place, understand? Like it or not, two o' you's gotta work t'gether."

Just as I was trying to understand why Oz seemed to be siding with that snake, I felt the rush of wind caused by the opening of the front door. Before I could turn to look, the unmistakable rhythm of a semi-automatic songbird sounded off: *CLACK-CLACK, CLACK-CLACK, CLACK-CLACK...*

I shouted, diving away from the line of fire, "Oz, look out!" With all the commotion going on, I noticed Amp was virtually unfazed. "Oz...Oz! You all right, old man!" I screamed over the sound of the gunshots. From where I was, only his legs were visible beside the cigarette machine but there were no signs of life.

Amp ordered, in a commanding tone, "Get that country some-bitch!"

As the setup became obvious, I summoned the assistance of my twin Smith & Wesson peacemakers. *CA-CLACK-CA-CLACK, CA-CLACK...* And screamed over the noise of the shots "Oz...Oz! You all right?" There was no noticeable movement from the once magnificent creature that now lay lifeless on the concrete floor. "Oz! Oz! Dammit man; can you hear me?"

I heard an unfamiliar voice beckon, "Willie, this Jerome."

I answered, "I know who the fuck you are! What I don't know is why the hell you let that fool, Amp, talk you into slitting your own damn throat!" and then returned fire, *CA-CLACK, CA-CLACK,*

His voice sounded as though he was almost pleading, "I ain't got no beef wit you, partner."

"If you've got a problem with Oz, then you've got a problem with me! And if he dies, you've got a problem to the grave!" I warned.

"Oh, ain't this a touchin moment." I heard Amp's voice above my head as he ordered from behind, standing above the table where I'd sought cover, "Now drop that shit and turn yo punk ass 'round."

I tossed the gun out onto the floor. "You know, you're a dead man," I said.

"Well that's gone be kinda hard for you since you gone be dead first," he said. "You just don't know it yet. Now throw out the other one. I know you be carry'n two."

I knew giving up my guns would mean giving up my life. But if I didn't hand them over, that coward would take my life. I could hear the faint sound of sirens as I slowly unhanded the second of the twins.

Jerome nervously yelled, "C'mon Amp, we ain't got no time fo this shit. Somebody done called five-o. We gotta get the hell outta here!"

Amp said, clenching his teeth as he turned to Jerome, "Man, I been itchin fo this shit fo a minute."

With him briefly distracted, I quickly went for the throwaway piece in the small of my back. It had been Oz who'd warned me to always keep at least one gun you can toss if you have to. "One that can't be traced, in case ya get in a sit'ation where ya gotta throw it down," he had said.

CA-CLACK, CA-CLACK, CA-CLACK. All I could see from under the table were Amp's legs, so that's where I put three shots from my backup .380 cal. semi- automatic.

"You son of a bitch!" I heard Amp's agonizing scream. "That punk muthafucka shot me. You's a dead bastard, Willie!"

I quickly grabbed the two 9mm partners previously placed on the floor and scurried over to check on Oz without much thought of where Amp and Jerome had ended up.

"C'mon Amp," Jerome called. "We gotta be out this bitch wit the quickness!"

Amp was preoccupied with pain. "How fast you think I can move wit two busted legs? Get yo ass over here and help me out this piece," he ordered.

The blaring of sirens got louder by the second. Amp threw his right arm over Jerome's shoulder and shouted obscene threats back at me as they made their way past the pool tables and out the back. My only concern was for Oz. Seconds later, there was a tug at my shoulder which caused me to wheel around and nearly shoot Tony, Oz's handyman, in his face.

Ducking and grabbing for the gun in one motion, Tony was focused on Oz's limp figure and questioned with a nervous anger in his voice, "What da hell goin on up in here?"

I yelled, "The Old Man's been shot!" while reaching for OZ. "It was that son of a bitch Amp who did this foul shit... him and that bastard, Jerome!"

Tony explained, "Yeah, I's almost run over by some dude damn near carryin him outta da back door when I come in. Ya know da boys in blue is gone be pullin up out front in a second?"

I answered, while trying to maneuver Oz's drooping mass, "Yeah, That's why you've gotta help me get him to the car!"

"But da cops gone be all over this place," Tony said. "Where we gone take him?"

"To see the bitching Statue of Liberty, Tone!" I snapped. "Where the fuck you think? I'm not going to let the man die waiting on a damn ambulance! By the time they decide whether they even want to come up here, his final arrangements will already be confirmed. Now bring your ass!"

Even with both Tony and me together, Oz's massive structure was difficult to handle. We hurriedly lugged him out the front and into my Impala just as the cavalry approached. Before the NYPD could circle their wagons in the rehearsed standard tactical formation, Tony was clawing the passenger's door wishing he'd never climbed in. We parted the two lead cars, causing them to seek refuge on the sidewalk with the rest content to follow suit.

Tony finally mustered enough nerve to say, "Man, if you don't slow this damn thang down, we all gone need doctorin."

I said, in a tone absent any emotion, "Any time you feel the need, Tony...feel free."

"Feel free ta what?" he asked.

While barely making it through an intersection without sideswiping a Snapple truck, I exclaimed, "Feel free to get the fuck out!"

While attempting to get the seat cushion out his ass, "That bitchin light was red!" Tony screamed. "You tryin ta kill us?"

Nobody, pedestrians nor other drivers, seemed to pay any attention at all to the hazard lights and blaring horn as we came barreling down Broadway. I almost clipped a tow-truck driver outside his double-parked vehicle negotiating the fee with the frustrated owner of a disabled red Porsche.

"Man, you need ta slow this damn thang down. I thank I'm gone be sick," Tony barked. "E'rythang I just ate 'bout ta be all in yo flo."

Already pissed at the entire situation, I warned, "Then I think you need to step your bitch ass the hell out. I'm not stopping."

Tony looked in the back seat and said with a pale stare on his face, "Bro, I thank he done..."

"Tony, I'm not trying to hear your shit right now!" I tensed at the thought. "He's not going to fucking die! I won't let him die!"

Tony rationalized while reaching his husky trunk over the back of the seat, "For real man, wit this, I don't see where you got much say in da whole thang." he stretched, trying to get confirmation.

Without so much as a word from Tony, I knew the exact moment Oz breathed out his last breath. It was as though someone had just hollowed my entire chest. I couldn't breathe, couldn't think, couldn't see anything but red.

I yelled over the sirens, simultaneously slamming both hands on the steering wheel with each exclamation, "Muthafucker! Muthafucker! Son of a bitch!"

"Man, you need ta..." Tony started.

Anger erupted from way down in the shaft of my Tony Lama cowboy boots, "I need you to shut the hell up, is what I bitching need, Tony!" as a single tear rolled down my face. "Just shut the fuck up, dammit. Give me a minute to figure this shit out!"

Tony uttered, while tearing up, "I mean, why you don't just pull over? Ain't no point takin him to da hospital," he paused, "He done already...." his words trailed off as though he was afraid to finish the comment.

I snapped back to reality just before slamming into a woman and her young daughter attempting to cross the street against the light. Seeing us barreling straight for them, the woman grabbed her daughter by the wrist and flung her forward out of the car's path. I snatched the steering wheel at the very last second to avoid the two. That action had me struggling to not run over the oblivious tourists and generally unconcerned pedestrians packed on the sidewalk like mackerel in a can.

I heard the voice of a woman selling incense and musk oils at a folding table, "MMMOOOVVVEEE! Get out the way!" she screamed. "Look out for that fool on the damn sidewalk! He must be done lost his bitching mind!"

There was a blind fellow on an old wooden crate with a cup begging for spare change. When hearing the commotion, his head snapped like he was at center court during a Venus and Serena Williams tennis match. He left cup, crate, walking stick, glasses and all, trying to make his way to turn the nearest corner, "People, git outta da damn way! Don't ya'll see that big ass ship comin on shore?"

When the car finally came to a stop seven feet inside the glass entrance of a clothing store on 103rd Street, I slowly reached to answer my cell phone which had been constantly vibrating like a battery powered sex toy since shortly after the chase began. "Hello."

I recognized a familiar voice, "Willie, this Ernestina!" she confirmed and continued without taking a breath, "Are you all right? I heard the license plate and description of your car on the scanner. I'm calling because I know somebody had to pry those damn keys from your dead hands to get away with your ride. The lead officer in the chase radioed just now that the car stopped at 103rd Street. If you need a ride, I can have a patrolman pick you up and take you to recover your car. With it being involved in a crime…"

"I'm already at 103rd street," I interrupted.

She was puzzled when questioning, "You where?"

My voice was monotone, without any feeling or emotion, "At 103rd," I repeated.

Baffled, she asked. "But how did you get there so fast? I thought they were just chasing the person who stole…" Her words faded and I heard a loud thump as the phone fell to the floor.

The nervous tension was obvious from the tremor in the officer's voice, "You, in the car; driver, turn off the ignition and slowly place both hands on the steering wheel." He said. "Passenger, slowly place your hands on the dash in front of you. Do not make any sudden moves."

The warning behind the words spoken was as clear to me as the barrel of the shotgun I was staring down. It was being held by some anxious rookie just three feet in front of the car. I knew if I so much as sneezed, he would paint the interior of the Impala with my brains. More armor-plated commandoes surrounded the car on all sides like sugar ants on a doughnut.

The commander ordered, "All right, you gone do this like I tell you, when I tell you. If you move without my instruction, you will be shot. If you don't move on my instruction, you will be shot. If you make any sudden move, you will be shot. If you don't move *as* instructed, you will be shot. Are we clear?"

My shirt was soaked with as much of my mentor's blood as perspiration. Still thinking about Oz in the seat behind me, I gently nodded my head to indicate an understanding of the rules of conduct just spelled out with painstaking clarity.

"Passenger," the officer continued, "Do you understand these instructions?"

Tony, like most New Yorkers, talked with his hands and immediately motioned to gesture with his right hand when I yelled without opening my mouth, "If you do that, you'll kill us both!" I said.

He froze, glanced out the window over his shoulder to see four police at the passenger's window poised with fingers on the triggers of their weapons. I think if Tony hadn't been so afraid to move, he would have passed out then and there. He cut a nervous wind that nearly lifted him off the seat. Without so much as parting his teeth, he said, "Youngblood, I'm gettin too old fo this shit. All my years on da block...ne'er been caught up in no shit like this."

With my mouth still closed, I said, "Tone, why don't you drop an anonymous note in the damn complaint box outside the manager's office? It's not like this shit was at the top of my to-do list for the bitching day either!"

"What da hell we gone do?" he quizzed. "It ain't gone be easy ta 'splain a dead man in da back o' yo car."

"That's just one of our problems," I said. "Right now, I'm more concerned with figuring out how to keep from joining him. You notice these bastards haven't moved, haven't said anything, and haven't done anything?"

Tony nervously scanned the scene as much as he could without turning his head. "What you reckon they waitin fo?" he questioned.

"Now, I know you're not that big a fool," I said. "What they're waiting for is us...for us to fuck up and do something they told us not to so they'll have reason to justify plugging our asses."

Tony was becoming irritated. "Well, what da hell they gone do, make us sit here in this hot-ass car all day? This bitch smokin wit da damn windows 'n shit up."

"You're going to shut your face and sit right here 'til sunrise tomorrow if that's what we have to do," I demanded. "How much love for two thugged-out undergraduate gangsters do you honestly think they have?"

Tony said, "I thought they job s'posed ta be ta serve 'n protect. That what our taxes pay 'em fo."

"Tone, in case you haven't realized it, their job is to protect tax-paying folk from muthafuckas like us," I said. "Just sit still and shut the hell up!"

He had a disappointed, somber look as he dropped his eyes and replied, "I don't 'preciate you telling me ta shut up, neither."

I heard the commanding officer over our bickering.

"All right fellas, which one of you is Willie Le...Beaux? Driver, I need you to crack your window about four inches; using the index finger and thumb of your left hand, drop your weapon out the car. Passenger, I need you to do the same. I only want one of you moving at a time. Driver, you first."

The knots in my stomach were so big it felt like there was somebody sitting on my lap. I began to remove the first of the three guns as instructed when my cell phone vibrated and nearly caused me to climb out through the roof. Lucky for me, the police officer at the side of the car where I sat was a terrible shot. I heard the gun discharge, *CLACK, CLACK*. The glass from the window shattered into what seemed like a million particles and covered both my upper thighs

Trying to keep from jumping out the other side, "FFFUUUCCCKKK!" shrieked Tony. "Man! What da... what da...what...FUCK! See Willie, I done told you, these muthas is tryin ta put us ta sleep!"

He must have shit his pants, but I was more concerned about the hole in the dash of my ride than the fact I'd almost taken one in the head. That is, until what had just happened registered. I clenched the steering wheel to the point my forearms cramped. Every run-in I'd ever had with any cop since being out of diapers replayed instantaneously in my mind. Every son of a bitch with a badge was, with that one incident, condemned to burn in hell.

"What the fuck was that?" I looked into the face of the lead commando, "We doing every damn thing we were told to do, exactly like we were told to do it! And you got this Rambo wannabe, trigger-happy mutha..."

The lead officer who had been ordering everybody around since the whole thing started shouted, "That'll be enough from you, mister!" he said. "Now, everybody, stand down. Let's not lose control and end up with more bodies than we got bags for."

That's when I realized how right Tony had been when he'd made the comment about them not wanting us to walk away from this. It seems, no matter what color the cop, wherever in this country you go, they don't take too kindly to being embarrassed, especially if you're a brother. With that, I knew this was not the time to be trying to push the envelope. Having a dead Black man in the back seat of my car wasn't an offense nearly as punishable as leading New York's finest on a high-speed chase all over Harlem. I reasoned that they were more concerned about the embarrassment than anything.

"I'm Captain Klein, Steve Klein; you boys can call me Steve," he directed. "Now let's everybody just calm down and I'm sure we can get through this. You boys wanna tell me your names? You, driver; why don't you start...what's your name?"

Already annoyed at the reference, I answered sarcastically. "You can just call me Boy. Like it's going to make a damn difference in tomorrow's headlines."

The captain was noticeably put off. He then addressed Tony on the other side of the car. "O…kay, passenger, why don't we try the same question…or you gone make us have to do this the hard way?" He asked.

"Uh, my name Anthony; but e'rybody on da block just call me Tony," he blurted out. "I just work at da lounge fo Mr. Oswald Jenkins. But I thank he dead."

Through clentched teeth, I said, "Tony, shut the hell up!"

He responded in defense of his comment, "Well, they gone know soon as they get us out da car…ain't like he can just decide ta get up 'n leave now, is it?"

"Fellas, ya'll wanna stop all the chatter with each other and focus out this way? I think I'm the one you should be explaining things to," Officer Klein protested. "Now, just who is this Oswald Jenkins, and where did you kill him?"

"We ain't killed no damn body!" Tony said. "It was them fools, Amp 'n Jerome that shot him. We's just tryin ta get him ta da damn hospital…'fore ya'll showed up."

Another officer shouted the warning, "There's a unknown suspect in the rear of the car…be aware. He's prob'bly armed!"

"Da mutha…da man dead," Tony yelled.

Officer Klein finally spoke up, "All right, enough; I want both of you out the vehicle…one at a time. Driver, drop any and all remaining weapons you might still have out the window in the same manner as the first. Then proceed to open the door with your left hand while keeping your right hand on the steering wheel in plain view."

I remember thinking to myself, *I know how to open a damn door!*

"Let's get this done today, mister!" He shouted. "I would rather not be caught up here after dark."

The words escaped before I could keep them from rolling off my tongue, "Bitch, you better not let me be the one to catch you up here after the street lights come on either."

Officer Klein snapped his head in my direction, "What the hell was that you said, son? You in no position to be making threats, boy. All right, enough o' this bullshit; get your asses out the damn car, right now. All right driver...no more pussyfootin around."

I proceeded to drop the second of the handguns to the pavement outside the car and even anteed up my little "throw away" .380 cal. from its hiding place. Reaching outside the door through the shattered window with my left hand so as to not have either out of plain view, I unlatched the door and moved to push it open.

I heard Officer Klein shout, "I said give up *all* the weapons before anybody exited the vehicle! Passenger, it's your turn now."

"He doesn't carry a gun," I responded before Tony could digest what the officer said.

Captain Klein condescendingly scoffed. "Yeah, sure, a criminal that don't carry a gun."

"I got three mo months probation," Tony said, "Three mo months on a two-year stretch 'n some shit like this gotta come up. Ain't that a bitch?"

"All right driver, let's keep it coming nice and slow... just like you started. Stand up, turn around with your fingers locked behind your head, and place your face on the hood," he ordered. "Passenger, once he has taken a position on the hood of the car, you do the same."

I had been in place as directed a good two or three minutes before Tony approached the front of the car. He leaned over but stopped short of placing his face on the hood. "That's gone burn."

Officer Klein instructed, "All the way down."

"This shit hot," Tony complained.

"Tony, the faster you get down here, the faster we can both get the hell up," I said.

Tony asked with much concern, "Ain't that shit burnin, man…?"

Before he could finish his question, four officers rushed in and slammed his head on the hood of the car. When he instinctively sprang up, they commenced to punch him in his side, back, and everywhere they could get a fist, billy club or boot.

I was yelling to make him understand that moving only gave the cops an excuse to continue the battery, "Tone, stop moving! Tony, just be still! Tone…"

The unwarranted assault by the officers continued until Tony lay motionless on the concrete.

I mumbled to no one in particular, "Sons of bitches…no good sons of bitches."

Suddenly, I felt a blunt object in my left side and heard a stern whisper from one of the officers. "I think you better shut up before I decide you was resisting arrest too," he said.

About then, I recognized a sound that was all too familiar when the voice identified, "Yes, I'm off duty. Officer E. Lady," she said. "I have knowledge concerning the suspect."

Captain Klein instructed her after requiring me to stand up and turn around with hands behind my back when they applied the handcuffs, "Proceed with caution, ma'am."

Once the cuffs were on, I turned slowly to the right, only to have my skin feel like it was still on the heated hood of the car when I realized Ernestina had slapped me.

An officer ordered, while two others grabbed Ernestina and nearly wrestled her to the ground.

"Ma'am, you can't be assaulting the suspect…" he said.

When I regained all my faculties and was able to shake the cobwebs, Ernestina's twisted face came into focus. Fortunately, she was still being restrained. She assured the officers, "I'm all right; I'm okay. You can let me go." When they released Ernestina, she marched over and positioned her face inches from mine. It was uncertain as to who was more anxious, the other officers or me. "Do you realize the trouble I could be in…the trouble I could've gotten into being affiliated with the right hand of one of the biggest criminal elements in all the five boroughs?" She asked. "How could you have put me out there like that? You knew from the beginning that I'm a police officer. Hell, I was on duty when we met!"

I couldn't put ten words together to complete a sentence, "I wanted to tell you. I mean I wanted to be out of…"

"You must think I'm as stupid as the idiot you played me for," she snapped. "You and I both know full damn well that once in, there is no getting out, unless you're the guest of honor at a damn funeral."

I tried explaining, "But I wasn't in like that," I said. "I wasn't involved with the usual operations and stuff they got into. Oz was a friend."

"Oh, please," she snubbed. "That's like being almost pregnant or sort-of fucking dead. Willie…either you are or you're not. So, which is it? Are you pregnant or just full of shit?"

The captain intruded, "All right, Officer Lady, is it?" He asked. "I don't mean to break up this little lovers' quarrel, but we got work to do. If your position here has no bearing on the circumstances at hand…I'm gonna have to insist you allow me and my men to proceed."

"Fine, carry on," she informed. "I'm finished."

As the cops turned me in the direction of a waiting patrol car, I called to Ernestina, "I need you to contact Moms and Poppy for me if you will."

She stopped, turned slowly toward me but never lifted her eyes from the pavement, and commented in a voice that sounded like a woman possessed, "I…am…so finished."

I was led away to the squad car and placed in the back seat. While waiting, I watched as an ambulance arrived to transport Tony to the hospital along with a second unit to pick up Oz's lifeless body. There were no waterworks as I sat watching. Even though a part of me wanted to break down and boo-hoo like a newborn, I couldn't bring myself to shed more than a single tear. For a moment, I resented my real father for never having allowed me to be in touch with my emotions as a youngster growing up in a difficult South. Sometime later, I found out Tony was D.O.A. at the hospital. It was rumored he had suffered a heart attack, though no autopsy was ever performed.

I was startled back to the present by the officer driving, "You done gone and got yourself in a whole heap o' trouble," he said. "They had to call the Police Commissioner off the seventh hole at the course. He don't like to be bothered on his golf day... My name Harry if you interested."

"Well, I'm not." My mind slowly drifted miles and years away, back to how it had all started with Oz. Now I wondered how it would continue without him...if it could. I was waging war within myself because I knew, if things continued, I'd have to be involved. The dilemma stemmed from the fact that I, for a long time, had not wanted any part of this world. The ride to the police station seemed to take as long as the years I was remembering.

I heard the security officer on the intercom as he instructed the patrolman, "Drive forward into the painted rectangular figure and keep your windows up."

Once in the painted area, a huge concrete door closed behind us and four jets began spraying the vehicle as if it was in an automated car wash.

My chauffer felt the need to explain something that was neither of any interest to me nor allowed to be shared, "Think about the kinda money they spend on new-fangled stuff like this; what it do is spray some stuff something like acid all over the car 'case some dummy might be hiding trying to sneak in and break some fool outta this place." Harry continued, "I tells 'em, they can put that cost to good use and pay all our asses a li'l more money at the end o' the week. All that money spent just to make a fool need to get a shower. It don't do nothing 'cept make ya itch real bad and burn a li'l bit. But I ain't s'pose to be telling you this stuff."

13

Retrieving Mine

Minutes that seemed like hours later, I found myself in what proved to be an interrogation room. Men in suits rotated in and out well into the following morning, taking turns rummaging the inner-most chambers of my mind… or so they were led to believe. I've been in the game long enough to know the standard "policies and procedures" right down to knowledge of how long they could keep me, and under what conditions. Granted, being caught with a dead man in the back of my car didn't win me any brownie points in their assessment for my Good Samaritan's award. But it would only be a matter of time before the whole incident was investigated and it determined neither of my guns was the one that killed Oz. That, accompanying the fact Tony had previously named other suspects, would be enough to give the hounds another fox to chase, provided they could get to him before I did.

It was exactly two days later, a coincidental forty-eight hours, when detectives informed me the story I'd spun them checked out. As well, there wasn't enough evidence to hold me on any of the litany of other charges they said were pending. They took the liberty to warn me against taking any trips out of town and the typical "keep looking over your shoulder" hook aimed at intimidating me. After signing what seemed to be a contract stating I wasn't mistreated, abused, denied my right to counsel, or any of the other rights on which they wanted to cover the city's ass, I was handed a large brown envelope with my name on it.

The grizzly attendant's raspy bark, peculiarly, made me think of a rugged mountain man in some obscure part of the Rockies. "Make sho e'rything in there that s'pose to be," he said.

Taking a quick peak, I determined there was something not contained in the package and called his attention to it, "This not all I had."

"What you thank missing?" he asked.

"Well, it appears I'm short about a hundred and forty dollars, for one. My gold rope chain and matching bracelet isn't here..." I started.

The Grizzly Adams look-alike cut in, "Well, that's all what stuff I was gave when you come in. You just have to file a report, I guess. That normally take a few weeks, but wit all that's been going on, could be long as a couple months 'fore they get 'round to looking into the whole thang."

Immediately, I felt perspiration begin to saturate the back of my shirt as I tried to avoid boiling over on his fat ass. "Never mind," I said. "It's not all that important anyway."

His concern was noticeably artificial, "You sho you don't wanna file no report?"

I ignored the question. "What about the three guns? They're not in the bag either. They're legal; I've got proper papers and everything on them."

Closing and locking the metal mesh window, "Not in New York City," he said.

"Wait a minute," I complained.

Never breaking stride, he smirked, turned the corner, and hobbled out of sight, "Guess you just have to file a report fo them too."

I walked away with clenched fists thinking, *This definitely isn't the place to blow a gasket. All they need is that one straw to break the camel's back. I've got too many other things to work out that are a whole lot more important at the moment than my stuff.*

The events of the past few days were replaying in my mind when I left the property room. Forging past all the fatigue, the hunger, the anger and frustration was the pain of Oz's fate. That had me focused on the fate of the two sons of bitches who had pre-programmed all the shit with which I found myself dealing.

Sam's Southern drawl was unmistakable as I exited the precinct, "Damn, dat ain't s'posed ta be da look on ya face comin outta 'dis place. Ya looks like ya's jest comin in," he said.

Looking up to see him decked out in his "taking care of business" suit, I questioned, "Poppy, how did you…?"

He explained, "Well some lady calls da house couple days 'go, tells me 'n Eunice 'bout all what go'n on; said dey's no point comin down 'fore now 'cause dey wadn't gone let nobody sees ya 'cept one o' dem lawyer fellas…say ya ain't even ask fo none."

"Well, it wasn't anything I couldn't handle," I said.

With his voice full of sarcasm and a coy smirk on his face, "Oh, so ya done been ta school 'n gots yo lawy'r license since da last time ya was at da house?" he asked.

"No. It's not a license," I corrected. "That would be a degree, a law degree…and no Poppy, I don't have one."

He was saddling his horse, "Well, if'n ya needs a good law man…"

I interrupted, "What lady called you?"

Wearing an expression that said he didn't approve of being cut off, Sam asked, "What'd ya say?"

"You said a lady called the house." I continued, "What lady?"

His fury eyebrows nearly touched in the middle of his forehead as he scowled, "No," he said, "She say her name Lady...E. Lady. I figure it ta be one o' dese folks from down here. 'Least she sound like da po-lice. 'Couldn't figure why da law care 'nough ta call da house." He shifted his weight to the other leg, "How dey knows ta call da house?"

"I know her Poppy," I volunteered. "She's a friend...or, was a friend, at least."

"Well, she call talk'n real nice...too nice ta be da po-lice," he said. "And ya say she yo friend?"

"Well, *she was a friend*, but something came up," I replied. "It's not like that any more."

He raised his head to make eye contact, "That ain't da way hit sound when she call da house. Sound like some real ser'ous stuff what was goin on wit her: Like when someb'dy be yankin dem heart strings."

The comment was more to myself than anyone. "I guess it was a little deeper than I thought," I mumbled.

"What dat?" he questioned.

"I said my stomach is in a knot," I covered. "You feel like getting something to eat?" I asked.

Sam looked at me and squinted as though trying to make out who I was while mumbling something inaudible, "Now I knows damn well dey done did somthin ta ya. Ya knows bet'er 'n fix ya face ta ask som'tin like 'at," he muttered. Heading for the front door of the police station, he directed, "Brang yo ass on here. I gots food at da house bet'r 'n any o' this shit dey sell'n down here. Come on up ta da 'partment...Eunice 'bout to go crazy anyhow."

As respectfully as irritation would allow, "Not today, Sam," I declined. "I need to pick up my car and get to the Village for a shower and change out these clothes. They don't work so well after the second day," I said. "Maybe I'll feel well enough to stop by tomorrow afternoon, if you'll have me."

Ignoring my comment, "Dat be fine," he said, "Food be ready when ya gets dere. Eunice be glad ta see ya, too."

"Yeah, and I'll be glad to get some real food...what's on the menu?" I asked.

He looked at me with that classic one-sided grin, "Well, since it'll be ya first meal at da house as a free man, I'll fix up whats'never ya wants," he said.

I was trying to fight my way out of the emotional hole I was in when I replied, "I think some fried chicken, corn, and mashed potatoes might work...and don't forget the cornbread."

He said, passing out the door, "I'll be sho 'n lets Eunice knows. So she be sho 'an git finished in her area o' da kitchen b'fore I gits started."

I had to go back inside to a different office where it took another half hour dealing with idiots in two additional rooms at the station before I finally got the information regarding what was necessary to pick up my car. Then it was still a matter of a two-hour subway ride, twenty minutes on the bus, a twelve-dollar cab fare, and a quarter-mile hike before I got to the place where I caught even more hell about picking up my car...something that legally belonged to me.

Right about the time I had myself convinced every employee of the crooked city was involved in a five-borough conspiracy—"You said, it was a Impala, right?" the slender kid with the Lou Rawls voice asked.

"Yeah, the charcoal-gray one," I said.

Shaking his head, he sghed, "Well, all I got in the computer is a burgundy Impala...no charcoal."

"Well, they should've brought it out here within the past couple days. It's the one that was involved in the high-speed chase through Harlem a few days ago," I explained. "It's missing the driver-side front window."

With an air of optimism, he briefly lifted his eyes from the keyboard, "I remember that car," he said. "They was unloading it when I got to work…kept on calling it a Monte Carlo cause it ain't the short-body style like the new Impalas," he explained without breaking his rhythm. "My name David."

"So how are you going to find it if they put the wrong information into the computer?" I asked.

"Well, it ain't a problem if you know what you doing," he said. "You just have to know where to look. Sometimes these fools gets lazy and don't care what they do. Had one car was lost somewhere out here nearly four years."

"Big place," I said.

David responded in the voice of a New York City tour guide, "Yep," he stated, "Seven hundred fifty thousand acres. They gone be outta room soon if they keep bringing cars out here the way they been doing."

My voice was a little more brash than I'd realized as the inquiry was quickly turning into a conversation I really wasn't interested in having, "Well, I'm not so concerned about the rest of them. I just need to know what I've got to do to get mine," I said.

David was noticeably bothered, "Just sign right here. You keep the white copy. I'll radio and tell 'em to bring your car 'round. By the time you get back out to the gate, it oughta be there…good day."

Without additional comment, I simply picked up my keys from the counter and started out. As I passed from the little office, there was a frail Jewish fellow entering the opposite door. He was debating with one of the drivers, "…And I'll have everything in pants brought up on charges in civil court if there's one scratch on my boy's damn car."

Politely stepping aside to let him pass, "Excuse me, sir," I said.

He then snapped at me, "And what in hell do you want?"

Wanting to be sure I'd heard him correctly, I asked, "Begging your pardon, sir?"

Pushing past me in the doorway, he mumbled, "Oh, just move out my damn way!"

Before I realized what was happening, I had grabbed the fragile stick by the neck, spun him around, and shoved his face damn near through the wall. David, behind the counter, immediately closed and locked the bars at the customer service window and began squawking on the two-way radio like a mother goose. I stood silently, looking at the older man, actually almost feeling sorry for him...until he opened his mouth again.

"You've just shit and stepped in it barefoot, you son of a..."

He never finished that statement. Without so much as blinking an eye, I caught him flush on the chin with a straight right and watched as he slid across the floor belly up. After finally coming to a stop, the fragile man looked up to find me straddling him, staring down at the blood trickling from his mouth.

Without raising my voice, I stated, "You have never met my mama...best you keep her name out your damn mouth."

I heard the clerk calling for the cavalry in a panic, "... Yeah, this...this is...this David, over at Gate J. I got a bit of a situation developing over here!"

While the attendant was summoning help, I politely reached down, picked up my keys from beside the scarecrow, stepped across him, and left the building to the sound of the little man's protest.

His voice echoed in the mostly empty space, "You don't know who the hell I am," he said. "Boy, I'll have your apartment building demolished and turned into a parking garage by the time you can get home."

I passed a silver six-hundred-series Mercedes with dark tinted windows parked directly in front of the door when I came out. Once past, I glanced back at the license plate to find out what state that damned tourist crawled over from. The personalized New York plates read *JUDGE-1*. I remember saying to myself, "OOOPS, Guess I might be barefoot by morning."

Just a couple short minutes later, I was already turning onto the highway when two of the facility's security vehicles came speeding past. "Probably looking for a Monte Carlo," I chuckled.

I accelerated to make sure there would be enough distance between the Barney Fife Patrol and me by the time they realized who was supposed to be the object of their chase. For most of the way back to the city I continued, periodically checking the rearview mirrow just to be certain nobody in uniform would sneak up on me.

14

Unmasked

More than six hours had passed since I'd left the police station with a "can't stop" agenda and a hunger pain that, by now, wouldn't stop. My navel and backbone had begun a pretty serious argument just prior to me leaving the station; by the time I'd finished at the impound yard, they had become engaged in an all-out war. In the Village, I was fortunate enough to find a parking space on the corner at the end of the street. Walking back to my building, I noticed Natasha in her usual position, perched atop the stoop.

As I finally started to make my way up the steps, Natasha asked, "Chu okay?" prior to casually informing, "Chu veen in nube."

Trying to be certain of what she'd said, I questioned, "I've been where?"

She let out an exasperating sigh, "In nube; on T.B."

Realizing the challenges of her communication skills, "Oh, you mean in the news." I determined, before dismissing the comment so as to avoid initiating a conversation, "Yeah, I was watching that channel too."

She asked with a look of genuine concern, "Ist eberting o.k.?"

"It'll be okay soon enough," I replied. "One way or the other, it will be."

She asked again, "Chu shzure chu okay?" as though expecting my response to be different. "Me caan kome hep chu veel better if chu vish."

I immediately replied, "No, not now Natasha; this isn't a good time," I reasoned.

"Me caan kome gib chu messaage," she pressed.

"What message?" I asked. "Who left a message for me… about what? And why would anybody have reason to leave a message for me with you?"

"No," She attempted to correct herself. "Me rubz chu beack."

Finally putting two and two together, I understood what she was trying to say as well as what she *was saying*. "I appreciate the offer Natasha, but I have plans," I confirmed. "A back rub is the last thing I need right now."

"Chu haab deate?" she asked.

I confirmed while entering the building, hoping that would be an adequate deterrent, "No…well, yes, I have a date."

For some reason, she wouldn't take no for an answer and assured in a sultry voice while following more closely than was comfortable, "Me be herve avter deate."

She nearly bumped into me when I turned abruptly, "Look Natasha, if you saw me on the news, you know this has already been one hell of a day. What I need right now is a long hot shower, some good food, and a little much needed personal time…alone!"

She pressed even harder, "But chu zay chu haab deate," and convicted, "Dat not avone."

I could feel myself getting irritated when I finally had to block the apartment door to keep her from following me inside. While pushing the door closed in Natasha's face, "Well, whoever I'm with tonight, it won't be you," I snapped. "Good night."

BBBRRRIIINNNGGG, BBBRRRIIINNNGGG, BBBRR... Moms' unmistakable voice condemned me when she answered, "Well, it's 'bout time yo ass called. Where is you at? We been s'pectin you o'er three hours. Where da hell ya been? You kilt somebody like them news folk said?"

"Maybe if you slow down with the questions, Moms, I'll have a chance to answer one or two of them," I interrupted. "You have my word that I'll come by tomorrow and explain everything to you and Poppy."

Unable to conceal the disappointment in her voice, she said, "But Sam said you's on yo way up ta eat wit us t'night. Why ya change yo mind? What done happen'd? You ain't done got in no mo trouble...?"

I cut her off, before she got on another roll, "See, there you go with the questions again," I said. "No ma'am, I ain't...I mean, I haven't gotten into any more trouble, and I didn't kill anybody...yet. I realize you and Poppy are due a lot of explanations...but not tonight. I just need to shower away this terrible day and get some rest."

Her concern was almost overwhelming, "You's sho ya gone be okay? If'n ya wont, I can fix ya some vittles 'n send Sam or Cherish down in da Vil'age wit it. Ya knows hit ain't good ta go ta bed hong'ry," she said.

I forced a grin, "You know Moms; I do eat other places besides Harlem. I can cook," I said. "Maybe not as good as Chef Johnson, but there are a few occasions when I have been known to beat up a pot or two."

Her voice took on a defensive tone. "I ne'er said ya can't cook," she replied. "Jest dat I knows ya done had it kinda rough past few days 'n I ain't know if dey's some'n at yo house ta eat. I done heared all kinda thangs 'bout dat jailhouse food 'n I can't 'magine ya feels much like cook'n."

"Thanks for caring Moms, but I'm fine," I said. "I'm sure if I look hard enough something will crawl out of the fridge that'll fill the hole in my gut."

Still not content with my answer, she insisted, "Willie, it ain't no pro'lem fo me ta git ya some'n ta eat. I can call ta see where Cherish at 'n I'm sho she won't…"

Trying to stop her long enough to get a word in, "Moms… Moms…Moms!" I called. "Really, I am fine. If worst comes to worst, I can always get delivery from the Cantonese place a few blocks over, but right now, I don't even want their company…I'll be just fine."

She finally conceded, "A'ight, if'n ya says so. Talk wit ya later, den."

"Yes ma'am, I say so. When is Cherish leaving anyway? Just tell her I said goodbye if I don't see her before she leaves. Later, Moms," I finished.

A quick makeshift club sandwich had to do for the moment because a couple turkey slices and a package of nearly outdated ham was all I found in the refrigerator that hadn't already sprouted legs and taken up walking. I summoned Coltrane and Billie Holiday to keep me company while swallowing the sandwich, then solicited the presence of Nancy Wilson before heading off for a highly anticipated hot shower. The phone rang as I stood outside the stall wearing nothing but the air around me while adjusting the water temperature. About two degrees below boiling was the normal setting, but I was in need of the type relaxation that required a somewhat hotter element. I decided to let the machine catch the call and stepped into my vertical sauna.

Nancy had sung every song on the CD twice already before I decided to begin lathering away the layers of dirt and blood. The blood, mostly belonging to Oz, had saturated through my shirt and Levis, causing my skin to take on a peculiar shade of burnt red. I smiled quietly to myself when watching the crimson-colored water find its way to the ceramic tile floor and down the drain. I chuckled at the thought, *Damn*

Oz, was you that dirty? Even yo blood got stains in it. By now, the temperature of the water was starting to get lukewarm; signifying I had overstayed my welcome. I quickly lathered and washed my hair before turning off the, by now, frigid water. Ms. Wilson could be heard knocking when the faucet was shut off. It wasn't long before a quick mental review of the Nancy Wilson CD led me to the conclusion that someone was actually banging on the door of my apartment.

"Hold on a minute, I'm in the shower," I said. "Be there in a second."

With that, it sounded as though the hammering intensified. Already annoyed, I yelled, "If it was that serious, there should've been a bitchin fire alarm. Give me a damn minute!"

The knocking continued, a little softer. *Thump, thump...thum...*

By now, I was straight pissed off and snapped at my neighbor while simultaneously flinging the door open, "Natasha, didn't I tell you earlier...!"

An attitude on steroids greeted me from outside my apartment, "And just who the hell is Natasha?" Ernestina asked. "And exactly what did you have to tell her?"

I stammered, "I...uuhhmm...how did...I wasn't expecting you."

She pushed a heavy platter-like plate into my still-bare ribs, upon passing into the apartment, "Obviously not. You always answer the door half naked?"

Still staring into the hallway, I noticed Natasha with her key inserted into the lock of their door. She looked back over her shoulder, opened her mouth just so much that the redness of her tongue fell over a full bottom lip, winked, and went inside.

Standing with the door open in disbelief, I mumbled in response to Ernestina, "Uh, yeah...I mean, no. No, I don't always answer the door in a towel. I was just coming out the shower when you knocked." I explained, before posing a question to more-or-less change the subject, "What's with the plate?"

"Your mom sent it," Ernestina specified. "Nice couple. They worry a lot about you though. Who's the female across the hall with the neck problem?"

I tripped over my tongue, "Who's who...where?"

"It's one thing if I can't see what you're hiding, but it's something totally different when you put the shit right in my damn face!" she accused.

Trying to head off a fight, I joked, "Oh, that's just my neighbor...she plays like that," I pretended to laugh. "So, you were up by Moms and Poppy...How did you find...? And how did you know where I live?"

She stated the obvious while taking a seat on the couch, "You're not the only one who can get things done, you know. I am a New York City police officer. And you are in New York City." Ernstina then warned, "And tell Ms. Neighbor that's no way to play...*somebody could get hurt.*"

Closing the door, I started to the bedroom, "Hang out here for a second; I'll go put on some clothes."

Standing up, "That's all right," she said. "I just stopped by to bring you something to eat like your mom asked. She said you were being hardheaded."

With a puzzled look I said, "Now, I know you didn't come all the way down here from Harlem just to bring me a plate. You went through the trouble you obviously had to for the purpose of dropping in like my apartment was on the way to wherever you were going. See, first of all, I know you don't do the Village."

"Don't flatter yourself," She cut. "I've been in this city basically all my life. *I can 'do' whatever the hell I want whenever and wherever I damn well please.*"

Intentionally putting her on the spot, I asked, "Okay, so what are you doing here?"

"If you must know," She stated, "I have a friend over in Tribeca. I came down to see him."

"Then you're definitely a little out of your way. Tribeca is a good hop from this area of St. Marks Place," I said. Then I questioned in a playful southern drawl, "Y'all wouldn't be down hur 'cause you's worried yo'self 'bout li'l ole me, now is ya?"

With a look so serious it was actually a little unnerving, "That's not funny. I'm not playing games with you," she said. "Hell, I don't even know who you are. You talking all sweet and making me fall" —she stopped mid-sentence—"making me risk losing my job on the force. I've been on that job eighteen years."

"Well, baby," I started.

She cut, to establish her point, "That's Officer Lady to you!"

I smirked. "You can't be serious. After all that we've been through…"

She was quite agitated at my reaction, "And just what the hell have *we* been through? You know all there is to know about me. My life is an open book, no guesswork. But what do I know about you other than the little I was exposed to by accident, happened to overhear, or catch on the news? All this time I think I know who I'm sleeping with and you turn out to be somebody I never should've given my damn phone number."

"You know it was more than that," I said.

She snapped, unleashing the built-up anger, "It was more than what? I'll tell you what it was…it was a conquest…an accomplishment…a feather in your bitching cap. Dammit, call it what it was… *It was just a FUCK!* Be real for once and call it what the hell it really was!"

"Look baby," I started.

With her arms folded across her chest, Ernestina barked, "And I've done told you about that baby shit! You can save that for bitches like your neighbor across the damn hall!"

"What the hell does she have to do with any of this?" I drilled. "You don't even know that woman. You two just met…

Hell, you didn't even meet; just passed by each other in the damn hallway."

"I might be slow, but I'm not stupid," Ernestina said. "Sometimes a woman just knows things. Like when some chickenhead has been closer to the hen house than she's supposed to be."

Feeling somewhat caged, "Oh, so now I'm your property?" I asked.

Looking for clarification, she questioned, "You're my what? You're nothing to me. Like I said, just a half-decent stiff one! You got yours, I got mine, now let's move the hell on to something meaningful."

"No…oh no! You referred to me as your property when you made the comment about a female being too close to the hen house. A house is property. So, that means you see me as yours," I clarified. "That's the reason you've got such a problem with ole girl across the way that you haven't even met. The one thing I am not is anybody's damn property."

Ernestina refuted my comment, "Oh come on, Willie, sounds like you've about convinced yourself that shit even makes sense," she argued. "You give yourself way too much damn credit."

I intruded on her thoughts, and went out on a limb addressing the things she wasn't saying, "Well, that doesn't compare to what you give me every time I think about that night at your place."

She took a step back and looked down at the towel wrapped around my waist. Her eyebrows did a little horizontal shuffle when noticing the petrusion a few inches below my naval. "That's nice," she uttered, before realizing her lower jaw hung open about four inches and attempted to redirect the comment. "I mean, good…it's good you don't consider yourself a piece of property," Ernestina said.

Noticing her lengthy glance, I asked bluntly, "Is there a problem? You look like you just saw a snake."

"Uuhhmm, something...like that," she whispered. "I was just looking at..."

I boldly stated, "It's not like this is your first time seeing me."

She concluded, in a much more inviting tone, "But this is my first time seeing it...I mean, you, from this angle. You're just...what is it that has you all worked up?"

"I've been trying to tell you all day that it wasn't just a fuc..." Before I could finish the thought, she had toppled me onto the couch, disregarded the loin cloth, and engaged in a sensual somba that had us exploring methods of re-arranging the furniture when thoughts of my neighbors prompted me to suddenly attempt applying some degree of rationale but Ernestina persisted.

As many times as I could remember having played that CD, Nancy Wilson had never sounded so good. It was like being at a live concert...the intensity of every note was magnified with extreme clarity. Nancy and I both raised our voices in unison on the final high note as my body deteriorated into a worthless pile of me. It felt like I had been in the gym for three hours. Every muscle in my body was like Silly Putty. I had unwittingly morphed into a mass of good-for-nothingness in the form of a lifeless lump of flesh and bone on the couch.

"How you feel?" she asked, with an impish grin. "Still stressed?"

"Woman, you nearly relaxed my ass into a coma," I said. "You're no damn good...you know that?"

"What, don't you feel good?" she prodded.

With a jovial air of sarcasm, I said, "Girl, you've done extracted all the feeling, anger, frustration, and everything else straight out my ass. I've got nothing left."

She playfully asked, allowing her bottom lip to protrude slightly, "You mean I done breakeded it?"

While shifting my body weight in effort to stand, "I think that would be an understatement," I declared.

By now, she was seated on the floor between my knees with her right arm encircling my left leg. Ernestina moved her left hand up and grabbed my helplessly exposed symbol of manhood along with his two ultra-sensitive companions and began her interrogation, "All right, now that you're totally relaxed and all inhibitions have been unmasked, give it to me straight. What's the real deal with you, Willie, or is that even your real name?"

Still trying to determine if she was really serious I playfully responded, "Come on, baby, those aren't toys to be handling like golf balls," I urged.

"Who said I was playing?" she countered. "There are a few questions I have, and you don't seem to be the type to volunteer the answers." Her voice and whole demeanor changed. Suddenly, she bore a strange resemblance to that doll, Chucky, from the movie *Child's Play*. "So I decided we should play a little game of truth or dare. You know, the one where I ask the questions and you tell me the truth because *I dare you not to.*"

I had never felt so vulnerable, "What the hell...?" The feeling of betrayal crept up my spine and slapped me in the back of the head so hard it nearly knocked me off the couch. "What the fuck has gotten into you? This shit isn't funny any more," I protested.

While tightening her grip on my family jewels, "All right sweetie, you've got two choices," she whispered. "You can either talk...or sing!"

The ordeal continued for more than forty-five minutes with me suffering Ernestina's badgering while she posed questions like an attorney in a courtroom. She delved into areas of my life I had no intention of ever remembering, let alone reliving. Everything from the abuse, neglect, and molestation I'd suffered as a child to the viciousness of a young adulthood manifested by the experiences of my adolescence. It was then she learned how I had been transformed from a caring, sensitive youth, into the distant, evasive social recluse I'd become...even the details of my association with the late

Oswald Jenkins. Suddenly, I noticed she had released her hold on me and was actually wiping tears from compassionate eyes. With an expression of genuine concern while trying to get a firm understanding of my mental state, Ernestina wondered about the next move.

She asked, "So, now you intend to take his place?"

"I...I don't know what to do. I mean, up 'til a few days ago I was looking for a way out this shit. Now, it's like I'm obligated to see it finished," I explained.

Her approach was more direct, "And where does that leave...us? You know, with all the stuff you just told me, one phone call and I could schedule you a fitting for a state-issued striped suit. *I am a member of the New York City police department, you know.*"

While cupping her small hand between my contrasting large palms, "Yeah, that's the one thing I've thought of every day since first meeting you. That's why I couldn't let you know...why I decided to get out," I said.

She slowly moved her hand away and looked me in the eyes, "But you're not out. Hell, you're in deeper now than you were when we met. I should have followed my mind that day in Harlem and ran like hell."

I wasn't certain whether my comment was more of an effort to convince her or myself, "Baby, I'm not the monster those other fools in the game are. I told you, I never even wanted to be in the game. It just happened like that."

Ernestina whispered, while lowering her head, "Well, from where I sit, nothing *just happens like that*," she said. "My grandmother used to say, you can always tell a zebra by his stripes. It's not like you can just shower the shit away."

"Well, it's a game I don't want any part of, but I have to play it out," I stressed.

As she pulled up on the cushion and stood to leave, "Then, I guess that answers my question about where it leaves us," she said.

There was an awkward, deafening silence for nearly five minutes while Ernestina straightened her clothes and captured a few strands of stray sandy-brown locks using the television as an improvised mirror. Without another word, she reached past me, still reclined on the couch, and picked up her petite but stylish Dooney & Bourke leather bag. She walked slowly to the door; head still lowered, and opened it without ever looking back. She uttered from a place that I never wanted to see her go while exiting my apartment, "You know, I am still a police officer."

It took a minute before I realized the door was still partially open. Retrieving the still-damp towel from the arm of the couch, I approached the opening to my apartment like a lion stalking its prey. As I reached to bump the door closed, it gently crept open to reveal Natasha's sultry green eyes peering in at me with her mouth watering like a famished feline over a fish aquarium. Before she even had a chance to form the words, I dismantled any attempt. "Not now, Natasha," I cut, "Not now. This definitely isn't a good time."

I closed the door, latched the two deadbolt locks, and leaned against it while thinking what a mess this saga known as my life had become. Images of Ernestina intruded on my thoughts while I was in the process of retreating to the bedroom. Entering my lair, I spoke aloud, "The one positive thing," as Nancy Wilson continued her blissful enchantment that eventually lulled my cares away and introduced me to the sandman.

15

The Family

I woke the morning after my encounter with Ernestina feeling like a prom queen who had been sexually assaulted on the date and dropped off at the bus station. Memory of my moving to close the door draped in a towel and having capitalized on the opportunity to burst Natasha's bubble, for which I realized she deserved an apology, was all I could recall of the previous night, but nothing beyond that. When the radio alarm had blared at seven fifteen, I found myself half reclined on the eight decorative pillows at the head of my massive four-foot-high queen-sized bed. The towel lay in a small bundle on the floor beneath my feet. I remember thinking, *It's a good thing there wasn't a fire or anything that would've caused an emergency evacuation during the night.* Vivid images of Oz and Tony's last day played, retracted, and replayed through my mind while I tried to muster the strength to get dressed.

I heard a solemn voice, "Damn, lost both those fools."

Looking curiously around the room, it was quickly determined the voice I'd heard was my own. *I really need to get the hell up out this place,* I concluded. This is the type shit that happens to fools just before they snap and kill up a bunch of folks for no real reason other than the fact *they just felt like it.*

I was thinking how nice things were down in Georgia around this time of year when the phone intruded on my tranquil thoughts of livestock, sugar-cane fields and small gardens you'd find at nearly every house outside the city limits. I took time to finish pulling my final pants leg over the shaft of my newly emancipated Tony Lama cowboy boots before meandering over to catch the phone on about the twelfth ring.

I answered in a careless tone to let the caller know I really didn't feel all that chatty, "Yeah, what's up?"

The unknown voice asked, "Who this?"

"Who the hell did you call?" I rebutted.

The caller identified in a harsh tone, questioning my motives, "Will, this Cherish, you always answer your damn phone like that? And why you don't have a machine?"

Already annoyed at her attitude, I refuted, "It's my damn phone...and I'll answer it however the hell I want to answer it...if I want to answer it."

"Whew, sound like somebody got up on the wrong side of the bitchin bed this morning," she sighed.

"Well, it's my damn bed too. And, if you must know, I haven't gotten up yet," I complained. "What the hell do you want, anyway? You didn't call me at 7:30 in the morning just to crawl up my ass, did you?"

Her bruised ego was accompanied by much attitude. "Well, Mom and Sam told me to call and find out what time you's comin up this way. And I did kinda wanna see you before I go, but the hell wit it now. You got yo panties all in a wad 'n shit," she said.

In effort to get more clarification, I asked, "Before you go? Go where?"

She reasoned, "I'm going back home to LA. I can't stay here forever. That's why I left this joint in the first place. 'Cause ain't shit to do."

Nothing to do in New York City, go figure, I thought. But knowing the type person she was, I realized Cherish could be bored if she were a matadore in the middle of a bull fight.

Hurrying to get my keys, I asked, "What time does your flight leave? Maybe I can meet you at the airport to see you off."

"At seven o'clock," she said.

While double-checking the time on my wrist, "Well, I could be wrong, but I think you're a little late for that one, sister," I said. "You couldn't make that flight if you were already at the airport."

"I meant six fifty-seven A.M.," she corrected.

"That's not any better," I determined. "There definitely isn't any point in even trying to catch that flight."

"No, no, *no*," she chanted. "I was tryin to tell you, tomorrow. My flight leaves at seven tomorrow morning."

"Oh, damn; I thought you were talking about leaving today. If you don't pull up until tomorrow, then we've got plenty of time. I'll be up that way all day," I said.

Her tone quieted a bit. "So, you comin up here to see Mom and Sam today?"

"Yeah," I said.

"But I'm interested in what you gonna be doin tonight," she hinted.

The little hell's angel sat on my shoulder whispering instructions in my ear. "That all depends on the night," I commented, with much insinuation. "Who knows, maybe I can drop you at the airport in the morning."

Her response was laced with optimism, "That sounds a awful lot like a invitation to spend the night," she said.

"You can call it whatever you want, but it's either you spend the night here or grab a gypsy cab from there tomorrow," I stated. "If I have to come pick you up in the morning, that means getting out around four-something to get you in Harlem, and then back over to the airport on time."

"You mean, I ain't worth the extra effort?" Cherish questioned.

"I'm saying, you all right, but I still haven't decided if I like you that much," I said. "There's no problem being up with you 'til four in the morning if things turning up the way they're supposed to be happening when things happening, but I'm not halfway trying to be out at four in the morning to come find your ass. You got me confused with some of those West Coast fools."

Cherish interrupted, to more or less shut me up, "Okay Will, you can save the fifty-cent sermon. I got the point. I'll have all my stuff t'gether when you get here." Still not the least bit dissuaded, she asked, "How long you gonna be?"

Securing the second deadbolt, I responded as Natasha's old man passed behind me in the hall, "I'm on my way out the building right now," I said. "I should be up by you within the hour…give or take a few."

Natasha's man, Uri, ordered as I left my door, "You need speak." It was difficult to understand his improvised English as he demanded while approaching me from behind, "You need speak, now!" I didn't even realize he was talking to me until I turned around and got caught in a choke hold. "You hurt me Natasha? Her say you hurt she!"

My cell phone tumbled to the floor. "Man, what the hell has gotten into you? I haven't even seen your girl."

I first rotated to the left and then, strategically to the right in attempt to break his death grip on my jugular. As I turned to face him, my right arm extended and introduced his nose to the heel of my hand. His head flipped back like a Pez dispenser and he stumbled backward into the door of their apartment. Although I wasn't fully aware of the reason for his assault, I had no intention of lodging a formal inquiry while he was still functional. The door had broken his fall but positioned him perfectly for a barrage of jabs and a couple left hooks, when the commotion summoned a slew of onlookers from their apartments. They were content to only stand in the entrances of the respective safe havens and observe without interference.

One elderly neighbor shouted, "It's about time somebody showed him how it feel to be smacked around."

"That's what he get for always whipping his ole lady's ass," came from another. "Now he'll have a chance to see how she feels the day after having her damn head beat in."

When I realized what was happening, my neighbor of three years lay motionless in the hallway with me standing above his limp lump. At the point I stopped pummeling Uri and stood fully erect, the nosey spectators disappeared as quickly as they had appeared, like fiddler crabs, back into their nests. As the heavy white oak-and-glass turn-of-the-century door swung open, I jerked around expecting an army of New York's boys in blue to rush in and give me a taste of what I'd just served Uri. Instead, I saw Natasha standing looking down at her life partner with a blank, emotionless stare before crossing the space that separated us. She gently reached up and palmed my left shoulder to keep her balance as the door was unlocked. My kept neighbor stepped over her motionless man, smiled, and disappeared into the dimly lighted space they shared. I reached down with blood-stained hands to retrieve my phone from against the wall where it had inadvertently been kicked during the ferocious exchange.

I reached to pick up the cell, "Hello...hello, Cherish, you still there?"

She responded before probing, "Uh, yeah, I'm here Bill. What the hell just happened? What was all that noise?"

I replied in a somber tone, "Nothing, just something I had to take care of for my neighbor; been putting it off for a while."

"Well, if you have something to do," she started.

"Oh no...I'm finished. Tell Moms and Poppy I'm on my way up...in about an hour or so."

Not content with the response, Cherish pressed, "You sure you okay Willie? That sounded like somebody was gettin they ass whupped."

"Cher," I said.

"Yes, Bill," she acknowledged.

I listed a matter-of-fact reply to signify the issue wasn't open for discussion before simply ending the call, "Be there in about an hour."

Leaving the building and proceeding down the steps out front rather hurriedly in the event one of the neighbors had found their moral conscience and decided to call the police, I stumbled at the step next to the bottom. Instinctively, I looked back over my left shoulder to notice Natasha staring out the window. She smiled a devilish grin and waved. I nodded without expression, then proceeded up the street, and over to my car. Not quite a block from where the Impala had been parked, I paused momentarily for a parade of five patrol cars with lights flashing, but no sirens, speeding off in the direction of my building.

I guess this would be a good time to take a vacation, I resolved. The police passed so quickly the officers didn't even notice me at the stop sign. Thoughts resurfaced about the recent situation at the impound yard. I said aloud, to my imaginary passenger, "Probably looking for a Monte Carlo."

At the passing of the patrol cars, I took time to search my music library and requested Miles Davis as copilot on the drive up to Harlem. While Miles did his thing from behind his horn, I handled my business from behind the wheel of the Chevy. We found our way over to the West Side Highway and up to 133rd Street in what seemed like record time. Parking in my usual place near the dumpster at the rear entrance of Mom's and Poppy's building, I saw Kenny, the usual security officer, climbing into his classic 1966 Ford Mustang. *Damn, that means I'll have to deal with that ass of a hole, John,* came the impulsive thought. I spoke, as we passed each other, "What's up Kenny."

"How you doing Will?" he responded. "You might want to raise your window, man. If you ain't got sense enough to lock the doors, at least let the windows up. Weather man said we supposed to get some rain."

"Well, it'll just get a good rinse on the inside; the window got busted," I explained. "I was going to ask you to keep an eye on it while I'm upstairs for a minute, but I see you're cutting out early."

Displaying an insincere frown, Kenny said, "Well, I would hang out a minute longer but I gotta get back home and set things up for my baby's birthday party...got a buncha little knuckleheads coming over to tear up the place. Holla at John. He in there."

Passing through the heavy door at the entrance, I couldn't help but go back to the first time I had the displeasure of making John's acquaintance. The thought still brought an ugly snarl to my face.

I heard a voice echo from behind the counter, "How you doing man? Will, right?"

While crossing the small lobby area, I replied, "What's up?" to hear, *BBBBZZZ*, the door's buzzer sounded as I approached.

John was explaining to a kid that looked like he was barely old enough to drive, "Dude ain't a tenant in the building but he be here on the regular. I think his folks live up on three or four."

With a frown on his face, the new kid started to interject, "But the regulations say..."

John came to my defense, "Look man, rules ain't all they is to a job; I'm telling you, dude all right," and then called to my back as I rounded the corner, "Take it easy, Will."

I echoed like sentiments, entering the long hall on the way to the elevators, "Make sure you do the same."

A few short minutes later, I stepped off the mechanical carriage on the fourth floor to discover Moms peering out into the hall.

She yelled back into the apartment, "He ain't up here yet," before questioning Cherish, "What time it was when he rung ya from da Vil'age?"

Moms' daughter yelled back from inside the apartment, "Oh come on, Mom. It ain't like I was ridin the second hand on the damn clock."

Eunice turned in the doorway to leave her back exposed while involved in an intense exchange with Cherish, "He say he comin straight here?"

"Yeah Ma, or that's what I think he said," Cherish concluded. "He'll be here 'cause he s'posed to take me to the airport tomorrow."

Eunice optimistically posed, "Oh, he plan'n ta stay ova t'night?"

"No, Mom, I decided to stay over by him," Cherish disclosed. "His place closer to the airport than here."

"I's figur'n he in da Vil'age," Eunice poked. "Dat ain't close ta L'Guardy Airpot.

Cherish insisted, "I ain't goin outta LaGuardia, Mom. You know I don't like that place. I flew in at JFK."

At that very moment Eunice was so involved in discussion with Cherish she didn't hear me sneak up behind her. I leaned over and clawed the back of her leg at the knee and yelled like a caged lion. Eunice instinctively donkey kicked me between my legs without ever looking back; catching me completely off guard. I fell to the floor like a ten-pound bag of potatoes and lay curled in the hallway in a fetal position. "Ouuuch, oh damn!" I shouted.

"Oh Willie, I's so sorry," Eunice cried, and then scolded me, "And what 'n hell ya doin sneakin up on folk like dat any ways! You gone be done mess 'roun 'n got yo fool self hurt."

"I just did," I grunted.

Moms continued chastising, "Ya's s'posed ta call when ya git here, anyways."

I spoke through the intense pain, "Well, that wouldn't do much for a surprise now, would it?"

About then, Cherish appeared in the doorway, "Look to me like you the only one that got surprised, dude."

Somewhat annoyed, I growled, "I oughta kick your…"

"What you oughtta do is get yo butt up outta that nasty-ass floor," she suggested.

Genuinely concerned, Eunice chimed in, "A'ight, both o' ya, dat's 'nough…Cherish, git o'er dere 'n helps da boy up!" she ordered.

She was still laughing at the thought, "Why I gotta help him up? You the one kicked him in his…thang."

I heard Poppy's roar, "What da hell all dat noise out dere?" he questioned, "Can't a man git no sleep in his own damn house?"

The *plop-shih* of Sam's house slippers could be heard outside the apartment as he made his way from their bedroom. He materialized at the table in the dining area wearing the trademark knee-length Bermuda shorts and a button-down pajama shirt that was never buttoned, exposing what looked like the skeletal remains of a pigeon he referred to as his queen's playground.

Eunice lashed him for his choice of attire, "Sam, why ya don't go git sum damn clothes on?"

"Oh, don't be modest, Mama. Dem sum big kids. Dey knows you's da reason da shirt comin off in da first place," he joked. "You'n tells 'em how I a'tacked ya in da room 'fore ya climbt outta bed dis morn'n."

"Dat's why you's jest wakin up, 'cause yo old ass can't do what ya used ta," Moms said.

Not to be outdone, Sam quickly retaliated with an impish grin while tapping his wife on her sizeable ass, "Well, I maybe not can't does likes I used to, but what's I does, I does it right mama," he said.

"Yeah, 'n den pass da hell out!" she said.

I commented to intrude on their moment, "Did you forget about the injured out here?"

Cherish retorted, "You'll be all right," before offering, "Just let me make you comfortable and take a look at your little boo boo. You want me to kiss it and make it better?"

Eunice was red with embarrassment. "Okay Cherish, dat's 'nough o' dat kinda talk now. We is still yo par'ents."

I gave Cherish a look that effectively conveyed my message and whispered, "We'll have to talk about you kissing the boo boo a little later. You did still want me to drop you at the airport tomorrow, right?"

"Eunice," Sam pretended to yell, "We's gonna have ta sep'rate 'em, dey in here skeemin up some'n."

Cherish's tone was a little too serious for comfort, "Aaugh old man, it ain't like it's nothin you ain't never done, wit yo old perverted ass."

"I don't knows what da hell you's talk'n. If Ida knowed what a r'sults was gone be when I met her, I ne'er woulda let Eunice takes off her damn clothes," he said. "She a'ready had six o' you muthas when we met...'n den I fucked 'round 'n finds two mo o' ya li'l crumb-snatchers."

Sensing an all out war, I cut in, "Okay kids, that's enough of the swordplay. There was supposed to be a reason I came to Harlem this morning."

"Yeah," Sam agreed, "Now dat ya mention it, dey's a whole lotta 'splainin you's s'pose ta do. I wanna know 'bout all dis gangsta 'n killin 'n shit been go'n on in da news."

Eunice said, coming to my defense, "I done told ya he ain't no gangsta and he ain't done no killin, likes he tells me. Tell 'em, Willie...likes ya telled me."

I was searching for the right words, "Well, no Moms. I'm no gangster and I didn't kill that man like the news said I did," I told her. "But, I have been involved in a lot of shi... stuff the past couple years. A guy by the name of Oz...well Oswald...that's his real name."

Cherish started to interrupt, "That's the nig..."

Eunice shouted a stern warning to cut her off, "Cherish...!" she yelled. "Ya knows we ain't gots no use fo dat kinda talk."

Cherish continued, "I mean, the dude they found dead in your ride couple days ago, ain't it?" she asked. "...Say they found him dead in yo shit."

I was questioning myself as to how any of their kids could be openly profane in the presence of Sam and Eunice but were not allowed to utter the infamous N-word without the risk of suffering dire consequences.

"Well, Will?" Cherish insisted.

"What Cherish?" I asked.

She specified, "The news said ole boy name was Oswald Jenkins," before asking, "But ain't that the dude I hear you be talkin 'bout lotta the time name Oz?"

I answered, "Yeah, that's right, but I didn't kill him," I reiterated.

Driving home her point, Cherish recalled, "But he was in your ride...*and he is dead.*"

Thinking of the outcome, "We've established that, but I didn't kill him. Tony and I, that's the other person who was in the car, we were just trying to get Oz to the hospital." I spoke with my head lowered, "And I would've made it if it wasn't for the damn police."

Cherish continued commentating, "The other dude was Anthony. They say he had a heart attack when he fell out the car at the scene."

I snapped; turning in her direction, "The hell they say; he didn't fall. That's a bald-faced lie," I said. "Those crooked sons of bitches beat his ass. They killed him right across from where I was standing. The bastards killed him on purpose."

Sam chimed in to offer his words of wisdom, "See, dat's why I be tellin dem fools like Junior; don't be stand'n 'round bullshit'n in da stowes 'cause dem folks don't be wont'n us in dese places no how. If'n he ain't mo careful, dey gone have his li'l ass downtown 'bout dat same shit."

"Poppy, I don't mean to make light of Junior's deal, but his stuff doesn't even register on the same scale as...well, it won't matter. Life is what it is," I said.

Sam input, "So, all o' dis time we thankin you's tryin ta get out ta Hollywood 'n you's hang'n out in Hellywood," before reasoning, "Ya out der wit all dem li'l devlish muthas; but from da sound o' thangs, dey ain't actin. Now, I don't needs none o' dat foolishness up in here."

I made my best effort at trying to reassure him, "It's all right Poppy. I got it," I said.

Sam stepped slowly in my direction and moved so close his head was practically resting on my shoulder while attempting to whisper, "I means, ain't no pro'lem wit me takin care o' myself," he said, "But ya knows I's gotta be doin alls I can ta make sho my queen gots nothin ta wor'y 'bout. Now, if'n I gots ta be wo'ried 'bout ya comin 'round 'n keepin huh all both'red 'n shit…"

My tone came across a bit more insistent, "Like I said Poppy, I got it. There has never been a time you and Moms were ever at risk. You know me better than that."

He responded, "Alls I knows is, she ain't real comfable wit all 'dis fool stuff been goin on wit ya in da news 'bout killin folk 'n bein in da jailhouse. It make huh real nerv'ous like." The expression on his face softened a bit as he lowered his gaze. "It ain't gots nothin ta do wit who I thanks ya is… ya knows you's a'ight wit us…but I can't be havin dis kinda thang gettin Mama all upset. She be wory'in 'bout ya. I seen huh mo upset o'er past few days dan I e'er seen huh both'red o'er any huh own flesh 'n blood. I ain't ne'er wanna tells ya dat ya can't be here, but I can't…"

I cut in to avoid the need for him to finish the sentence, "You don't have to Poppy…it's understood."

I realized he was having a more difficult time trying to say it than I was trying to imagine how things would be in New York without the family I had come to know and love. At that point, there was nothing more that could be said.

I then asked Cherish without taking eyes off my adopted father, "You about ready to go?

Knowing he was still the point of my focus, Sam never lifted his eyes, "Y'all young'ons be careful out der now, ya hear?"

Even though I'd heard the same words from him a number of times before, there was something that sounded different about the way he said it. This time, it sounded so final. I extended my right hand and, without uttering a word, we shook to confirm the unspoken, but understood, agreement before Poppy retreated to the safety of his bedroom. I found Moms in her comfortable place at the counter near the kitchen sink and gave her a brief but sincere hug before turning toward the door.

"Cherish, where you put your bags?"

She responded in a way that spoke of her not fully understanding the situation, "They back there in the room at the end of the hall, your old room," she said.

Moms made her way from in front of the stove, "Ya ain't leavin, is ya Willie?" and had followed me halfway down the hall, "But ya jest gettin here. I thought we's gone have dinner. Ain't ya hongry none a'tall?"

Sam appeared in the hallway and stepped in front of his wife, "Eunice, lets da boy go. He gots bidness ta tend," he said.

The disappointment in her voice took front position, "But I's fixin da food fo us all ta eat…'n he jest come a minute a'go. Where ya gotta be gettin off ta in sech a hurry? Cherish, where is you makin 'em take you?" she accused.

She turned to her mom with a look of disgust, "Why it's always gotta be my fault?" Cherish protested. "I can't *make* him do nothing… Hell, he a grown ass man!"

I spoke up from the back bedroom, coming to Cherish's defense, "It's not that, Moms. There's stuff I have to do before I leave."

Eunice yelled from their bedroom, "Oh, is ya go'in ta Californy wit Cherish? Cherish, ya ain't tells me dat."

"Because I didn't know my damn self," Cherish said.

"No Moms, I ain't... I'm not going to California with Cherish," I explained. "Just figured maybe this would be a good time to drive down to Georgia and see my folks."

"Well, what 'n da world fo?" Eunice whined. "We said somethin ta make ya wanna leave?"

Sam spoke up, "Dammit woman, 'cause dey's his real mama and daddy; dat's why. Since when man gotta have a freakin reason ta go see his folks? 'Cause Dat's where he come from."

Scowling in Poppy's direction, I addressed the comment to my overly sensitive Moms, "No ma'am, you guys didn't do anything to make me want to leave. I'll just give New York's finest something else to think about while they try to figure out where I went...and how," I said.

"Now don't ya go's gettin yo'self in no troubles," Poppy input. "Ya knows dey done told ya not ta be leave'n town. Dem folk be watchin ya like da damn Chinaman watches ya in his jewry stowes. Now don't be givin whitey no 'scuse..."

I interrupted, "Like I said, Poppy...I got this." And then, turning my attention toward the front of the apartment, I spoke a little louder, "Cherish! You want to help a slightly disabled brother out?"

She called back, "What you mean disabled? Ain't nothin wrong wit yo legs."

In the most sincere tone I could fake, I said, "I'm serious. I took a shot to my leg earlier."

I ain't see you limpin when you come through..." she debated my claim, "You took a shot when...to which leg?"

I cut her off, "The third one," I laughed. "The one I might need you to take a look at later."

Poppy called from their bedroom, "Y'all mus thank we's stupid," he said. "We might be old, but we's a long way from be'n dead; I keeps tellin ya."

Moms chimed in, "A'ight Cherish," she said. "We is still yo parents."

Coming down the hall to grab the smaller of her two suitcases, Cherish commented as she rolled it past her parents' bedroom, "Come on Will; you gone be done got me in trouble."

Knowing their daughter, Eunice spoke up, "He ain't able ta getchu in no mo troubles dan ya wanna gets in."

"All right, Mom, don't start your…" Cherish began.

I intruded to cut her off, "Cherish, they *is* still your parents!" I said, mocking Sam and Eunice before saluting them. "Come on, let's get you out of here and on your way back to LA. Later Moms…Poppy!"

We rode the elevator to the basement in total silence and proceeded out the building to my ride. I don't know what was on Cherish's mind but I was still in the car with Oz and Tony two days earlier, feeling the warmth of Oz's blood and noticing the temperature change from warm life to dead cold; seeing every blow the cops had delivered to Tony's already helpless body even after he fell, lifeless, to the concrete.

A heart attack, they said. "Yeah right; I got yo heart attack," I mumbled.

"What'd you say?" questioned Cherish.

At the realization of not being alone with my thoughts, I asked, "Do what?"

"You said something. I didn't hear you," she persisted.

"Oh, it was nothing," I explained. "I was just talking to myself."

"Will?" she asked.

"Yeah, what's up?" I responded.

Cherish said, "I got a question," then paused, prolonging the assault.

"Okay. Are you going to spit it out, or choke on it?"

Capitalizing on the opportunity to take a stab at me, she questioned, "I'm just curious, what you could possibly tell yourself you don't already know?"

Without responding, I cut my eyes at Cherish and turned up the volume on the CD player to the point she couldn't hear herself think.

16

The Difficult Goodbye

'd driven a full four or five blocks after increasing the stereo's volume before Cherish finally reached to turn it down.

She asked, "Why you come this way? Don't you usully go West Side Highway to the Village? Ain't that way faster to get back?"

I responded, "We're not going to the Village. Not right now."

"Then, where we goin? You know somebody live over this side?" she drilled. "I been livin in Harlem all my life and don't come here no more than I got to. Who you know over here?"

Cherish's jabbering was constant the entire ride over, until the car slowed and left the street. I stated without feeling as I turned into a fenced lot next to a huge sign that read *Tyler and Son's*. "Funeral parlor," I said, "Wait here."

Cherish began her protest, "You gotta be outta your damn…"

I repeated in a dry tone without looking her way, "Wait here."

Appearing to dissolve into the leather seat, Cherish replied, "Leave the radio on...please."

I noticed the side door to the building propped open with a small block of wood, so I entered what turned out to be the room where the bodies were embalmed and prepped before being dressed. There were two nude corpses atop stainless steel tables with clothing draped over their legs. I couldn't help but stare at the exceptionally pretty female and, without thinking, the words, "To die for," escaped my lips.

I was startled by a deep voice from behind, "Interesting choice of words."

While trying to mask my uneasiness, I posed, "Excuse me?"

The ghoulish mortician introduced himself, "My name Edgar. Your comment...interesting choice of words, considering she was the victim of a murder/suicide. The guy next to her was the one killed her...then hisself. We didn't get the other body. Dude she was caught with come from Upper East Side...Jewish realtor."

"I...uh...my name Willie," I stammered. "That's a real shame."

He warned, "You know, ain't nobody s'posed to be back here. You trespassing," then reconsidered, "But I guess it be a'ight. Can't say I get much company...none that can talk anyway. Who you come for?"

"What makes you think I came for anybody?" I questioned.

He replied, "Well, for one, 'cause I know sneaking in mortuaries ain't what you do to pass the time."

I finally disclosed, "Umm...Oz...Oswald Jenkins. I'm looking for Oswald Jenkins."

Edgar instructed, "He in that room to yo left...over there." Before questioning, "What...you family? 'Cause only family s'pose to be allowed in there to see him 'n that other fella."

"Well, you can say he's my brother, but we not actually related," I replied.

Edgar half grinned as he pointed me in the direction of the adjoining room where the made-up bodies of Oz and Tony lay in caskets positioned beside each other. "I knows what you mean. Sometimes folk ain't even blood kin treat you better than yo own," he said. "I ain't s'pose to do this, but the family ain't here yet. I give you five minutes. Then you gotta get out…through the side like you come in."

Moving to where the bodies lay, I said to myself while standing between the two caskets, "Just like they lived…Side by side."

I was reminiscing for what seemed only a second when Edgar's head appeared in the doorway nearly half an hour later. "You gotta get outta there," he whispered. "The family coming in. I didn't see 'em when they got here, so they right…"

A scream came from a dark-complexioned heavy-set woman who'd appeared in the doorway, "Oh Lord! It's him; the man that had my brother dead in his car!" she said. "You killed my brother!"

Edgar directed, to no avail, "Excuse me ma'am, you not s'posed to be back here. No clients s'posed to be in this area. Please wait out front."

The woman insisted, "But he the one killed my brother."

"I didn't kill him," I defended.

"Ms. Jenkins," demanded Edgar, "You and yo family gone have to leave now."

She spoke with a condescending tone, "The name is Mrs., if you don't mind; Mrs. Harriston, thank you very much," and then started shouting directions at the other family members. "Somebody call the police. I want that hoodlum arrested! How they let him outta jail? Will somebody call the damn police?"

A vaguely familiar voice mumbled, "Ain't no point calling the cops Mama," but remained hidden amidst the group. "He ain't wanted for nothing."

I realized it was Oz's nephew, Marcus, who I had pinned against the building with Amp's truck when he and his partner tried to jack us for Oz's money. I squinted and searched the small crowd of relatives until his heavy form materialized in the entrance to the room.

His mom insisted, "But he...that's the man from the news...he..."

Marcus volunteered a defense on my behalf while yelling over her screaming, "He worked for Uncle Oswald!" he clarified, "For the last two or three years, far as I know."

Oz's little sister seemed to want somebody, anybody to be accountable. "Marcus, you sure you know what you sayin? I mean, how did your uncle end up dead in this man's car...and why was the police chasing him?"

Her son reasoned, "It's like he said Ma. Guess they was just trying to get Unk to the hospital. I mean, if Uncle Oz... uh, Uncle Oswald was his bread and butter, what sense it make for this fool to kill him?"

The comment struck me rather peculiar. I couldn't figure out whether Marcus was speaking defense or damnation. At this point, it really didn't matter one way or the other, as long as I could get out that proverbial lions' den without having to fight my way to the door. All eyes were on me as I passed slowly through the crowd of still dissatisfied hyena who were already itching for blood...no matter whose blood it happened to be. I whispered when briefly making eye contact with Marcus as I approached the entrance beside him, "Thanks man."

"For what...I still owe you, fool. This just ain't the time or the place for no bullshit," he warned.

Nodding in agreement, I softly replied on my way past him, "You right, but it's never the time or the place to threaten me...watch your back."

Climbing into the car, I interrupted Cherish scanning radio stations to keep herself occupied. "Thought you was gonna need my help when I saw the hit squad goin in the buildin 'while ago," she said.

The skepticism in my voice did well to establish the point, "And just what the hell were you going to do, run in there and force me to fight all of them for the both of us?" I asked. "Thanks, but no thanks; you did the best thing."

She unknowingly confirmed, "But I ain't do nothin 'cept sit here and listen to the radio."

I smarted back, "Like I said, you did the best thing."

"Well, it's just my opinion, but I think the best thing woulda been to just keep on drivin down the West Side Highway and not stop by this place. But that's just my opinion," she said.

I responded, while pulling out into traffic, "Well, you know what they say about opinions…like assholes."

When we drove up the street approaching my apartment building nearly forty-five minutes later, the unmarked police cars might as well have been neon green with platinum shields painted on the sides. Fortunately, they didn't recognize my *Monte Carlo* passing them.

"Where you goin Willie? You done drove past where Eunice said yo place is. You move to another buildin without tellin us? Three parking spaces was right in front," Cherish said.

"Maybe one will still be open when you come back around," I replied.

"Come back 'round…me…from where?" she questioned.

"When you drive the car back around the building to park it; I can't get out here," I insisted.

"Why not…you still live here, right?" she questioned. "What's goin on Willie?"

"Well, New York's finest sitting out front watching the place," I said.

Cherish continued, "Where? I ain't see nobody."

I attempted what proved to be a futile explanation, "That's the whole point…you're not supposed to."

She asked in a nervous tone, "So, what you gone do? If I go to jail, I'll miss my flight tomorrow."

"Well, I need you to let me out, then drive the car back around front and go into my apartment," I directed. "Whatever you do, no lights, no television, or anything that'll let them know somebody's there. That way, you'll keep us both from going to jail."

Cherish unwisely tried to reason, "I ain't understandin why you hidin if you ain't done nothin. Didn't they ar'eady let you go?"

I explained, pulling into an alley blocks from my apartment building, "There's a big difference between being released and being let go. They released me all right, but that's far from letting me go."

Cherish still wore a look of uncertainty, "So where you want me to park...and how you gone get upstairs wit the Po Po sittin out front?"

Pushing the button on the remote to open the trunk, I assured, "I'm going to get in the same way you're going to; through the front door. Now, come around to the driver's side."

We met at the back of the car where I lifted the trunk lid and began sorting through the contents of a canvas duffle bag.

"Hold this a second," I said.

Cherish paused to question, "You ain't gonna shoot nobody is you?"

Straightening the dreadlock hairpiece and donning a pair of dark glasses, "No silly, I just need to get dressed," I said.

"What the...if you knowed how you look," she laughed.

Before trying to instruct her, "The most important thing is, I don't look like me," I said. "Let me show you which keys fit which locks."

"I'm pretty sure I can figure that part out," she insisted.

"All right, but you don't want to be standing in the hall fumbling with keys to what's supposed to be your apartment. Wait for me just inside the door so I can walk you through the place. It might be a little difficult for you getting around with no lights," I said.

Climbing into the car, she partially lowered the window, "Why is it I get the feeling you kinda used to sneakin 'round in the dark?"

I smirked and looked out into the street, "You go, I'll be there shortly."

Leaving the alley, I walked opposite the direction Cherish had driven and turned left at the next street. After another two blocks, I made a second left and walked five blocks, and then back over two to approach my building from the direction opposite the way she would have driven. I strolled past, within inches of one officer seated in his car at the end of Bleecker Street.

"Excuse me," he called.

My heart seemed to lodge in a parched throat as I responded with my best Caribbean impersonation. I asked, "Yeah man, what can me do ya fur?"

The officer asked, "You got a light on you?"

I even modestly impressed myself with the impromptu response, "Naugh man, me no smoker...only pure breath o' da Cre'ater go in des lungs. Dat cancer stick kills ya, man."

"Yeah, thanks anyway buddy," he dismissed.

Sweat could be felt rolling down my spine as I continued walking; realizing I'd just passed the proof-of-identity test. Approaching the steps at the front of my building, I noticed Natasha in her usual position atop her perch. I nodded at the top of the steps thinking she was none the wiser.

As I passed and opened the huge wooden doors, "Gute oukfit," she quietly commented. "I keeped chu zeecret."

This was not the time to try and figure out how she had recognized me. The last thing I needed was to become involved in a conversation with her. I continued without breaking stride until outside the door of my apartment. Pausing momentarily to be certain no one was looking; I quickly disappeared into my lair.

"Damn, it took you long 'nough," Cherish greeted.

I quieted her, "Shhh." I whispered, "Nobody's supposed to be in here. We've got to move away from the door. Hold on to my belt."

In a sensual whisper, she asked, "How the hell you know where you goin?"

I clarified, making my way around the end table and couch, "To my room; it is my apartment, remember?"

I felt a slight tug at my waistline when she asked in a warning tone, "You think that's safe?"

Proceeding through the kitchen and into the hallway, I flatly stated, "I'm not in any danger, but you can crash on the floor if it would make you feel more comfortable."

She prodded, while playfully slapping me on the shoulder, "What, no offer for me to sleep on the couch?"

I confirmed, as we approached the bedroom door, "My couch is for sitting..."

"I know, I know," she cut. "The table is for eatin and the bed is for sleepin."

I sang in a suggestive whisper, "Among other things."

"Things like..." she prodded.

Before Cherish could finish the question to which we both new she'd already determined the answer, I turned and led her to the side of the huge bed, gently kissing her shoulders, neck, and face until I had mapped my way to succulent full lips. She let out a subtle moan as one hand found its way inside her blouse. Strategic motion of the forefinger and thumb of my right hand witnessed the clasp in the front of her bra retreat and leave eager subjects to fend for themselves. Layer after layer gingerly subsided until she stood wearing nothing but the French-cut thongs once guarded by the cotton/polyester blend of her miniskirt. The soft gray glow from the half moon filtered through the partially opened Venetian blinds past the sheer curtains, and outlined the silhouette of grace personified.

I questioned to be certain, "Are you all right?"

She slowly exhaled, as I lifted and gently placed her in the queen-sized chamber of pleasure, "I can't...can't see," she said.

As I reached into the drawer of the night stand and summoned protection, I whispered, "You don't have to...just feel."

Her body methodically tensed, relaxed, stiffened, and softened with an intense rhythm that had me exploring the boundaries of ecstasy for the next forty minutes. Simultaneously, we both reached the pinnacle of pleasure and let go a masked yell that had each of us wondering if we could have been heard by anyone outside the apartment.

I asked again, "Are you okay?"

She quietly panted, trying to catch her breath, "You bad."

I pretended to sulk, "I'm not bad," I said. "I just do bad things."

"That you do," she confirmed. "So bad 'til it's good."

"Speaking of good," I teased, "Where you learn...?"

Cherish joked, "I watch a lotta movies."

I whispered, "Yeah, right," prior to inquiring, "You going to join me for a shower?"

17

No Place like Home

Three a.m. the day after Cherish boarded the plane at JFK headed for Los Angeles found me in the driver's seat of the Impala on I-95 about sixty-five miles south of Savannah, GA. Fatigue urged me to stop after over eighteen consecutive hours of driving, but the desire to reach my destination compelled my Chevy to continue on its journey. About the time I tired of the company from the library of musicians housed in my CD case and gave up on finding a decent radio station some three and-a-half hours later, what used to be familiar ground seemed to have crept up on me virtually without notice. About twelve miles outside Valdosta, the old wood-framed house stood as it always had, in the middle of a tobacco field, at the end of a country dirt road that had no ditches for drainage. As the sun topped the tree line, I drove up in the front yard at the pump house on the left; near a garden that had been planted every year since I was a child, but seldom properly tended. We had always jokingly referred to it as the weed patch.

Once I'd cut the car's engine I heard an insistent voice, "Who dat out dere?" dad questioned. "I say, who dat?"

I answered in a hurry, when recalling the fact my old man was never more than two steps from his trusty shotgun. "It's Willie," I said.

"Who ya say?" he questioned.

I wisely identified, "Its Willie, Pop...your son, home from New York."

A scream came from the kitchen window, "Oh my goodness; Lord, if it ain't a miracle! Will, whatcha do'n back here?"

The high-pitched voice of my one shade-darker-than-Caucasian cousin, Tammy was still as unmistakable as ever. Although we were billed as relatives, Tammy's opinion allowed that there were enough branches between fourth cousins on the family tree to warrant a romantic relationship. It was her who had taught me how to French kiss at the point I first discovered the difference between boys and girls. But that was when I was a lot younger and a lot curious. I responded, trying to maintain balance after she'd bolted off the porch and into my arms, nearly knocking me onto the hood of the car. "The last I heard, this is where I grew up. I like to think of it as home."

Another familiar voice came from the corner of the house, "Ya did 'til ya left."

I turned to see my mom, as spry as she ever was and joked, while reaching to embrace her barely four-foot tall petite figure. The embrace had her feet lift off the ground, "Well, who is this pretty young thing? You better be careful I don't kidnap you and take you back to the city."

A solemn voice cut into the moment. My dad complained, "I don't reckon she gots no mo bidness in dat city dan you do."

I commented with just enough sarcasm to not be disrespectful. "Well, I'm happy to see you too, father," I said.

"Hmmph," he grunted. "Dat be no pro'lem if'n ya cared 'nough 'bout da place you's a'ways say'n is yo home."

"C'mon Ed, da boy jest gettin in," Mom defended. "'Least let 'em get cleaned up 'n fill his belly 'fore ya'all start slappin each other 'round."

Tammy chimed in, "That's right. He gots a lotta 'splain'n to do 'bout what he been up to in the Big Apple....ain't that what them turist folk calls it.....the BIG APPLE?"

"Yeah, something like that," I said.

Dad's voice was filled with the contempt he didn't bother trying to conceal on his face, "Prob'ly back 'cause he need someth'n."

I tried to sound convincing, "And no, I didn't come because I need something."

"Or 'cause he run'n from someth'n," Dad concluded.

Mom's irritation took front position, "All right now, that's 'nough." She directed the both of us, "You gits yo stuff outta da car, 'n you gits back in dat house if'n ya don't means no good," the pint-sized powder keg ordered, while shaking a finger at Cousin Tammy, "And you git yo butt back in dere 'n finish da cookin so we can all eat."

"Yes ma'am, I'm a-go'n," Tammy conceded.

In my old bedroom, I found things exactly as they had been left almost five and a half years before. Like I had gotten up, gone out to tend the animals, and was just returning to the house. Everything, that is, except the small twin bed on the wall opposite the door. It was positioned in front of the large floor-to-ceiling window. The first order of business was to remove the board just below the window frame that allowed access to my hiding place. That's where two spare nine millimeter handguns, identical to those taken by the New York police, were kept. After strapping them on and replacing the board, I was standing reminiscing the many nights and early mornings when that window had served as a portal. It had unknowingly granted me unauthorized access to a world beyond the tobacco patch and corn fields. Suddenly, my thoughts were demolished when a squeal shattered the memory glass.

Tammy's soprano rang out, "That there my bed."

I tried to not make it obvious that she'd startled me, "Do what? I mean, excuse me?"

Tammy began explaining, "I been stay'n wit Aunt Martha 'n Uncle Ed since my mom passed away 'bout three years ago."

"Aunt Joyce died?" I interrupted. "And why didn't anybody tell me?"

"Well, ain't nobody knowed how to git in touch wit ya 'an Uncle Ed said ya prob'bly won't come to the fun'ral no way."

I felt the temperature of my blood start to rise, "Who the hell does he think he is to decide for me how I'm supposed to feel? That was some foul..."

My old man interrupted, "I's yo daddy boy," he said. "... And I don't 'preciate no cuss'n in dis here house. Ya ain't in da city now. Thangs still don't work here da way dey does up dere where ya been liv'n. Or maybe ya done fo'got ya roots?"

I was suddenly irritated at the mere thought of his presence. My mind wrestled with the fact that he'd taken it upon himself to decide the level of compassion I would have for a family member. The reply was intentionally harsh, "So what, you can't come into the room and take part in conversation? That's what normal people do. Why you sneaking around hiding behind walls and shi...and stuff?"

"One thang fo sho; e'ry one o' dese is my walls and if'n I don't got noth'n ta say ta ya, I jest ain't got noth'n ta say. Just ya 'member, e'ry one o' dese is my walls," he declared, "E'ry sangle sol'tary one o' dem."

I instinctively prodded, "You don't have anything to say to me, but you can lurk around spying, trying to find dirt to throw in my face the first chance you get? That sounds a lot like a ruler's behavior," I said. "That is what you always say, right? You're the king of this house...your castle?"

He warned, in a twisted country philosophy, "Well, I guess ya done gone off ta dat city 'n gotta good whiff. Seem ta me you's smell'n yoself...Jest ya be careful ya don't git out dere too fer dat ya can't git back, now."

My voice was lased with an irritated sarcasm as it required more effort than I was willing to expand to simply avoid cursing him. "Don't you worry yourself father dear, whatever I might be occasioned to get myself into, I have certainly learned to get out, no thanks to you," I said.

The scowl on Dad's face was more defined as one brow raised a couple inches and the corners of his mouth angled downward. He snorted louder than the old red bull fenced out behind the barn. "Figers ya take dat at'tude...like ya ain't ne'er git noth'n from me...I ain't done noth'n ta makes ya da man ya thanks ya is; many a time ya planted yo foots under my table 'n sucked down my grub..."

I protested, "Why does everything have to be about you and yours? You act like nobody ever did anything around this place except you," I said, before stating the obvious. "There were many days I worked my ass off to put stuff in those pots so food *could be* brought to the table...where we all planted our feet."

He began to chastise, "I done told ya 'bout..."

I snapped, "And I'm telling you!"

Mom appeared from the hallway beaming at us both with a look that was beyond interpretation. In classic fashion, her voice never exceeded a whisper but served to immediately establish order.

"And I's tellin both o' ya...stop dis fool talk, now. Y'all actin like ain't ne'er been nobody right 'cept yoselves 'n ain't ne'er been nobody wrong 'cept e'rybody else. Now, I tells ya, da past jest well be left whey it is 'cause ya sho can't ca'ry nothin 'bout it wit ya, 'cept fo da ed'cation it brung. Hell, I can'ts see why'n da world ya'd wanna drag da past witcha thru life no ways."

Trying to prove his manhood, my father scolded, "Martha! Ya might wanna mind yo tongue!" while shaking a crooked finger at me. "Da boy ain't eb'n back a hour 'an ar'eady dis-rupt'n thangs."

"Hell ain't no cuss word," Mom said. "It's all o'er dat Bible you's al'ays throwin at folks…"

I took offense and argued back, "Now, just how is what she said my fault? I'm not holding a gun to her head."

Tammy had excused herself midway though the exchange between my father and me and now re-appeared with an announcement that the food was ready. That was her way of attempting to usher in a sense of calm in the tense situation. "If'n alls y'all gone do is fight the whole time Willie home, ya gone need to eat so's ya can keep up yo strength," she said.

"Don't bother to prepare much for me, Tammy. In fact, don't take up anything; I've suddenly lost my appetite," I said. "I think it might do me well to just take a ride into town."

Tammy sounded disappointed, "But Will, I fixed pork sausage, scrambl'd eggs 'n toast the way Aunt Martha say ya liked; 'an all fresh from the back yard…'nclud'n the sausage."

"Well, you obviously weren't cooking it for me," I said. "You were already in the kitchen when I came up. Besides, I try to limit the pork. Once in a while is okay, but not more than twice a week."

Dad grunted, "Hummph, furst, he too good fo us country folk…and now our country cook'n ain't good 'nough fo him neither."

"Well, if you must know, it has been a proven medical fact for years that eating too much pork can have an adverse effect on your blood pressure. I had pork chops before leaving the city."

"Yeah," dad interrupted, "Jest go ta show ya what dem fancy city docters knows. Folk in dese parts been eat'n pork 'long as an'body can 'member."

I stated in false agreement, "Yes sir, you're right." Then detailed, "But that's the reason people around these parts don't see much past sixty…if they're lucky; the reason why forty or fifty always been considered old; because people never expect to see much past that."

My dad launched a verbal assault, "Dem's yo peoples ya talk'n 'bout...ya oughta have mo r'spect," he said. "Dey's a sight better bunch o' folk dan you's e'er gone 'mount to. Ya walks 'round wit dat city-folk talk like you's bet'er 'n rest o' us. Soun'n likes one o' dem yanks, 'an ya acts dat way too."

"So, that's what it is? You've always blamed me for getting a decent education," I accused. "It wasn't me who decided to go off to Atlanta for five years because you couldn't take care of your son during the time Mom was sick!"

My dad snapped at the thought of what he considered his one demonstrated act of failure, "Ya ain't gots no bidness toss'n 'round what done been gone o'er!" he argued. "Ya ma had da cansur and da doc say she had ta go in da hosp'tal. I ain't knowed nuth'n 'bout tak'n care 'o no young'n."

"Well, if you must know, I've got plenty of respect for my people. It's just ignorance and stupidity with which I have a problem," I corrected. "Like I have much respect for you, but..."

Mom cut in, to keep me from finishing the thought, "You sho ya ain't hongry none a'tall?" she asked. "I means, ya been ridin all night 'n most o' da morn'n. Why ya don't let yo Cusin Tammy fix a li'l sumthin fo ya?"

By now, I was standing at the sink watching Tammy near the stove while secretly admiring the Daisy Dukes, shorter than shorts, she wore. It was no secret the thong-cut shorts exposed enough of her ass cheeks to almost be considered X-rated. I found it rather peculiar that Dad didn't openly protest the nature of her costuming as he did everything else. That is, until I realized Tammy's shorts were most often the target of his increasingly frequent blank stares. I had to admit, since arriving, I'd been mesmerized on occasion myself. There were times that the branches on the family tree were sometimes farther apart than at others. Mom's insistence interrupted my enjoyment of the shade from one of the limbs on that same tree.

"Will, did ya heared me?" she asked.

My uneasiness at the notion of having been caught with my mouth open was rather apparent. Tammy noticed the fact that I had noticed her and our eyes met momentarily which left me with the feeling of having been caught with my hand in the cookie jar.

"Uh, no ma'am; I mean, yes ma'am, I heard you, but I don't...uh...want any sausage and eggs."

The insinuation in Tammy's tone confirmed speculations that she'd noticed my gaze if no one else had. "Ya sho they ain't noth'n ya wants to eat?" Tammy smirked.

The embarrassment had to be apparent, "No, I'm good."

Tammy passed me on her way to sit at the side of the table and seemed to go out of her way to briefly come into contact as she rested her hand on my shoulder while taking a seat. "To be d'termined," she whispered.

There was a lump in my throat and I suddenly felt the need for fresh air, "I'll be right back," I advised.

"If'n ya gives me a minute, I'll ride ta town wit ya. If'n ya don't mind," Tammy suggested.

"Well, I mean, if you don't have anything else to do," I said.

"She gots dishes," Dad interjected. "No sense leav'n da kitchin in sech a mess."

Mom interrupted in effort to save the moment, "Ed, r'lax a l'il. Po chile been workin all morn'n and she done a real good job wit fixin dinner yesttidy night. Let dem kids go catch up on thangs. It been a great while. I takes care o' the kitchin," she said.

It hasn't been that long, I thought to myself. But the way those shorts complimented what signified Tammy as a full-blooded Black woman had me considering things that shouldn't even be an option. The mere thought of "climbing the family tree" would be a violation of the most sacred of codes in my parents' book.

Moments later—"Okay Will" —Tammy sprang up from the table and tossed her dish into the sink. She committed, "Gimme a minute to brush my teeth 'n change shoes; then I bees yo's the whole day."

I thought to myself, *She has no idea the implications of that statement,* but the expression that accompanied the comment as Cousin Tammy passed from the sight of her aunt and uncle, told me she did. I informed her while making my way from the kitchen to escape any further comment from Dad, "All right, I'll be waiting for you outside," I said.

Coltrane had been keeping me company in the car for nearly forty-five minutes before the passenger door popped open. In slid Tammy, outfitted as though she was on her first date.

"Looks like you changed a little more than just your shoes," I commented. "I was beginning to think you'd reconsidered going."

A discrete wink came from behind a mischievous grin, "What? Pass up this chance," she asked. "'Sides, what I's wear'n ain't match these shoes."

"O-Kay, and you had to put on pumps with a skirt to go riding? Who's going to see your feet if you're in the car?"

"C'mon Will, ya been liv'n in the fashion cap'tal o' the world 'an ya tell'n me ya ain't know a woman always need to look her best," she defended. "Maybe I jest wanna looks good fo ya. I mean…while…while I's wit ya."

I commented, without looking in her direction, "For some reason, I don't think looking good is ever much of a problem for you."

Tammy grinned like a three year-old in a candy store, "Be careful, that almost sound like a compl'ment," she said, before asking, "Ya really mean that?"

I remarked, in a rather matter-of-fact tone, "Well, I'm not in the habit of saying things I don't mean."

She blushed, "Oh…well, thanks."

"You're welcome," I responded. "Now where are we off to?"

She pointed out, "Since ya the one b'hind the wheel, that'd be a d'cision fo you, ain't it? Ya mighta been gone a few years but thangs ain't change that much," Tammy said, "They did open up a new lounge, place called Harry's...'an they's talk 'bout a new mall in a couple years. But don't nobody knows fo sho if that gone ever happen. Place jest ain't got 'nough folk fo noth'n like that."

As the car began to slowly move forward, "The way I figure, that's a decision for somebody other than people like you and me. I try not to get caught up in the whole politics thing," I explained. "Why are we going to a lounge on a Sunday afternoon? I thought this was still a dry county."

"It s'spose to be," Tammy said. "But Harry half-brother wit the mayor. E'rybody knows they's sell'n a'cohol, though. Folks jest looks the other way. Where ya thank the police chief be e'ry Sundy from church?"

"Well, it's all about money anyway," I replied. "Something people like us don't have near enough to make a difference. How far to the lounge?"

Reaching to adjust the volume on the CD player, she asked, "What's that?"

"Coltrane," I replied. "The unofficial master himself."

Searching my thoughts, she asked, "No, I mean, what it is folk like us don't got 'nough of?"

Turning the volume back to the level it was before she'd changed it, "Presidents...the good old dead ones," I replied, before stating, "Like you said, I'm the one behind the wheel."

Following a lengthy deliberate silence, she finally directed, "The other side o' town...off Main Street." She pouted about me having turned up the CD player, "I's thank'n we's gone have a chance to talk 'bout stuff."

"It's not like I'll be gone by the time you wake up in the morning. There'll be time to play *twenty questions* soon enough," I assured.

My cousin frowned amidst the confusion, "I ain't got twenty...jest two or three quest'ons," she said.

I'd began laughing before realizing it, "The phrase *twenty questions* is just a figure of speech," I explained.

"I don't see noth'n so funny," Tammy scolded.

I laughed, pushing her forehead with my index finger, "I do...you."

An eerie hush accompanied us for the rest of the drive to the lounge excepting periodic directions from Tammy and the Jazz Master commanding respect from the CD player.

18

Re-introduction

As we pulled into what appeared to be an excessively large parking lot that surrounded a small concrete-block structure, Tammy recognized two females approaching the entrance. My observant cousin motioned at the larger woman who was first through the door.

"You r'member her?" she asked.

I responded, while trying to find a parking space, "No, didn't get a good look. I'm the one behind the wheel, remember?"

As the female turned to face the girl directly behind her, Tammy stated, "When ya sees her, ya'll gone know."

I was completely caught off guard at the sight of someone I'd known before leaving Georgia years ago, "My goodness. Is that...?"

"Ya gots it," Tammy said, "Queen Bee in the flesh... Yo prec'ous ex, Kimb'ly Will'ams"

"What the hell happened to her?" I gasped. "She used to be two winks from perfect."

There was no sympathy in Tammy's voice. "That what birth'n kids do if'n ya ain't care 'nough fo yo'self to take care o' yo body."

"She's got kids?" I asked.

My cousin seemed rather pleased to update, "Three of 'em the past two years; set o' twins...'an a l'il girl, gotta be 'bout six months by now."

I blurted out, without thinking, "Damn, she done got big as a barn."

Kimberly and her friend were still in the foyer area when Tammy and I entered through the glass door. Her friend obviously, recognized me though I didn't know her.

"Well, hey stranger. Kim, look what the buzzards dropped at the city limits," she said.

"Oh my gosh! Nancy, can you believe your eyes? If it ain't the walkin dead!" Kimberly acknowledged.

I simply nodded in recognition while attempting to pass between them and the wall, "Ladies," I said.

Both Kimberly and Nancy immediately made eye contact with Tammy and simultaneously questioned, "And who might this lucky lady be?"

I opened my mouth to answer but Tammy cut in, "A ver'y good friend o' his."

Kimberly responded, "Well, pardon my frankness, but you don't sound like no Northerner I done e'er heard." Before directing her attention back to me, "Willie, we's all told you went up to New York or someplace like that."

I began to explain, "You're right about that part, but only half right in the assumption that Tammy's my girl. She is with me, but actually lives here...in the county. She stays several miles outside of town."

"I been what they call, homeschooled," Tammy interjected.

"That's the reason you don't look familiar," Kimberly said. "This place ain't so big I don't know e'rybody in town."

"Yeah, 'an e'rybody knows you, from what I hears," Tammy responded.

Nancy extended a hand, simply disregarding her friend's inquiry, summoning Kimberly's attention to the far corner of the lounge. "Well it was certainly nice to meet you. We gotta be going," she said.

She and Nancy hurried toward a table where two gentlemen were seated. "Willie, you and yo…friend…have a good time," Kimberly called back.

"Nice to see you too, ladies," I said.

"Now, ain't you glad ya ain't stay tied up wit that?" Tammy asked.

I commented in defense of my ego, already poised for the attack I knew was coming as she watched the two women cross the small opening on their way to meet the two guys. "Well, when I was with her, she didn't look like that," I said.

"Ain't make no ne'er mind," Tammy replied. "If'n ya *was* still wit her, that what she look like now….'an ya'd be catch'n hell."

"You're going to be catching hell if…" I started.

"If what?" Tammy presssed.

"Never mind, it was just a thought," I said.

"Well, if'n it worth thank'n, it gotta be worth say'n," she urged.

I attempted to dismiss the abandoned remark, "No, I shouldn't."

My cousin continued to prod, "Maybe I's want'n ya to."

Realizing where the conversation could be headed, I said, "That's part of the problem."

"What pro'lem?" she drilled.

"I might want to as well." I tried to withdraw and steer clear of the temptation, "Maybe this would be a good time to change the subject, talk about something a little less intrusive."

"Intr-u-sive?" Tammy questioned.

"It means...never mind," I dismissed again, before concluding, "I just think we'd better find another topic of discussion."

She continued in pursuit of the issue, "What's the mat'er? Ya ain't skerd is ya?"

As realization of the fact she was intentionally tempting me registered, I asked, "Scared of what?"

"Of li'l ole in'ocent me?" Tammy poked.

"Something tells me you aren't as innocent as you want people to believe," I challenged.

With the look of a chesshire cat, she responded, "I knows ya'd likes to know."

"Like I said, this would be a good time to change the subject," I concluded.

Reluctantly, "Well, if'n we gotta," she agreed.

"Yes, we better," I insisted. "Before we get too far gone."

She continued playing, "Where's we go'n?"

Tammy was being down right mischievous by this point. I knew the edge was a little closer than I was comfortable walking. There was a sneaky suspicion she had intentionally played the role to get me off from the house where we'd be alone. *Sneaky suspicion, hell,* I thought, *You know damn well that's what you were hoping for all along.* Then, I spoke aloud and engaged in an all-out debate with myself. In a tone more stern than I realized, I said, "Now, all that isn't any of your damn business."

From behind a mask of confusion, "What all ain't my bidness?" Tammy questioned. "I's jest say'n how good it is to be here wit ya."

"Doesn't matter. I was someplace else," I offered.

"Where, back in New York City?" she questioned. "I knows ya prob'ly gots someb'dy there... One o' them gorg'ous model types, I bet. I means, who can blame 'em? It won't make no sense none a'tall ta leave a good cut o' meat on the chopp'n block....'an you's a sirlo'n in my book."

I was desperately trying to avoid yielding to the temptation and scratching that itch my cousin had. It was one thing
to reminisce about days long gone and the adolescent things
we did but, at our ages now, foolish choices are accompanied
by consequences.

"Okay Tammy, that's enough. I think maybe it's time we
get back. Mom and Dad will wonder what happened to us,"
I said.

She addressed my fictitious concern, "Well, they knows I's
out wit ya," she said. "I ain't gone ne'er be much mo safe than
I is now."

I continued to debate with myself: *If they know like I know,
you're not all that safe...not as safe as you'd want to believe.*

"We can't stay jest a li'l while longer?" Tammy pleaded.
"I ain't ev'n had my first glass. Ya knows, ladies drank free 'til
one o'clock in da aft'rnoon on Sundays."

"Well, you could probably finish the drink a lot faster if
you ordered one. All this time we've been sitting here jawing,
you could've finished one for you and me both," I said.

"What, ya in a hur'y to git back out to the house?" she
inquired. "Ya got someth'n in mind ta do?"

I reconsidered, and suggested while standing to my feet,
Get me one of those, will you? On second thought, I guess it
wouldn't hurt for us to stick around a little longer."

Tammy stated, "Well, they brangs 'em only one at a
time...'an they's fo the ladies," before inquiring, "Where's ya
go'n?"

She was so attractive when she pursed her lips in apparent
disappointment. My mind traveled a thousand miles to places
I knew it shouldn't as I placed a ten-dollar bill on the table
at my seat.

"To the men's room...do you mind?"

She half-jokingly offered, "Not a'tall; ya need some help?"

Logical reasoning pushed the words of my libido aside
just before they jumped from already parted lips and I simply laughed, before turning and walking away from the table.

"No, I think it's manageable. Besides, you don't have any business lifting such heavy objects," I said.

Several minutes later, I returned from the bathroom to notice one fellow sitting in my seat which he had moved within inches of Tammy's. There was another man standing to the left of him. They both looked like hungry hounds sneaking up on an unsuspecting rabbit.

I announced approaching the table, "Excuse me, guys."

I heard Tammy's squeal, as she pointed in my direction, "There he is." She said, "That's my man right there. Will, this Todd 'an stand'n up is Ter'y...they brothers."

"What's up?" I nodded. "Mind if I get back to my chair and my drink?"

In the process of standing, "Not a'tall," Todd said. "We's jest keepin ya lady comp'ny. Someb'dy look good as dis li'l filly gots no bidness bein left by theyself."

"Actually, she's not..." I felt a sharp pain in my leg, "Ouch! What the hell...?" When I cut my eyes at Tammy the look on her face told me I'd get worse than that if I didn't play along. "She's actually not by herself with guys like the two of you around," I said.

As he hoisted his pants, "Well, we's jest holdin ya place man," Todd said. "So nobody come 'an desturb da li'l lady."

Suddenly, I was getting an uneasy feeling, "And I appreciate that...more than you realize."

"What he say'n is," Tammy interjected, "I's got this thang 'bout be'n left by m'self fo more 'n a few minutes. But he back now...I be's a'ight."

"Okay sweetness, but if ya thanks ya might..." Todd insisted.

At first, the situation was a bit humorous, but now it was borderline disrespectful. *Never mind who the girl is; they don't know if she's my girl, my wife, or my daughter*, I was thinking to myself. Standing back to my feet, I said, "All right boy scouts, the babysitting job's over. She already told you; the two of you can ease on up and go find somebody else to play with."

Terry, the larger of the two, finally spoke up, "Seem ta me the li'l fella gots a pro'lem wit you 'n me bro. He ain't too pleased wit us protect'n this li'l pearl o' his."

Todd nodded in agreement as he moved to a position opposite Terry while I noticed he'd grabbed a pool stick. Sensing what was about to transpire, I moved slightly to my left and turned to the point that they were both more to the front of me than one in front and the other behind but Tammy was still oblivious to the storm brewing.

"Baby, ya mind run'n o'er 'an git'n me 'nother drank whiles ya up? Jest car'y my glass 'an tell Hal b'hind the bar I's want'n 'nother fuzzy navel...he be know'n who it be fo," she asked.

I said without taking my eyes off the brothers, "Maybe you should go over and get it yourself."

Her words trailed off as she began to realize what was happening, "Aaww baby, I thought ya said t'night gone... be...my...night." She eased through the already small space separating Terry and me, "On sec'nd thought, maybe I's be bet'er to go 'an sees Hal fo myself. Want me to git someth'n fo ya h-o-n...? Guess not."

Todd stepped closer, "Maybe I should jest go help the li'l lady wit huh drank."

I sidestepped and slid into his path before suggesting, "Maybe she doesn't need your help."

"Now see Terry, that right there what done hap'ned ta all da good colored folk in da South. Dey takes a trip to da city 'an next thang ya knows, dey comes back thankin dey good as us wit one o' our women hangin off dey arm."

It was then that the whole situation fell into perspective. The chivalrous redneck brothers had made the same incorrect assumption about Tammy as was most often the case with strangers who assumed she was Caucasian. As I wondered whether Tammy had been close enough to hear Todd's feeble attempt at identifying what he felt was a problem, the question was answered.

Suddenly, Tammy rested her hand back on my shoulder. "Ex-cuse me! What did ya jest say, mister? I have ya know they's folk in my fam'ly blacker 'n yo belt! Hell, if 'n most o' ya ofay Whites from the South dig far 'nough thru the roots o' them fam'ly trees, I'm sho they'll be some com'on sprouts in both our o'chards."

I spoke without allowing my attention to be taken off the two sorry excuses for men standing in front of me. "Tammy, calm down. Nothing you say at this point is going to make a bit of difference. Especially now that they're embarrassed to know you're not one of them," I said.

From behind me, Tammy snapped, "Heck, 'an I thanks the Lord I ain't! I's better 'n the both o' dem put t'gether."

Just then Todd, the closer of the two, stretched out his hand to grab at Tammy over my right shoulder. "Why ya li'l bitch! I oughtta…"

"The worst thang ya can e'er do," my old man used to always say, *"is let some fool git c'ntrol o' yo space."* I reached across with my left hand to swat Todd's arm while cocking and clocking him with a good stiff right jab. He fell back like a sack of mud.

A lady who looked too young to be dating yelled, "Oh my goodness!"

The guy across the table clutched his date's purse to keep it from falling to the floor and exclaimed, "Fight…fight!"

From the corner of my eye, I could make out a large form rushing in the general direction of where I now stood. I dipped at the waist to avoid Terry's wild swing and simultaneously scooped the pool cue Todd never had an opportunity to use from the floor near where he'd fallen. As I stood erect, Terry caught me in a most unaffectionate bear hug with arms that looked like small saplings. The pool stick flopped to the concrete floor. His death grip had me fighting to maintain consciousness when I saw what amounted to nothing more than a blur over his left shoulder. Suddenly, my lungs filled with air again and the room slowly stopped spinning. When I finally regained focus, Tammy was already at the table gathering our things while still clenching the pool cue transformed into a battering ram she'd used to get Terry's attention.

"Tammy…you all right?" I asked.

"I's do'n bet'er 'n yo butt," she said before commanding, "Let's git outta this place 'fore somebody gits it in they head we done took a'vantage o' the fact these two is so stupid. I got the keys. I'll drive."

"Just one second," I cautioned. "You did good to clock that fool over the head, but let's not get carried away, now."

"You's in no shape ta drive," she said.

"I'm fine," I debated.

Given her response, my cousin seemed to have gotten a grip on more than just the pool stick. "No…ya ain't…This no time to fuss 'bout it. We gotta go…now!"

About then, I noticed the bartender and several of the regular patrons gearing up for a frontal attack. As they gathered at one end of the bar, Tammy pulled me in the opposite direction toward the exit. "Willie, this def'nitely ain't no time to be try'n to prove yo manhood. We gots ta git outta here b'fore the real trouble show up!" Tammy warned.

One of the patrons questioned, "Did somebody call da po-lice?"

Another shouted, "Block da doe. Don't let 'em git out!"

Tammy was practically dragging me to the door while I was more concerned about the beer we'd left behind. "You're leaving the drinks," I protested.

"Ya bet'er git movin or I'mma leave yo ass too!" Tammy shouted. "Them beers ain't gone save yo ass…'an I ain't wait'n fo ya."

As she and I came around the corner in the area leading to the exit, it was as if someone had constructed a wall behind us after we'd entered the building. Only this wall was wearing Wrangler jeans and boots. Suddenly the man's eyes showed as bright as the headlights on a half-ton Chevy pick-up truck and he appeared to be looking right past me with people in his general vicinity screaming and running for cover.

The woman collecting money at the door shouted, "Look out!"

One of the bouncers yelled, "Dis bitch done gone crazy!"

When I paused long enough to glance to my left I almost broke to run my damn self. Tammy was there waving a stainless piece of iron that bore a strange resemblance to a .380 cal. handgun I'd once owned.

"What the hell are you doing?" I coughed. "Never mind, I see what you're doing. The question is, where in hell did you get that thing? Do Mom and Dad know you've got that?"

She ordered, "Will, this ain't e'xactly no time to play *twenty fuckin questions*! Now git yo ass out that door!"

Without another word, I dashed out the door trying to keep Tammy from running me over. We turned the corner and hurriedly scampered to the Impala, ducking down in the seat as several police cars made their way into the lot.

Tammy urged, reaching for the keys, "Why we ain't go'n?"

While still clutching her hand on the ignition key to prevent her from starting the car, I said, "Because they don't know we're in here. Nobody in the place knows what we're driving and if we move now, that would be reason enough for the police to stop us," I explained. "Besides, with the tint on the windows, they can't see inside anyway...long as you hold still."

"Sound like ya done this b'fore," Tammy discerned.

"I read something about a situation like this in a book once," I dismissed.

While sucking her teeth, "Yeah, right," she remarked, "That yo story 'an ya stick'n to it, huh?"

Checking to be sure the coast was clear before reaching over and starting the car, I commented, "Yep, something like that."

"Where we's off to now?" Tammy asked.

"You're the one who wanted to drive," I said. "Any place has to be better than being caught here. Now let's move!"

She posed again, in an elevated tone, "But where we's go'n?"

"Someplace other than here, if you're as smart as you pretend to be!" I said.

She scowled, while simultaneously slapping me on the shoulder, "Hey! What the hell that's s'pose to mean?"

I finally demanded, "It means drive the damn car Tammy!"

Startled, she slammed down on the gas and the rear tires on the Impala began singing a high-pitched tune that would carry us out the parking lot and onto the main street. Tammy drove straight to the country without ever looking in my direction for the entire ride home. Except for the melodious taunting of Coltrane resuming his duties from inside the CD player, it was like sitting beside granny in church...without a sound.

I directed Tammy, as she arrived at the house, "You can pull up on the left...around the pump house to the back."

"Well, Uncle Ed don't take too kindly to folk park'n back o' the house," she informed.

"How so? His truck was just back there yesterday," I said. "I can park outside my room window to remove things from the car...and put the shit back that you just threw all over the place."

While simultaneously opening the driver's door, "That's 'cause he say it's his house, his truck...'*an his grass*," Tammy concluded, exiting the car and leaving the engine idling, "Ya can move it 'round there yo'self if'n ya want; I's done," she stated.

Without looking in her direction, I simply eased over behind the wheel, adjusted the volume on the sound while repositioning the seat, and dropped the car into *Drive* to park it outside my bedroom window.

19

Link to the Past

Dad spoke aloud, as he barged through the screen door with packages filling both arms, "Tammy, where dat boy? Tells 'em ta git out dere 'an help takes dat stuff outta da truck."

She nervously confirmed, "He ain't in here Uncle Ed."

My father began his interrogation, "What ya means, he ain't here? Ain't y'all come home t'gether earli'r?"

"Ed, I tells ya dat when ya pull up li'l bit ago," Mom interjected. "You's so busy on my case 'bout dem darn chickens…"

"Martha! I done told ya 'bout ya words, now!" he snapped back. "Where dat boy done git off ta now, Tammy?"

"He ain't gone off nowheres," Tammy said.

Her uncle was noticeably irritated, "But, ya say he ain't here."

She attempted to clarify, "No sir, I say he ain't *in here*.

His annoyance became increasingly apparent, "Child, stop all dat fool talk 'an come straight outta ya face. Where da boy at?"

"He out back," Tammy mumbled. "Wash'n his car. He parked there when we come in little while a'go, 'an he out clean'n it."

Tammy saw Dad's brow twist like it was about to separate from his face, "He do'n what!" as he started toward the door, "On my grass?!"

Coming through the door with my hands full of groceries seconds after his comment, "...Washing my car," I interrupted.

The old man about blew his top, "'An what da...on my cuss'ed grass!"

I mocked condescendingly, to intentionally bait him, "Careful Pop, you know there's no cussing allowed under this roof."

"Now, ya ain't been 'way from da house so long ya done fo'got I don't a'low nobody park'n on my grass," Dad recovered.

"Well," I started, "I figure that little part of the yard, right there beneath my window, is mine...since it is under my window. As much pushing as I've done with that lawn mower over the years, *all of it should be mine*."

Mom cut in to quiet him, "Now don't da two o'ya start dat fool stuff agin. Will, if ya knows ya daddy don't likes nob'dy parkin on da grass, why ya go 'n park dere? 'An Ed, it ain't like him bein dere long 'nough ta wrainch off his car gone kill dem weeds. Lord, I tell ya, two grown-ass young-ons."

Dad barked a warning, "Martha...!"

"What Ed!" she cut back. "What da hell pleasure ya gits outta always screamin my gosh-darned name?

Uncharacteristic of my old man, he stopped in his tracks, lowered his gaze, and found his way to the closest exit to get away from the petite powder keg simmering in the middle of the kitchen. She then said in a near whisper, "Will."

My response was a bit more timid, "Yes, ma'am?"

She simply stated, "Go moves ya car off da grass."

While continuing to remove items from the bags on the counter, "Yes ma'am," I replied.

Her voice was even softer, "Will?"

I answered again, "Yes ma'am?"

"*Moves da car, now!*" Mom finished. "I ain't gone tells ya no mo."

I immediately turned and started toward the door to discover Tammy standing with a bewildered look on her face. It was no secret that my mom was wired emotionally backward. The more upset she became, the softer her voice. In short, no one ever had the nerve to test the little stick of dynamite beyond a whisper.

"I can moves it fo ya if'n ya want," Tammy suggested.

Mom stopped her, "Tammy."

She knew Mom's tone warned of treading lightly, "Yes ma'am, Aunt Martha?"

Mom quietly suggested, "Ya gots plenty thangs ta do."

Tammy conceded, "Yes ma'am."

My ego was somewhat bruised when I passed out the door, but common sense advised it was nowhere near as bruised as my ass would be if I so much as thought about changing words with that little woman. She might've been small in stature but could take the average man on her worst day. That was no secret and my father was always content to leave Mom to deal with herself when she got the least bit twisted. He talked much trash until she actually opened her mouth.

Outside in the car, I sat sifting through the case of CD's until coming across a familiar companion. Within a few seconds, the legendary Muddy Waters was coaxing me back toward town. I was thinking how riding solo had me right back in my comfort zone when the cell phone chimed as the tune "Blues and Trouble" ended.

I greeted in a dry tone, "Hello."

My cousin inquired, "Where's ya go'n?"

I could taste the salt in my mouth, "What?"

"I means, what ya gitt'n ready ta do?" Tammy cleaned up the question. "I's jest wonder'n if'n ya gone be back time fo dinner."

I instructed her, trying to avoid the query, "If I'm not, just put my plate in the oven. I'll eat when I get home."

"Want comp'ny?" Tammy questioned.

"No, you've got things to do," I said. "Besides…"

"B'sides what?" she asked.

"Oh, nothing. You just have plenty to do at the house, and I wouldn't want to disrupt the process," I said.

Through her innocence, she inquired, "Disrup what process?"

"Oh get off it Tammy. You can't tell me you're so thick headed that you haven't noticed the way Dad's been riding my ass since I showed up here."

There was a sudden silence that lasted for almost a minute before she retorted into the phone, "I ain't gots no aprec'ation be'n called thick headed; I gots ta go," she mumbled, just as the line went dead.

I held the phone momentarily in disbelief before falling back into the groove of Muddy Waters' "Kinfolks Blues." In classic fashion, I dismissed the issue, cranked up the volume, and set out to literally drive my troubles away.

Dusk found me nearly three hours later, parked outside Harry's, the lounge where trouble had found Tammy and me earlier today. The dark tinted windows of the Impala provided perfect cover as I, otherwise, wouldn't dare show my face in the place again so soon. I sat in the car taking "*coping with shit*" lessons from Muddy and a number of his friends for what seemed like days before recognizing two faces from my previous visit. Only, this time, they were without the presence of the beef heads that had accompanied them in the lounge this morning. As the two of them exited the foyer, walking to the parking area, I pushed the door open just enough that the dome light illuminated the car's interior. It created a soft glow against the canvas of darkness cast by the tint, which inevitably summoned the attention of the two passers by. I pretended to be looking for something in the floor of the car.

"Well, you either done got a hell-uv-a-lot more stupid than you used to be, or a lot more brave," Kim said.

"Excuse me?" I pretended.

While signaling her friend, Nancy, that it was okay to leave, Kimberly said, "I ne'er knowed nobody ta return to the scene so soon after they committed a crime."

While simultaneously scoping the surroundings for any sign of the guys, I reasoned, "Maybe that's because there's no place else around here interesting enough to find any trouble."

"That what ya wonts, Willie…ta gits in some trouble?" Kimberly taunted, as she adjusted herself in the passenger's seat and closed the door. "Ya know, they says that's all I is."

I sarcastically responded, "Well, I'm pretty good at getting out any trouble in the middle of which I might find myself."

Running her right hand up my thigh to clutch the semblance of me as a Neaderthal of the male gender she discovered already in the process of waking, I was somewhat surprised when Kimberly simultaneously thrust her tongue down my throat, "That a fact?" she asked.

Moments later found me pulling off the highway north of town, "I think this is the address. It looks like the place you described but there's not much light out here."

Kimberly was in the midst of a stroll down memory lane but redirected her thoughts long enough to utter, "Go 'round back, pull off left o' da driveway 'an drive 'round b'hind da house."

My mind took me back to a place that seemed a hundred years ago, where fantasies of a small house and white picket fence had me convinced of the day she and I would return home together.

Kimberly's question demolished the picket fence and brought me back to the rear of a run-down double-wide mobile home with concrete blocks stacked to simulate steps, "Well, ya jest gone sit there wit ya eyes poppin out yo head or ya gone come inside?" Judging by the trodden path, I determined I wasn't the first to receive those instructions. "Be careful goin up; I ain't had nob'dy come ta put up no rail," she whispered.

I informed in convincing fashion, "That's all right, I can manage."

"Thru da door 'an turn right…that be my room," she directed, before casually informing, "I gotta go up front 'an check on da kids; I's be back witchu in a minute."

I went into a room with only a night light for visibility and a king-sized bed that left just enough space to slide between it and the wall. Slightly startled by what turned out to be a large stuffed animal on the bed but bore a strange resemblance to a man in the dim light, I let out a slight yell when the phone vibrated on my hip. I refused to answer it.

Seconds later, Kimberly appeared at the door. "What's da pro'lem? Why is ya makin all that fuss? I do got li'l 'ons in da house ya knows…"

I began standing, "You know what, maybe this isn't the right time."

Stepping into the room and closing the door behind her, "Its likes dey says, ain't no bet'er time dan right now," she replied.

Sitting on the side of the bed near where I had been, Kimberly tugged at my belt buckle and brought the fly of the Levi's full flush to her face. Methodically, she loosed the restrictions of the button-fly 501s and seemed to gnaw through my Hanes like a pit bull. In a matter of seconds, reason had me convinced it would be okay to let her continue *this time.*

Just over half an hour had passed in less time than I could imagine with me feeling the way I'd not felt in more time than I wanted to imagine. There were mixed emotions ranging, from guilt to condemnation, with me reasoning there wasn't cause for either but still unable to make that thought make any sense.

"Now, ain't ya feelin lots better?" she posed.

"Well...uh...yeah," I stammered. "But what about... well...you?"

She whispered, "A'ways da consid'rate one. No, I's okay. B'sides, my husband'll know 'an he won't like dat."

"You got a damn husband!"

"Yeah, sho nuff does...ya seent him this morn'n. Truth is," she said, illuminating the LED face on her watch. "He oughtta be pullin up out front in 'bout..."

At that very moment, a deep voice sounded from the front of the house and my heart skipped a beat when I heard, "Hey guys 'an gals. Wheres ya mama?"

A little person responded, "She back dere gettin ready."

Just then, Kimberly stepped to the door, "I gotta go. Waits a minute 'fore ya sneaks out da back...Bye!" She disappeared into the hallway. "Hey babe, what's up? You's a li'l bit early ain't ya?"

The burly voice joked, "Thankin I's gone sneak in early 'an catch ya wit dat other fella!"

She playfully responded and laughed the comment away, "Ya almost did."

I was less than three feet from them on the other side of the bedroom door about to piss my pants and quietly commented to myself, "If you only knew, brother man...if you only knew."

The sounds of the front door closing and her man's truck leaving the driveway were two of the most relieving noises I'd ever heard. Eventually, the only sound audible was the ten o'clock news from channel four on the television. I peeked from the bedroom, crept to the back door of the house, and eased out unnoticed. The only thing moving faster than me getting out of that yard was my heart, which still hadn't stopped racing.

I spoke to my reflection in the rearview mirror after several minutes on the highway, "You have done some stupid shit in your life, but this tops it all."

That was about the time I noticed the patrol car that continued to follow me almost halfway to the house before turning on the lights and pulling me over. I would have made a run for it, but I knew for as long as he'd been there, the plates had already been checked and probably my life story reported back over the radio.

20

The Fullness of Time

The officer cautiously approached the side of the car with a hand resting on his still holstered revolver. In an instant, my mind replayed all the tall tales, horror stories, and accounts of police brutality I'd heard depicted throughout the years of my relatively short lifetime. The fact I was driving a car with a New York license plate didn't help matters in the least either.

From behind mirrored sunglasses, the officer barked, "License 'an registration please…"

While secretly wondering why the shades after sundown, I wisely conceded, "Yes, sir."

He began what I perceived as the skillful art of prodding, "'An I needs ta see yo inshorance card, if'n ya got one."

I started, "Now if I didn't have…" and then, remembering where I was, simply made note of his name tag prior to respectfully responding, "Yes sir, Officer Overstreet."

He collected the requested information, before turning toward his cruiser, "Wait here."

The officer was gone before I could respond…not that he would've cared to hear what I had to say anyway. While waiting for him to return, my cell phone began vibrating. I reached to turn it off but remembered the call missed during the time I was at Kimberly's place. I looked to realize it was a 212 area code which meant New York.

I answered and requested in one breath, without allowing the caller an opportunity to speak, "Hello…let me call you back in a few minutes."

"Willie! This Ernestina!" I heard.

The officer was returning, "Okay, but I'm dealing with a situation right now."

"I know; that's why I'm calling. Let me talk to the patrolman," she directed.

I insisted before quickly ending the call, "Listen, I don't know how you know what's happening but how about you call me back in a minute so he won't think you're somebody I just snatched out my ass. I've got to go!"

The officer approached, "Mr. LeBeaux, look like we might got a li'l bit of a pro'lem," he started to explain. "It seems yo vacation gone have ta be sorta cut showt. Ya knows they's a war'ant out fo ya in New York City?"

"Well, sir, that's what I wanted to talk to you about. You see…" Just then, my cell phone began buzzing. "Uh… Sir."

More bluntly, I felt, than was necessary, he asked, "What is it, boy?"

"Well, I started to explain that I was waiting for a call back from my parole officer in New York. You might want to talk with them. That should be the call ringing in now but I don't want to make any sudden moves or anything," I said.

Apprehensively, he directed, "Go 'head, but slow. 'An keeps yo hands in plain sight."

"Hello," I answered. "Yes ma'am Ms. Lady. There's an officer here right now who was just explaining about the warrant.

I told him you, *my parole officer*, should be calling back about the mix-up in the paperwork."

Fortunately, the policeman couldn't hear Ernestina chewing me out about having left New York in the first place, "I should let your ass go to jail and be brought back here in chains!" she snapped. "You're going to owe me big for this shit...got me sticking my neck out for you...again!"

I assured her, "Yes ma'am, I sure would appreciate it if you could explain things to the officer and I'll be on my way back to New York just as soon as he turns me loose," before turning toward Officer Overstreet, "Here, sir, she wants to speak to you."

He took the phone and casually walked to the back of my car for what seemed like an hour before returning. For a moment, I was more concerned about the usage of minutes on my calling plan than the possibility of ending up in jail.

Officer Overstreet returned. "E'erthin seem ta be in order, but you better git yo butt back up ta New York City 'fore I find out diff'rent. Don't let mornin find yo ass in my county, ya hear?"

"Yes sir, sir," I uttered. "I'm on my way back right now."

I drove the rest of the way to my parents' place in total silence while thinking of the fact I'd just had two close calls in less than an hour...different circumstances, but still too close for comfort. Things were definitely starting to heat up on the home front.

As I eased up the dirt lane that symbolized our driveway, I saw Tammy seated in one of the two antique straight-back rocking chairs positioned on either side of the front door. She was wearing an old oversized button-down Oxford, sitting with her right leg hanging over one arm of the chair. I couldn't help noticing the pink lace as I caught a glimpse before reaching the top of the steps.

"Did ya find what ya's look'n fo?" she questioned.

Much more abrasively than I'd realized, "Says who I went looking for anything? Maybe I just needed some fresh air," I responded.

She assured me with a slight attitude, "Well, air ain't ne'er gone gits no mo fresh than out here 'way from all the folks 'an dust in town."

In effort to intentionally raise suspicion, "That depends on where in town you go," I smirked. "Some places a lot more inviting than others."

She cut, "Maybe if'n folk pay more 'tention, they'd know when the inv'tation been 'stended," then added, "Uncle Ed 'n Aunt Martha told me to tells ya they's gone over ta Valdosta."

I rhetorically inquired, only to receive the answer I'd expected, "What in the world for?"

She rationalized, "Don't know. Ne'er ask; they don't of'er ta takes me so I figer it ain't my place ta ask where they's go'n, *or what fo.*"

I tried to avoid the possible opening, "And the purpose of me knowing that tidbit of information was…?"

Lifting her leg to give me a brief flash of the lace under-wear, "Jest so's ya knows." She smiled.

I felt the sweat rolling down my spine and asked to inten-tionally steer clear of the path down which I knew she wanted me to travel, "You already ate?"

Her comment was a little more direct than usual, "Yeah. Yo's in the ov'n like ya had asked 'fore ya left," she instructed.

I simply stated, before opening the screen door, "Thank you, Tammy."

She winked, while pretending to fan herself with the lapel of the shirt and exposing just enough cleavage to say she hadn't intended to provide a glimpse, "After ya finish eat'n, I's think'n ya might wanna have some de-sert."

Excusing myself into the house I responded, "Yeah, maybe I'll think about it."

"Don't think too long!" she teased.

Once I finished downing some of the best homemade chicken and dumplings I'd ever eaten, I started the water before going into my shared room to get clean socks and underwear. When I returned to the bathroom moments later, I found Tammy reclined in the oversized tub wearing only the country well water.

Pretending to be unfazed, I commented, "I thought you said you already took a bath."

"No, I says I done ar'eady ate," she corrected, "Now I's think'n 'bout someth'n sweet, fo de-sert."

"You know we're cousins," I said.

She began to explain, "Not fo real, we ain't. Uncle Ed 'n Aunt Martha don't know I heared 'em one night they's on the porch talk'n 'bout how I's 'dopted or someth'n." It was honestly difficult to tell whether she was more disappointed or confused. "Someth'n 'bout I's born to Aunt Martha second cous'n, 'an my mom, who really my cous'n but I a'ways calls her my aunt, 'dopted me. So that make Aunt Martha 'n me third cousins, I think. Any how, it ain't like we's no blood kin 'an if'n we is, then it ain't close 'nough ta make no ne'er mind."

At that point, I was confused and crossed the bathroom to the window in order to conceal the effect her being naked was having, "Well, they don't know that you know what you do know, and I'm not supposed to know," I said.

"So, ya ain't wont me?" she pretended to sulk.

I managed to get my tongue out of the way long enough to form a complete sentence, "I never said that. I mean, who wouldn't…want you?"

Tammy stood in the tub, stepped out onto the floor, and walked to where I leaned against the wall, water trickling from her flawless body. Placing her bare breasts against my chest, she leaned forward and whispered in my ear, "Does ya *wont me?*"

The words refused to cross my lips, "I…I…"

Tammy pressed, while taking the index finger of my right hand into her mouth, then gently caressing my wrist and pulling me to her. She let go a somber sigh, and leaned closer to whisper in a voice that sounded like silk on cotton, "Well...does ya?" she questioned, "*Does ya?*"

The only words I could formulate were, "Ahhh...uhhh... Damn."

"I's tak'n that as a yeah," She asserted. "That's '*cause I wonts you, for real.*"

My heart damn near leaped out my chest with her words being a defibrillator that nearly overwhelmed anxious senses. It wasn't like I had never been approached by a pretty female before or even that I hadn't considered Tammy in a number of situations, but the sensuality she utterly exuded at that very moment totally took me by surprise. It was the closest thing to what I could imagine an out of body experience would feel like. I watched me bend slightly to take her into my arms.

"Ye...Yes," I murmured. "Yes, I want you. *You know I do... always have.*"

"Ya knows I's a'ways been yo's," she sighed. "Ev'n from way back when we was kids; I knowed...wonted...'an waited."

More surprised than anything, I questioned, "You've waited?"

"Yeah Will, I's been wait'n fo ya all these years," she stated.

I questioned in disbelief, "Are you saying...?"

"Ya gots ta ask?" she prodded.

I let go a nervous sigh, "You're a...a...?"

Tammy finished my thought, "*A virgin.*"

I nervously questioned, "Are you sure about this?"

She half seriously responded, "What...that I's a virgin?"

"No," I said. "That part I know you're certain of. Are you sure you want me to be the one you...you know?"

"Will," she whispered.

"Yes," I answered.

"I knows ya done this b'fore," she commented.

"Yes, it's no secret I have," I admitted.

"Does ya use'ly ask s'many dog-gone quest'ons?"

I couldn't find the words, "Well...no. But I don't normally...well, I've never..."

Placing her index finger to my lips, Tammy insisted, "Shhhhh, ya talks too much."

I was wrestling with the morality of the whole issue, "But I just want you to understand..."

Her finger was, again up to my lips, "Shhhhh," she said. "I knows alls I needs ta know."

How we got from the bathroom to the bedroom was a mystery to me. The next thing I knew, we were on the bed with moonlight from the window perfectly encasing Tammy's flawless form. Her kisses, passionate...her body, inviting. I was captivated by the look in her eyes generated by the soft touch of my lips over succulent flesh seasoned with lilac-scented bath oil. She sighed, tensed, moaned and released with every gentle caress. Her body stiffened when I moved to a point below her navel.

"Relax," I whispered.

She instinctively questioned my motives, "What...is...ya do'n?"

"Relax and enjoy," I urged.

Moments later she shrieked quietly, "My body moved to meet hers. "Ooooh," she grimaced as I eventually found that sacred place.

I forced the question, knowing there could only be one truthful answer, "You want me to stop?"

She commented while passing the protection she'd obviously found in the console of my car, "Ya don't wants ta stop."

Applying the personalized shield, I all but pleaded, "You want...me...your first time?"

"Ya talk'n a'gin," she said. "Too much. Jest do what ya knows how ta do 'an let me d'cide if'n I likes it...now hesh up, 'an does what ya does. I wonts it ta be da most wond'rful pain I e'er done felt."

Moving into position, "Invitation accepted," I said.

Forty minutes later found me breathless, exhausted, and Tammy unusually rejuvenated. "Ya ain't gots ta stop," she said.

I gasped, in utter disbelief, "Yes...I do."

"But I's need'n more," she pleaded.

"What you need, sweetheart, is some formed plastics and a few C-cell batteries," I half-joked.

She was seeking clarification, "Some what?" she asked. "I ain't und'rstand'n."

"Never mind. *You shouldn't understand*," I said.

"What I needs wit bat'ries?" she insisted.

I couldn't bring myself to be annoyed at her innocence, "Never mind, sweetness. Let it go."

In a more sincere tone, she asked, "What...I's done did someth'n wrong?"

I quickly responded, to dismiss her concern, "Tammy, just let it go...it was nothing. You didn't do anything. At least, not wrong anyway."

21

Day of Reckoning

Sunlight through the floor-to-ceiling window greeted me when I was awakened earlier than anticipated. It was the sound of Dad's truck pulling up outside the house that prompted me to move. That's when I felt something heavy on my chest and remembered what happened last night. "Oh shit!" I exclaimed.

Tammy was startled to consciousness. "What's ailing ya, Will?"

I unknowingly directed, "My folks just drove up! You've got to get out of here!"

With a look that came from somewhere beyond confusion, "Where's I'm gone go to?" Tammy asked.

I nervously began explaining, "Look, if my parents find you in my room…"

"But this room mine's too," she said.

Gathering my senses, I corrected, before instructing in a panic, "Okay, hurry, get off my bed. Quick; back to yours!"

Tammy stood up but remembered how we had left the bathroom and started toward the door, "I's gotta gits our stuff!" she said.

My knees nearly buckled, "*You might want to put on some clothes your damn self before going out there!*"

She stopped to look down at her naked body as if it wasn't a part of her, "Oh shit...what is ya done did?!"

"Why does everything always have to be about what I did? I think we both had a hand in the events of last night," I defended. "Here, get into your bed...under the covers. I'll take care of getting our things out the bathroom and draining the tub."

"Hur'y," she ordered. "They's git'n outta the truck!"

I dashed across the hall and quickly gathered the clothes from the floor when I heard the front door open.

Mom's voice sounded as she entered the house, "I gess dem chillin is still sleepin."

The disdain echoed from dad, "Hmmph, 'an dis time o' da day."

"Well, Ed, seben-thirty ain't all that late no more. Dey's still plenty time ta git thangs done 'fore da day all gone," Mom offered. "Most da real work finished 'til next plantin seasin anyhow."

They passed down the hallway right by the bathroom door with me, like a statue, standing behind it.

Dad was positioned outside our room door, "I still ain't fo sho if I'm lik'n da idea o' dem two in da same room... Dey ain't young-ons no mo," he said. "Why dey gots ta push up da doe?"

Mom planted a seed without knowing how fertile the soil was, "Ed, git on 'way from dere 'fore ya wakes dem chillin. I knows dey's all growed up...but...I figers it can't be all dat bad if'n da two o' dem does git t'gether."

My old man questioned, walking into their room and pushing the door to close it, "What be so bad, Martha?"

I heard Mom as their door swung closed. "We's, a'ways talkin 'bout how she need ta find huself a good man 'an, well, he ain't a bad boy. 'Sides, maybe that be reason 'nough fo 'em ta comes home from dat city fo good," Mom presented.

I heard Dad protest from the other side of their room door, "Dat ain't no kinda right," he said. "Dey's kinfolk."

Lodging a rare difference of opinion, "Only 'cause dat's what dey's a'ways been told," Mom said.

My old man didn't like the idea, "Well, ain't no time fo dat kinda talk," he said en route to their bathroom. "I gotta gits some r'lief from dat Mex'can food we ett fo dinner."

I took advantage of the opportunity to sneak into our room and crawl back into my bed while dropping the arm-load of clothes into the closet.

Tammy mouthed silently, "Did ya gits e'ryth'n up?"

In like fashion, "Yeah....and drained the tub," I confirmed.

With a serious expression, she asked, "What 'bout da wrap'er?"

"Wrapper...what wrapper?" I questioned.

She said, in a hushed yell, "Da wrap'er fo that thang!"

I continued the quiet debate, "Tammy, what the hell are you talking about? What wrapper for what thing?"

Tammy let out an exasperating sigh, "Da one fo that thang ya used ta put on yo thang!"

I felt a panicked heart kick at my rib cage trying to jump out my chest, "Oh damn! Where did you leave it?" I asked. "If my old man finds that shit...Damn!"

Tammy looked at me with the biggest Cheshire cat grin and commented while displaying the wrapper between her fingers, "Sweetie."

I pretended to yell, "Ooh! That wasn't funny worth a damn! You know that one's going to cost you."

Just then, we heard Mom at the door, "Will...Tammy."

It gently came open while we both pretended to be asleep. I watched Mom through one squinted eye as she crossed the room to my cousin's bed, paused, then reached to pull the second blanket up to cover Tammy's shoulders.

Mom said while covering Tammy, "Chile gone catch huh death…can't b'lieve dat gurl sleepin like dat all night…night time git pretty cold in dese parts dis time o' year," and exited without another sound.

It was nearly ten-thirty before I meandered into the kitchen for some much needed nourishment. I didn't feel like breakfast and wasn't sure what I wanted for lunch. I resolved to pick through the leftovers and see what I could create that might be interesting.

I spoke more to myself than anyone, "New York has gotten me spoiled. Definitely no Chinese takeout in these parts," I whispered.

Mom's voice summoned me from behind the opened refrigerator door, "Well honey, if'n ya gives me time, lunch be done in a bit."

Somewhat startled, I popped my head up like a prairie dog from its burrow, "Ma'am?"

"I's sayin lunch be done shote-ly," she repeated.

"That's okay, Mom," I explained. "I'm really not all that hungry anyway."

"I sees," she sighed. "Den dat 'splain why ya all up in da ice box in yo bed clothes…'cause ya ain't hongry?"

"Well, I can eat but I'm just not much in the mood," I said.

"Now, if'n dat ain't 'bout da dangdest thang I done e'er heared. Ya hongry, but ya ain't in da mood ta eat. What's dat, some *ole city foolishness?*"

"No ma'am, it's just that things are usually always moving so fast that you stop to eat when time allows you the chance," I said.

"Well boy, ya ain't been gone so long ya done furgits dat 'round dese parts, we eats when our belly tells us to," she established.

Tammy's soprano intruded on my feeble attempt at explanation, "Maybe he gots more'n 'nough ta eat last night, Aunt
Martha."

"Well, what wuz it ya fixed fo 'em Tammy dear? I ain't
seent no lefto'ers in da ice box 'cept da ones dat was ar'eady
dere," Mom questioned.

"Oh, Auntie, I fixed him up someth'n ta eat real special
like."

Mom asked unknowingly, "It musta been real good. Will,
ya ett e'ery bit?"

My jaw hung like a possum from a tree as I stood with
my mind trying to find a way to close all the doors Tammy's
comment could have possibly opened, "Uh...ma'am?"

While making eyes at me, "Yes'um," Tammy answered.
"He say he watn't hongry none a'tall when he first gits back,
but he ett up e'ry bit, even after he ett da chicken 'n dumpl'ns,"
she said.

"Well darlin, ya gonna spit out what ya say'in 'an tell me
what it is ya fixed or y'all jest gone keeps it sec'ret?"

I searched for the words, "It was...uh..."

"Well, it ain't rea'ly gots no name, Auntie," Tammy said.
"But I can writes down da n'gredients 'an maybe..."

"You can't do that!" I yelled.

"Why da heck not?" Mom asked.

"Yeah Will, why da heck not?" Tammy snickered. "Aunt
Martha 'an me be do'n stuff like com'n up wit new ways fo
fix'n grub all da time. T'was da one wit da beef 'an veget'bles,
Auntie. I jest added some mo ingred'ents."

"So Will, how ya liked it?" Mom asked.

I picked up on Tammy's diversion, "Uh...well, I liked it
fine, Mom. I liked it just fine." I said. "It was just the way I
prefer it."

"But I thought ya say ya ne'er had nothin like it 'fore,"
Mom quizzed.

Tammy saved me again, "He mean when I puts in a li'l
moe season from when he first taste it."

"Well Tammy, ya be sho 'n keeps all 'em rec'pees t'gedder fo when we d'cides what we's gone does wit all o' dem," Mom directed.

Tammy was talking toward Mom's back with her at the sink but looking directly at me, "Yes ma'am, it sho be a shame to let someth'n so good get'way, won't it?" she asked.

Attention was momentarily diverted by the sound of Dad's truck in the yard.

I started, while moving from the line of Tammy's seductive gaze, "Speaking of getting away," I said, "I plan on leaving later tonight."

Mom responded without looking up from what she was doing, "Will, why ya tellin me dat? Ya knows ya ain't gots ta tells me yo bidness…ya comes 'n goes as ya please. Ya ain't been a chile since long 'fore ya left here."

"No ma'am. I mean, I'll be leaving for New York," I clarified.

I heard the knife she was using to cut the chicken fall into the sink. Almost instantly, mom composed herself. "But ya jest gits here two days 'go Will. Did somethin happen ta make ya not wanna be here wit us?" she asked; her voice full of concern.

Moving around the table closer to where I was standing, "Why ya gots ta be leave'n so soon?" Tammy asked.

I commented with as straight a face as possible, "Well, there are some things I didn't have a chance to finish before I came down, so I've got to get back and take care of them," I said.

Tammy eased up close to me and whispered, "I done someth'n? Ya wasn't happy wit me?"

"Yes, of course," I responded.

Mom spun around from the sink. "Did Ed said somethin ta ya? What fool talk he done spat outta his face now?"

"No, it was no big deal," I assured.

"It wasn't?" Tammy snapped.

"But ya jest says it was," Mom countered.

"Now hold up! I can't keep up two conversations with two different people at the same time. The answer to your question, Mom, is no. Dad hasn't said or done anything I wouldn't expect him to say or do. And Tammy, the answer to your question is: yes, I was satisfied."

"Tammy, ain't nob'dy complainin 'bout yo cookin," Mom defended. "He done say ta ya da food good."

The look of bewilderment on Tammy's face told more than Mom needed to know, "What cook'n ya talk'n 'bout, Aunt Martha?"

Now Mom was confused, "What? Da same thang I figer we's all talkin 'bout. Where yo head at, chile?"

I tried to bring things back to order, "Okay, everybody stop! I can explain…"

Coming through the kitchen door, my old man demanded, "Gosh danggit, ya damn well bet'er, mister!"

My mom was in awe, "Ed, what 'n God's cre'tion done got inta ya?"

I could feel Dad's beam searing my skin through the T-shirt I wore, "Now dis ain't gots noth'n ta concern ya right now Martha. Dat boy knows what I's talk'n 'bout." he said. "Boy, jest what it is ya feel'n a need ta 'splain?"

"Pop, what do you mean?" I questioned.

Dad was noticeably irritated, "What mat'er is what you's mean'n. What bidness ya gots com'n back hure brang'n troubles wit ya?" he asked.

Mom was shaking like a leaf in a storm, "What troubles Ed?" she asked. "Will, what troubles ya done gone 'n gits yo'self in?"

"Well, Mom, that's what I was tryin to explain," I began. "The thing I have to go back to New York and take care of…"

My father's brows nearly met in the middle of his forehead, "Da thang ya gots ta takes care…? How's ya s'pose ya gone take care o' be'n wonted fo killin a man?"

Mom wailed, "Oh my Lord! Ed, what nonsense dis ya talkin?" She then turned to me. "Will, what he talkin 'bout…

killin a man?" And back to my dad. "What foolishness ya sayin Ed?" By now, Mom was hysterical.

"Martha, I's o'er ta da feed stowe where I tells ya I's gone be ta pick up dat new futilizer stuff dat ya puts ta da dirt 'tween plant'n seasins..." Dad started.

Mom's patience was gone, "Ed, if'n ya don't git dat thought outta yo head in a hurry, I's gone goes in dere 'an gits it out m'self."

"Any how I's back o' da feed when dese two fellas comes in talk'n 'bout one o' dem fancy set ups I's mentien'n 'bout gitt'n fo da CB rad'o...one o' dem scan'ers dat lets ya list'n in on what da po-lice be say'n..."

"Ed!" Mom snapped.

My old man detailed, "Well, dey's in dere talk'n 'bout some feller by name o' Will from 'round dese parts dat gone up ta New York City 'an kilt someb'dy 'an den he come back...dey say dey's a war'nt out fo his a'rest fo run'n from up dere."

Tammy stood silent, mouth hanging open, with eyes that shone like two full moons and when I faced her, she simply whimpered, "My Lord!" and fell to the floor like an old wet dishrag.

Immediately, I dashed to where she had fallen but before I could get to her, Dad stepped between us, "I thanks ya done 'nough." He bent, gently scooped Tammy into his massive arms, turned, and started toward the couch.

In an effort to explain, "But, Dad," I started.

Without ever looking back over his shoulder, he muttered, "I's thank'n ya done plenty 'nough, Will."

I turned to my mom, "But, Mom, I didn't..."

"Martha!" That was enough to silence us both as Dad stood erect, "Boy, I say ya done 'nough now!"

My mom stood silent with cupped hands, dropped her head, and began walking in the direction of Tammy and Dad as she passed me, "Jest git Will," she whispered. "Jest git."

The old man's gaze never left me as I crossed the kitchen and walked within a few feet of where he stood, motionless.

Tammy slowly regained her composure as I passed through the den toward what had become our bedroom.

She stretched out her hand, "Will."

Dad gently pushed Tammy's arm back, "Gurl."

The three of them were in virtually the same positions when I returned from the bedroom after gathering the few things I'd brought with me, "I'm gone," I said to no one in particular, with no response from either of them while I continued toward the screen door.

Mom stood and Tammy sat; both with tears streaming down their cheeks but dared not make a sound in the presence of my dad, who'd morphed into what resembled an evil taskmaster overseeing the duties of two subjects. I stood at the door for a moment and looked at the three of them while imagining myself attempting to offer a suitable explanation. It was then that realization registered; there was nothing I could say that would sound anything close to justifiable; let alone, right. My exit was to the sounds of the two women, one the caretaker and the other who had become the caregiver, openly displaying displeasure in the moment but wisely maintaining their respective positions. I was down the steps and into the car in what seemed the blink of an eye. Pausing long enough to consult my many traveling partners until the infamous BB King agreed to ride shotgun…and so, we began our journey back to the Apple.

The End